'This book is a gripping thriller, but it is also so much more. An exploration of family, of female strength, of ageing and death, relationships, community and where we fit in the world. There is so much depth and ideas to mine, but it is also pacy and darkly comic in places' A Little Book Problem

'Blackly comic and full of bathos ... I raced through the book with all its twists and turns. Cannot wait for the next one, as there's a cliffhanger or two at the end' Rambling Mads

'A darkly comedic thriller that will lighten your day, make you smile, make you sigh and tug at the heart. A book from a brilliant storyteller that will keep you engrossed to the very last word' Books behind the Title

'Doug Johnstone's books are sharp and engaging ... It really is brilliant to read a book that portrays women so wonderfully. I love the dry wit and dark humour, and think it matches perfectly with the characters and their jobs' The Wee Book Reader

'The story and characters are so fresh and unique that I find myself surprised and unable to predict the outcomes'
The Twist and Turn Book Blog

'They're delightful books, filled with light, humanity and love – even amidst the corpses and embalming fluid. I hope this series lasts for many, many more books' Blue Book Balloon

'A glorious mixture of black humour, drama and mystery with strong female leads and a beautiful Scottish setting. I really hope we will be reading more about them soon'
Intensive Gassing About Books

'*The Big Chill* is a dark and enthralling read that kept me on edge. I could never fully relax as throughout I seemed to be waiting with bated breath for what these women were going to come up against next' By the Letter Book Reviews

PRAISE FOR THE SKELFS SERIES

'A new series from the criminally underrated Johnstone. His warm portrait of the tough, indomitable Skelf women is gripping and blackly humorous' *Observer*

'This enjoyable mystery is also a touching and often funny portrayal of grief, as the three tough but tender main characters pick up the pieces and carry on: more, please' *Guardian*

'MUST HAVE' *Sunday Express*

'Flawed, funny, brave – and well set up for a series. I wouldn't call him cosy, but there's warmth to Johnstone's writing' *Sunday Times*

'An engrossing and beautifully written tale that bears all the Doug Johnstone hallmarks in its warmth and darkly comic undertones' *Herald Scotland*

'The bitter humour around the subject of death has the sardonic sting of Evelyn Waugh's *The Loved One*' *Financial Times*

'Johnstone keeps the plot and character development moving at a steady pace. The descriptions of the novel's Edinburgh settings are well done, and the many intriguing plot twists make *A Dark Matter* a difficult book to put down' *Scotsman*

'Johnstone's fantastic new novel concerns a family of female undertakers who find themselves caught up in murder and mayhem' *Independent*

'Doug Johnstone is for me the perfect free-range writer, respectful of conventions but never bound by them, never hemmed in. Each book is a different world, each book something new in this world' James Sallis

'That rare book with heart and smarts to lift it above your average crime novel' Stuart Neville

'This dark but touching thriller makes for a thoroughly enjoyable slice of Edinburgh noir' Mary Paulson-Ellis

'It's a tense ride, but what is most enjoyable is seeing the complexities of the relationships between the three generations of women unfold as they help and impede one another and deal with their grief in their own particular ways' *Big Issue*

'Doug Johnstone is one of Scotland's best writers ... This is a novel that cements that position. Dark, engrossing, impossible to put down. In turns a crime thriller, a family saga, and a page-turner, this book has everything!' Luca Veste

'Premier-league crime writing' Martyn Waites

'Doug Johnstone is a noir heavyweight and a master of gritty realism. This may be his finest novel yet' Willy Vlautin

'*A Dark Matter* is the first in an entertaining and dramatic family crime-thriller series; more, please! It is compelling and darkly humorous with enough intrigue and suspense, secrets, lies and revelations to fill a grave' The Tattooed Book Geek

'Deliciously chilling, with a wry humour running throughout. *A Dark Matter* is toxic, unsettling and just perfect. I loved it and recommend it highly. Bravo Mr Johnstone!' Random Things through My Letterbox

'This is an outstanding novel; quirky, complex, with humour and real heart – I absolutely loved it. I believe this may be the start of a series? Oh I really do hope so' Tales before Bedtime

'*A Dark Matter* is everything I hoped for – dark and shocking yet imbued with a very real sense of warmth and compassion, I loved it' Hair Past a Freckle

'Complex, dark and utterly fantastic ... *A Dark Matter* is an original and gripping read, I can't wait to see if there's a second book' On-the-Shelf Reviews

'Proper top-notch crime writing. Pure brilliance!' By the Letter Book Reviews

ABOUT THE AUTHOR

Doug Johnstone is the author of eleven previous novels, most recently *A Dark Matter* (2020). Several of his books have been bestsellers and two, *Breakers* (2019) and *The Jump* (2015), were shortlisted for the McIlvanney Prize for Scottish Crime Novel of the Year. He's taught creative writing and been writer in residence at various institutions over the last decade, and has been an arts journalist for twenty years. Doug is a songwriter and musician with five albums and three solo EPs released, and he currently plays drums for the Fun Lovin' Crime Writers, a band of crime writers. He's also player-manager of the Scotland Writers Football Club. He lives in Edinburgh.

Follow Doug on Twitter @doug_johnstone and visit his website: dougjohnstone.com.

The Skelfs Series
A Dark Matter
The Big Chill

**Other titles by Doug Johnstone,
available from Orenda Books**
Fault Lines
Breakers

THE BIG CHILL

DOUG JOHNSTONE

ORENDA
BOOKS

Orenda Books
16 Carson Road
West Dulwich
London SE21 8HU
www.orendabooks.co.uk

First published in the United Kingdom by Orenda Books, 2020
Copyright © Doug Johnstone, 2020

A catalogue record for this book is available from the British Library.

ISBN 978-1-913193-34-8
eISBN 978-1-913193-35-5

Typeset in Garamond by typesetter.org.uk

Printed and bound by CPI Group (UK) Ltd, Croydon CR0 4YY

For sales and distribution, please contact info@orendabooks.co.uk
or visit www.orendabooks.co.uk.

This one is for Val, Mark, Chris, Stuart and Luca.

1

DOROTHY

Dorothy felt at home surrounded by dead people.

She breathed deeply as Archie drove the hearse through the cemetery gates and along the rutted path that ran round the edge of the small graveyard. Like most cemeteries in the city, Edinburgh Eastern was hidden from public view as much as possible, an anonymous entrance on Drum Terrace, high stone walls enclosing the space. One side was flanked by terraced flats, another by the back of the Aldi on Easter Road. Behind the opposite wall she could see the corrugated-iron roof of a trade wholesalers. Looming over the graves on the south side was Hibs' stadium, more dirty corrugated iron, a grid of green support beams around the top like a crown.

They crawled round the cemetery, past a graffitied shed, then a skip full of rotten flower bouquets, cellophane shimmering with dew, ribbons flapping in the breeze. She wished the guys who ran this place were more considerate, mourners didn't need to see the business side of death.

Dorothy had been in the funeral business for forty-five years, it was all she knew. She glanced round at Susan Blackie's coffin in the back of the hearse, the family car following behind. She looked at Archie, deadpan face, shaved head, neat grey beard. She'd known him for a decade, considered him a friend as well as a colleague, but that had been tested by what happened six months ago. She had uncovered horrifying secrets in her family and the business, and they were still dealing with that. The one thing that gave her peace was this, looking after the dead.

They reached the open grave and pulled over. Dorothy eased out of the passenger seat, her seventy-year-old muscles letting her know that yoga wasn't enough anymore. She stretched her back, angled her hips, small movements so as not to draw attention. A funeral director should be anonymous, if people noticed you, you weren't doing your job properly.

Archie got out and opened the back of the hearse, removed the wreath from the coffin and placed it to the side. There was comfort in all of this, the correct way of doing things, deference in the way they moved. It was hard for young people, but the older you got the more natural it felt, creating the smallest ripples possible. Dorothy had had her share of ripples recently and she was happy to be back in still waters, helping others pay last respects.

The Blackie family emerged from their car as more family and friends coalesced around the grave. Very little was said, it was almost telepathic, a hand on a shoulder, a tilt of the head, the body language of grief.

Archie and the young driver from the other car rolled the coffin across the rollers and out of the hearse, enlisting the Blackie men to carry it to the grave. They laid it on the plastic grass next to the hole, a large mound of damp dirt to the side. It was rare these days to bury people rather than cremate them, even rarer for the whole ceremony to take place by the graveside. But Dorothy liked it, it was more honest, more connected than seeing a shrouded coffin sink inside a plinth in a cold chapel.

She stood with her hands clasped as the funeral party stood around the grave. She looked at some nearby gravestones, recent additions, engraving still sharp, lots of flowers and photographs. The Skelfs had buried some of these people and she wondered how the bereaved were coping. Were they dealing with it better than she was with Jim's death? It was half a year now, and it was true what she'd told others for decades, the sharp pain did reduce, replaced by an aching throb. Background emotional noise that gave life a bittersweet edge.

The young Church of Scotland minister said a few quiet words to Gordon Blackie and his sons. They were working-class Scottish men, buttoned-up and stoic, there would be no wailing and gnashing of teeth today. Plus, Susan Blackie had suffered dementia for years so it felt like she'd left them a long time ago. Death was often a relief, though it was hard to admit that.

The minister began the familiar intonations of the ceremony. Susan's life was remembered, our fragile nature in the face of the almighty was given a nod. The minister was in his twenties, floppy black fringe that he kept touching. Dorothy wondered how someone went into that profession fresh from school or college. But then she had entered the funeral business at the same age.

She looked around. The oak and beech trees were coming into leaf, the rejuvenation of spring. But there would be no rejuvenation for Susan Blackie. Nevertheless, Dorothy couldn't help feeling something, a sense of rebirth, a chance to make the world new again.

The highest branches swayed in the breeze, pigeons and crows perched and watching. Dorothy heard the shush of Easter Road traffic mixed with the minister's words. His voice didn't have the gravitas for funerals yet, not enough experience. The Blackie men stared stony-faced at Susan's coffin, as if they could lower it into the ground with sheer willpower.

Dorothy heard a police siren, faint but getting louder. She listened for the change in pitch, the Doppler effect Hannah had explained to her, when the source of the sound travelled away instead of towards you. But it didn't change, the wailing just got louder, making the minister pause his eulogy.

There was an almighty metallic crash and Dorothy spun round to see the iron cemetery gates buckle and spring from their hinges, clatter into the stone pillars either side and collapse as an old white Nissan careened into the graveyard and pummelled along the gravel path on the south side, rising into the air over bumps and swerving between graves. It was moving at maybe fifty miles per hour, engine a high whine, as the siren got louder and a police car thundered through the cemetery gates in pursuit.

The Nissan braked and swerved at the bend in the path, fishtailed into a headstone, which fell like a domino. The car straightened and sped up, the police car copying its trajectory round the bend, running onto the grass. The Nissan glanced off two more gravestones and ricocheted across the path, the gravestones tearing chunks from the front bumper, denting the driver's door.

It was a hundred yards away from the hearse, the family car and Susan's coffin. The Blackie party stood with eyes wide, Dorothy the same, the minister with his mouth open.

The hearse was blocking the path but the Nissan kept racing towards them, bouncing along, clattering against headstones and thumping over grassy mounds. The police car was behind, lights flashing, siren screaming.

The Nissan was almost at the hearse now as Dorothy felt someone pulling her, Archie was yanking her arm. She stumbled towards a large memorial stone just as the Nissan rushed past her, swerved away from the rear of the hearse, scattering mourners, the Blackie men jumping out of the way. The car clattered into the gravestone next to Susan's coffin, bounced into the air, then its front end dipped and it landed with a sickening thud halfway in the empty grave, its rear end hanging in the air, wheels spinning.

The police car skidded to a halt a foot from the hearse and its siren stopped. The sudden quiet was disorienting, as Dorothy straightened and ran to the Nissan. She went past Susan's coffin, which seemed unscathed, to the driver's side of the car. She hauled at the crumpled door three, four times. Eventually it opened and she leaned in.

Behind the wheel was a dishevelled young man in dirty clothes, with longish hair and an untidy beard. He wasn't wearing a seatbelt and there was no airbag. He had a long gash across his forehead, which was leaning against a crack in the windscreen. Blood poured from his ear. He was dead, Dorothy knew that look better than anyone.

She held the door open, staring at him, as a young police officer arrived behind her. He looked at the Nissan's driver, eyes wide. He'd obviously not seen as many dead bodies as Dorothy. His face went pale.

Dorothy heard a noise from the back seat. She leaned in, heard the noise again, a whimper. She spotted him, a small border collie with one eye. The dog climbed forward from the back and licked the driver's head wound, tasting its owner's blood. It whined and shrank away.

Dorothy turned to the young cop, who was shaking.

'What the hell?' she said.

2

JENNY

'Cheers.'

Jenny smiled at Liam as they both hit their drinks, a double Hendricks for her, a pint of Moretti for him. Maybe they should've been on champagne, given they were celebrating his divorce, but who pays pub champagne prices? Anyway, divorce is always melancholic, Jenny knew that well. Mingled with the relief was the admission of defeat. You weren't good enough to make the marriage work, even if the other person was a piece of shit and you were well rid of them.

She looked around The King's Wark. Ancient, rough stonework, large fireplace, mismatched wooden tables and chairs. Just a handful of drinkers this time of day, suits from Pacific Quay on early lunch.

'So you're young, free and single again,' Jenny said, deadpan.

Liam pulled at the skin under his eyes. 'I haven't been young for years.'

'You're younger than me.'

He did look tired, the divorce had taken its toll over the last six months. But he was still handsome, those green eyes, the flecks of grey through his black hair. He still looked after himself.

He smiled. 'That's not hard.'

'Hey.' She faked outrage, punched his shoulder, felt the solid muscle.

She looked around the pub. 'Nice touch, coming here.'

'This is our place.'

It hadn't been a conventional way to meet. Jenny was hired by Liam's now ex-wife, Orla, to find evidence he was cheating. Jenny had just started working for her mum, helping out at both the

Skelf's funeral director's and private investigator's. She had no idea what she was doing, but she followed Liam to his artist's studio round the corner, then sat in this pub watching him. Which is where she saw Orla's failed sting attempt – she'd hired an escort to seduce him, to entrap him so that Orla could file for divorce. Jenny sprung a trap of her own, got evidence that Orla was fucking her gardener, which she presented to Liam. Again, right here in The King's Wark.

It wasn't the most auspicious start, but Jenny's own marriage to Craig began with true love and wound up with her husband lying and cheating, so maybe this was better.

'Thanks for everything,' Liam said.

Jenny shook her head. 'It was just a few pictures.'

'I'm not talking about the evidence,' he said. 'I'm talking about us.'

Jenny looked away. It was embarrassing how open Liam was. Maybe because of his creative side he was in touch with stuff that Jenny and most of her generation kept hidden. She was raised to shrug and say 'whatever', hated direct emotional engagement. That's what made her bad at the funeral business. She should be helping Mum right now, but she found it difficult to handle the emotions that spilled over at funerals. And anyway, Dorothy and Archie would have everything under control.

Liam took her hand and she resisted the urge to pull away. Ever since Craig, she struggled with this. Maybe she should go to therapy like Hannah, to help her cope. But therapy wasn't in her DNA, the idea of talking to a stranger about the fucked-up things in her head made her teeth itch.

'How's Hannah?' Liam said, as if reading her mind. Maybe it was obvious she was constantly worried about her daughter. Fuck, who wouldn't be? Hannah's dad had killed one of her best friends, and tried to kill Jenny and Dorothy too. When Larkin said your mum and dad fuck you up, did he have that crazy shit in mind?

Jenny sighed. 'I don't know.'

'She'll be OK.'

'I wish I had your confidence.'

'I have plenty of confidence in your family, less in myself.'

'God, I'm fed up telling you.'

'It's fine,' Liam said, smiling. 'We have confidence in each other, just not ourselves. That's Gen X, right?'

He was so honest it was painful. How had the world not crushed this man already? Six months after finding out his marriage was a sham, he was here in the pub smiling and joking. When Jenny's divorce came through ten years ago, she curled up in a ball at home for years afterwards. Craig moved on to a new woman, new family, new life. How do you square that shit away?

Liam took a drink and narrowed his eyes. He knew her already, what her moods were, when she was shrinking into herself.

'Hannah and Dorothy will be fine,' he said. 'You're the strongest women I've ever met. If anyone can handle things, it's the Skelfs.'

Jenny drank and shook her head, felt the burn of the extra gin in her tonic. She needed that edge to hold on to. Hannah was seeing a counsellor, Dorothy seemed to have found peace in the funeral work. But where did that leave Jenny? A dead dad, a murderous ex-husband, no home of her own, working two jobs she couldn't do very well. She looked around the pub and out of the window. It was a beautiful spring day and the Water of Leith was shimmering in the sun. She had a handsome, smart man with her, and she had her family.

She turned back to Liam and made a face. 'So today is the first day of the rest of your life.'

Liam rolled his eyes. 'Today is always the first day of the rest of your life. Until you die.'

'Cheery.'

Liam raised his glass. 'Cheers.'

They drank, and Liam put his glass down.

Jenny leaned in and kissed him, squeezed his hand on the table, tried to feel sexy, wanted. She pulled away and drank.

He smiled. 'What was that for?'

'Just a Happy Divorce kiss.'

He sipped his pint, keeping his eyes on her. 'I should get divorced more often.'

'I wouldn't recommend it.'

They were comfortable with this level of flirting and banter. They'd been seeing each other for the last couple of months, ended up in bed a handful of times, but hadn't discussed what this was yet. Jenny was scared that if they did it would vanish in a puff of smoke. They were both licking their wounds, for God's sake. But Jenny wanted to be seen, still wanted to be a sexual being, wanted to turn him on. And he certainly turned her on.

She thought about what he'd said before, that today was always the first day of the rest of your life. She liked that. At least until you die. But she lived around death every day, bodies in the embalming room, the viewing rooms, the chapel. Deceased and bereaved everywhere you looked in a funeral home.

Jenny watched Liam drink, delicate movements, considered, unassuming. She suddenly wanted to take him home to bed.

'Let's get out of here,' she said.

'And do what?'

Jenny's phone rang in her bag as she took a final swig of her gin. She fished it out. 'Hey Mum, how was the funeral this morning?'

3

HANNAH

The counsellor's office was annoyingly jaunty, bright yellow seats, a lurid green desk. Outside the window Hannah saw the Meadows, students soaking up sunshine on the grass, mums with little kids in the play park, tennis players thwacking balls across the courts. To the right was Bruntsfield Links and she could just make out the Skelf house beyond that. The irony of it, while undergoing counselling she could see the place she chased her dad covered in blood.

Out the other window of Rita's corner office was George Square and the dome of McEwan Hall, where Hannah would graduate in a year's time, maybe. Recent grades were not good. She could've taken a year out, given everything that happened, but she would've gone mad with nothing to keep her occupied.

'What are you thinking about?' Rita said.

Hannah turned. The counsellor was about the same age as her mum, purple hair chopped short, black frilly top, leggings, Doc boots, biker jacket on the back of her chair. Hannah wondered how she came to work for Edinburgh Uni, talking students through their crises. Most of them would be stressing over exams, depressed about breaking up with a boyfriend or girlfriend, confused about their sexuality. Hannah could trump that.

'You mean apart from the fact my dad killed my friend, who was carrying his baby, then tried to kill my mum and gran?' she said.

Rita gave her a look like a kicked puppy.

'I'm sorry,' Hannah said.

Rita held out her hands. 'It's what I'm here for. You've been through a lot. Anger is reasonable.'

Hannah shook her head. 'I'm not angry, that's the thing, I'm just tired. So fucking tired.'

Rita nodded and crossed her legs. 'Again, totally reasonable. I'd be tired. Anyone would be tired in your situation.'

Hannah's girlfriend, Indy, had floated the idea of therapy or counselling a month after everything happened with Craig, when it was clear Hannah was struggling. Dorothy suggested a private shrink but Hannah refused. They cost a ton of money, and Hannah believed that talking to one person about your shit was the same as talking to anyone about it. Would a psychiatrist wave a magic wand and make it all go away? So here she was talking to an ageing rock chick who no doubt had a bunch of her own unresolved shit to deal with.

Hannah had never told Rita they had a view of the crime scene from her office window. Normally Hannah liked talking, she'd grown up connected to the world in a way Rita's generation could never grasp. But she didn't want to talk about this. What difference did it make? Mel was still dead, her dad was in prison, and everyone still carried the scars.

'Have you heard of the many-worlds interpretation?' she said.

Rita tilted her head. 'No.'

'But you know about Schrödinger's cat?'

Rita frowned. 'Something about a cat in a box that's alive and dead at the same time.'

Hannah smiled. 'Kind of. It's quantum mechanics. On a subatomic level, a particle is in an indeterminate state until it's observed. So what if you scale that up? Put a cat in a box with a flask of poison and a radioactive source. If the source decays, a quantum event, the flask breaks and the cat is poisoned. But until you open the box you don't know whether the source has decayed, so the cat is both dead and alive.'

'OK.' Rita dragged the word out.

'It's a paradox, but there's a way out of it.'

Rita waved a hand.

'The many-worlds interpretation says that whenever you open the box, the universe splits, so in one universe the cat is dead, and in a parallel universe somewhere, the cat is still alive. That happens with every observation.'

'Right.'

Hannah looked out of the window at her gran's funeral home in the distance. Indy was working at reception there, waiting for Hannah to finish, waiting for her to move on with her life. Waiting for a snog.

Hannah turned to Rita who was fingering a big hoop earring. 'So do you think, in a parallel dimension, Mel is still alive, about to have a baby, my half-sister?'

'That's an interesting way to look at it.'

Hannah sighed. 'There's a problem. Say *you* were inside the box instead of the cat. Then you would observe if the source decayed and the waveform collapses. You'd be dead. That's quantum suicide. But the many-worlds interpretation goes the other way. Since you can only observe outcomes where you're alive, by definition, then you stay in the universe where you keep surviving. Quantum immortality.'

Rita was frowning, lines across her forehead. 'You've lost me.'

'If you always end up in the universe where you survive, doesn't that mean you can do anything you want?'

'I don't think that's helpful.'

'Maybe that's what my dad thought,' Hannah said. 'Maybe he thought he could just do anything he liked and get away with it.'

Rita sighed. 'It doesn't take quantum physics for men to think they can get away with stuff.'

Hannah smiled. She imagined being a cat in a box, waiting to die. 'And I'm half him, that's the way genetics works.'

'That's not how life works.'

'Are you sure?'

'I'm nothing like my parents.' Rita smiled as something occurred to her. 'Let me tell you about my mother.'

'What?'

'It's a line from *Bladerunner*. Ever seen the original *Bladerunner*?'

Hannah shook her head. 'Just the recent one.'

'They catch a replicant and interview him, ask about his mother. He says "let me tell you about my mother" then shoots his interviewer under the desk.'

Hannah smiled and lifted her hands. 'No gun.'

'You're not a replicant,' Rita said.

'But I don't know that, they had implanted memories, right? If that's true, can you erase some of mine?'

'If you erase your memories, don't you erase yourself?'

'I don't know.'

Rita smiled. 'This is more like an ethics class than a counselling session. We've kind of gone off topic.'

'Did the replicants have morals?' Hannah said.

'I think they were programmed into them.'

'So they couldn't do whatever they wanted.'

'No more than any of us.'

Hannah shook her head as her phone rang.

'Sorry,' she said, pulling it from her pocket. 'I'd better take this.' She pressed reply. 'Hey, Mum.'

'Something's happened,' Jenny said down the line.

4

JENNY

Jenny handed cash to the taxi driver and stepped out. The sight of the house gave her a trill in her stomach, like always, throwing up childhood memories. A three-storey Victorian block with low additions to the side that housed the embalming room, body fridges, coffin workshop and garage for the hearse. The funeral business she'd escaped from decades ago, only to be sucked back in six months ago when her dad died. So she was living here again, haunted by memories, haunted by the thousands of dead who'd passed through the place.

She went in the side door and through to reception, where Indy was at the desk. Hannah's beautiful girlfriend, just one of the strays Dorothy had accumulated at the funeral home over the years. She'd turned up four years ago to arrange her parents' funeral, wound up helping out around the place, a natural at dealing with people, Hannah included. She'd dyed her hair again since Jenny last saw her, a green that set off her dark skin.

'Archie told me what happened,' Jenny said.

Indy shook her head. 'Crazy.'

'Where's Mum?'

Indy nodded upstairs. 'In the ops room. She's fine.'

Jenny headed up. The ops room was where they ran the funeral and PI businesses, but it was also their kitchen and dining room, where she'd had countless family meals. She reached the doorway and saw Dorothy at the sink, spooning cat food into a bowl.

'Mum, Archie called me, are you OK?'

Dorothy turned and smiled, placed the bowl at her feet with one hand touching her back.

Jenny went in and stopped when she spotted the dog.

'Who's this?'

The collie snuffled at the food, then a couple of licks and it began eating. It looked up between bites as if the food might be taken away.

Dorothy crouched and tickled his ear. 'I don't know his name, no collar.'

'Where did you find him?'

'In the car.'

'What?'

'The accident this morning, you said Archie told you.' Dorothy stood up and reached for a cupboard, took out two glasses and a half-empty bottle of Highland Park. 'I need a drink.'

She poured two measures, handed one to Jenny, then sat at the table.

Jenny watched her movements, slow and careful. She hadn't been the same since everything with Craig. He'd stabbed Jenny in this room, then beaten and choked Dorothy, who'd stabbed him in self-defence.

Jenny was left with a large scar on her belly and night terrors. Dorothy's bruises took a long time to heal. Before, despite being seventy, she had energy, moved with grace. Now she was tentative, as if the world could really harm her, aware she wasn't going to last forever. It broke Jenny's heart to see her mum like this.

She sipped her whisky, pulled out a chair and sat, placed a hand on her mum's. 'What happened?'

'Archie saved me,' Dorothy said, looking out of the window.

Bruntsfield Links was putting its spring show on, the trees filling out and dancing in the breeze, a few souls sitting on the grass, happy to be through another winter. The ancient dead buried below were pushing up new grass, her dad's ashes down there too amongst the plants and flowers, worms and bugs.

Jenny looked from the window to the two large whiteboards on the other wall. One for funerals, the other for PI cases. The funeral one was busy, half a dozen jobs on the slate, bodies in the fridges downstairs or waiting to be collected, or already embalmed and waiting for the final send-off. The PI work had been steady recently too, mostly marital stuff, which Jenny found she had a knack for since Liam.

Jenny turned to Dorothy. 'He said there was a police car chase?'

Dorothy exhaled. 'That's right.'

'In the graveyard?'

'Yes.'

'What the hell?'

'That's what I said.'

'Are you OK?'

'I'm fine, Archie pulled me out of the way. No one in the Blackie party was injured, including the deceased. But we've had to postpone the funeral, the grave is a crime scene.'

'What were they thinking, chasing him into a cemetery?'

Dorothy took a drink. She never used to touch whisky before Jim died, it was always his drink, but she'd claimed it as her own since he was gone, maybe the taste was a memory.

'The man in the car died,' Dorothy said.

Jenny shook her head. 'Why were they after him?'

'Car was stolen, that's all.' She drank. 'I think he was homeless. The car had a sleeping bag and an old backpack in it.' Dorothy nodded at the collie. 'And this guy.'

'Why is he here?'

'Where else could he go?'

'The police should deal with him.'

Dorothy smiled. 'The police officer was just a baby, poor thing. He was in shock. I had to make him do breathing exercises. Then I got the dog out of the car, put him in the hearse. The police don't want to deal with a dog.'

'But the dog might belong to someone.'

Dorothy nodded. 'I've spoken to Thomas about it.'

This was her friend, a police inspector over at St Leonards.

She'd helped him bury his wife a few years back, he'd helped her with PI cases since.

Dorothy drank again. 'I'll look after him until we find his home, if he has one.'

There was a hiss from the doorway and Jenny saw Schrödinger there, back arched, staring at the collie. The ginger cat was another of Dorothy's strays, she attracted those who didn't have anywhere else.

Hannah appeared in the doorway and scooped the cat into her arms. Schrödinger stayed alert, eyes on the intruder.

'Gran, are you OK?'

Dorothy sighed. 'I don't need any fuss.'

Schrödinger squirmed from Hannah's arms and landed on the rug. Jenny saw where they'd tried to clean up the blood from that night. The rug was red and patterned so the blood was easy to hide.

'Who's this guy?' Hannah said, pointing at the collie.

Jenny looked at her daughter. Her black hair needed a wash and she looked tired. This had been hard on everyone, Hannah most of all.

Jenny took a sip of whisky. 'He belonged to the guy driving the car.'

'Belonged?'

Jenny glanced at Dorothy, who was staring out of the window again.

'The driver died,' Jenny said.

'Holy shit.' Hannah stroked the dog, Schrödinger hissing in the doorway.

'Take it easy,' Hannah said to the cat. She looked up. 'So we've got this guy until we find his family?'

'If he has one,' Dorothy said.

Hannah checked for a collar, tickled under his chin.

'He got a name?'

Jenny shook her head.

Hannah stood and thought, looked from the dog to the cat.

'He can be Einstein,' she said. 'Einstein and Schrödinger never got on.'

Indy appeared at the doorway with a look. 'Someone's downstairs.'

'A funeral?' Dorothy said.

'No.'

'A case?' Jenny said.

Indy shook her head and threw a look of apology around the room, landing on Hannah. 'It's your stepmum, Han, she wants to speak to all of you.'

For years Jenny had built up Fiona as a nemesis, the perky little blonde who lured her husband away. That was insane, of course, Craig was the one having an affair back then, and anyway, Jenny was lucky the way things turned out. She'd thought about Fiona in the last six months, how it would be for her, her husband in prison, a murderer, a cheat. Worse still, he and Jenny had been fooling around before all the craziness. They were all tricked by the same man, so Fiona wasn't the enemy. But that still hung in Jenny's mind, anxiety creeping up her spine at the thought of the woman downstairs.

'Bring her up,' Dorothy said, touching her forehead.

Hannah held the kitchen worktop, breathing deep, eyes closed.

Jenny heard footsteps, and there she was. Fiona was beautiful, same age as Jenny. She was small but expertly put together, both her figure and her smart suit, like a successful solicitor with an edge of sex appeal.

'Come in,' Dorothy said, waving a hand.

Fiona hesitated, looked at Hannah.

Hannah lived with Jenny after the divorce, but she'd spent weekends with Craig, Fiona and Sophia, her cute wee half-sister.

'Hi, Han,' she said.

'Hey.'

Fiona looked around. 'So this is where it happened?'

She meant Craig's face-off with the Skelf women.

'The crime scene, one of them at least,' Jenny said, then regretted it. Mel had died, fuck's sake, this wasn't a joke.

'It can't have been easy to come here,' Dorothy said. 'Would you like a drink?'

She waved the Highland Park in the air. Jenny wished her mum wasn't so calm. It was irrational, but Jenny wanted to hold a grudge against someone, and Craig was in Saughton Prison, so Fiona would do.

Fiona nodded and entered like a deer into a clearing. Jenny imagined her in rifle crosshairs.

'How's Sophia?' Hannah said.

Fiona scratched at her neck. 'OK. She doesn't understand, misses her dad.'

That made Jenny think, the ripples in all their lives.

Dorothy handed Fiona a whisky and she took a gulp. Jenny saw bags under her eyes, a nervous twitch in the corner of her mouth. She was thinner than Jenny had seen her looking on social media.

Fiona looked at the whiteboards, scribbles and scrawls, deaths to be negotiated, mysteries to be solved. She took another drink, stalling.

'How are you all?'

'The wounds have healed,' Jenny said. Her hand went to her scarred stomach, touched the skin underneath her T-shirt.

'I didn't mean that,' Fiona said.

'Why are you here?' Jenny said.

'Jenny,' Dorothy said.

It took Jenny back to being a kid, the reprimand in her mum's voice, a shiver of shame up her neck.

'This isn't easy for anyone,' Fiona said. 'He refuses to sign the divorce papers, he's still my fucking husband, think about that.'

Jenny thought about it. They both had daughters by the same bastard, they should be sisters-in-arms. But it wasn't that easy.

Fiona took a drink. 'I wanted to tell you in person. He's

changed his plea. From guilty to not guilty on the grounds of diminished responsibility.'

Hannah's grip on the worktop tightened, she rocked back and forth. 'Are you serious?'

'He's claiming he was crazy?' Jenny said.

Fiona shook her head. 'I couldn't believe it when the solicitor told me.'

Hannah pushed herself away from the worktop and balled her hands.

'But he admitted it,' she said. 'He admitted it all to the police.'

Fiona shrugged. 'Says he wasn't in his right mind. He's pushing for a quick trial now too.'

Jenny couldn't get her head around it. 'After all this time? What's he playing at?'

Dorothy had been silent through all this. 'He can't think he has a case.'

Fiona swallowed hard. 'It's not about that.'

'Then what?' Hannah said.

Fiona looked around the women. 'He wants to see us in court. The solicitor thinks he'll call us all as witnesses.'

'But we'll testify against him,' Jenny said. 'He must know that.'

Fiona downed the remains of her whisky, shivered from the hit. 'He doesn't care,' she said. 'He wants to punish us.'

5

DOROTHY

St Leonards police station was a bland modern brick block sitting amongst student flats in the Southside. Dorothy saw Salisbury Crags to the right, the cliffs leering over the southern part of the city. She went inside the station and waited at reception, but she'd barely sat down when Thomas appeared.

She was struck, as always, by how he carried himself – upright, confident but never arrogant. It couldn't be easy, being a black man in a Scottish police force was as rare as hens' teeth, but he walked as if he knew his place in the world.

'Dorothy, are you OK?' Still the trace of Swedish in his voice despite living here for twenty years. That was another reason she liked him, they were both immigrants in this strange country with its black humour and deep-fried food. Now they were both widowed, another thing in common.

He pulled her in for a hug, more than perfunctory, and she let herself be held, sank into it. Eventually she pulled away. 'Don't fuss.'

Thomas looked her in the eye. 'I like fussing over you.'

He was fifteen years younger than her but there was something unspoken between them. Never acted upon, she'd been happily married until six months ago. Since then she'd felt untethered from her previous life. Maybe it was time to do some tethering. Who was she kidding? She was seventy years old, that stuff didn't happen to women her age.

'Come through,' he said, holding the door.

They went up to his office, a better view of the Crags from here. It was kicking on for sunset, the sky was a bruise behind the blade of the cliffs, a few dots moving on the skyline, tourists up for the views.

Laid out on a table against the far wall were the joyrider's belongings. The grubby sleeping bag and the rucksack, its contents alongside.

'How's the young officer?' Dorothy said.

Thomas shook his head. 'He'll be OK.'

'He was in shock.'

'Understandable. But he was to blame too.'

'Don't be hard on him. He needs support.'

Thomas shrugged. 'He'll get it. But there will be an enquiry. He didn't follow procedure.'

'What happened?'

Thomas leaned against his desk. 'He saw the car parked somewhere it shouldn't have been. Ran the plates and realised it was stolen. When he approached the vehicle it took off, so he went after.'

'Through a graveyard?'

Thomas rubbed at his forehead. 'He's only been with us a few months.'

'Poor guy.'

'Dorothy, he could've killed you, or anyone else at the funeral.'

'He didn't, though.'

'Only through dumb luck.' Thomas waved at the table of stuff. 'And if he hadn't kept after him, our joyrider would still be alive.'

Dorothy walked over to the table. The sleeping bag was filthy and ragged, the zip broken, a hole where the stuffing poked out. She ran a finger across it.

'Do we know who he was?'

'No ID in his possessions. We've compared his picture to local missing persons, no match.'

'DNA?'

'A sample is in the system, but if we don't have him on file we won't get a hit.'

Dorothy looked at the rucksack. It was a decent brand but ancient, frayed around the zip, worn through at the corners, stains on the material. She looked over its contents, a filthy jumper, skanky boxer shorts and socks. Heroin works, syringe, belt, spoon, cotton wool, lighter. All used. An A6 notebook with puckered pages from water damage. A single photograph of him with a woman.

She picked it up. He looked younger, no beard, light-blue eyes. He wore a hoodie and crucifix, one ear pierced. The woman was the same age, early twenties, short blonde hair, sharp nose. They were up a hill, a view of Edinburgh and the Forth spread out behind them.

'Arthur's Seat?' Dorothy said.

'I think so.'

Dorothy flipped the picture over but there was nothing on the back.

'You could put this out, see if the woman comes forward.'

Thomas nodded. 'If the DNA doesn't come through.'

'He was homeless.'

'Looks like it.'

'So maybe check hostels and social care.'

Thomas took the picture and studied it. 'We don't have the resources, you know that.'

'If he was a murder victim or suspect, you would.'

'This wasn't murder, it was an accident. A stupid, avoidable accident.'

Dorothy opened the notebook. A manic pencil scrawl. She narrowed her eyes and tried to read. Words about hate, conspiracy, the system keeping people down. It wasn't sentences, just ramblings.

'Can I take this?'

Thomas frowned. 'One of our guys has been through it. He doesn't think there's anything to identify him.'

'Still.'

'OK, but don't lose it.'

Dorothy smiled. 'And can I get a copy of the photograph?'

'I'll email it.'

'Is his body at the City Mortuary?'

Thomas nodded. 'Post-mortem is tomorrow. I'm not expecting much but toxicology might throw up something.'

'Can I see him?'

Thomas still had the picture in his hand. He looked from it to Dorothy, sizing her up. 'You know Graham Chapel down there, right?'

'Of course.'

'Tell him I said it was OK.'

'Thank you.'

Thomas put the picture down then placed a hand on Dorothy's elbow, his face softening. 'What's your interest in him?'

'Are you serious? He literally crashed into my life.' Dorothy touched the edge of the notebook. 'We all come from somewhere. I want to know who he was.'

Thomas gave her elbow a rub then let go. 'I get that. But remember last time you got your teeth into something like this. After Jim ... passed. You can get carried away.'

She'd called in favours with Thomas to work out her dead husband's secrets, only to realise they were worse than she could've imagined. And Thomas didn't even know the whole story – only her girls and Archie knew what really happened.

'That was different.'

'Was it?' Thomas said.

'It was personal.'

'And this isn't?' Thomas gave a sceptical smile. 'He almost killed you.'

Dorothy looked at the photograph again.

'I just want to know who he is.'

6

HANNAH

She stared at her laptop screen. She'd got the title, 'Melanie Cheng Memorial', and the cursor blinked at her from the next line. Anxiety swelled from her belly to her chest, and she breathed deeply and looked out of the window.

The view was out to the back of the flats, a patchwork of small lawns, a cluster of birch trees, and thirty other living-room and bedroom windows. She was reminded of that Hitchcock film Gran liked, imagined seeing a murder across the road. But all she could see was an old man bent over a stove, a young couple building Lego with their son, students staring at phones, their faces lit like figures in a Renaissance painting. Everyone getting on with life, the little disappointments and triumphs, the small gestures of comfort or annoyance, the incremental moments of time that accumulated into experience.

She felt stuck in comparison. For her, those moments weren't accumulating, they were slipping away, one flash of panic to the next, one depressive slump bleeding into another, the constant anxiety. And this blank page in front of her wasn't helping.

'You don't have to do it.'

Hannah turned to see Indy in the doorway, her face a balance of love and worry. Hannah felt her own twinges of love and worry. She was sick of feeling shit because of what happened, and Indy had been so supportive through everything. But it was crap that she had to be supportive, that Hannah needed nursing, when all she wanted to do was throw Indy onto the bed and kiss her, or go to the park and have a picnic, or sit in a café over brunch and taste each other's food.

'I do,' Hannah said, looking at the screen.

Indy came over and placed her hands on Hannah's shoulders. 'It's too much stress.'

'I want to do it. We're supposed to celebrate Mel's life and we were her best friends.' Hannah put a hand on Indy's. 'How do you do it, how do you cope?'

'You know it's different. With me it's just grief, with you it's more complicated because of your dad.'

Hannah had done the reading, on top of the grief there was guilt that her dad had killed Mel. And survivor guilt too, that she was alive when her friend wasn't. She was to blame, of course, because if she had never been friends with Mel then Craig wouldn't have met her. But how far back do you go with cause and effect? She preferred the quantum world, where cause and effect were looser, time didn't run at the same rate, where her friend was still alive and nursing her new baby.

Indy leaned down and kissed Hannah, and she felt a shiver. She was glad she still got that, despite everything, that she was still turned on by her girlfriend.

She pulled away eventually.

Indy pointed at the laptop. 'Just speak from the heart. Whatever you say will be great.'

It'd taken six months for the physics department to get around to this memorial for Mel, and Hannah was surprised they'd done it at all. It was complicated by departmental politics for a start. If they did a memorial for Mel, did they need one for Peter too? Hannah presumed they didn't want to go there, given he was having an affair with one of his students, was thrown out by his wife, suspended by the department, then hanged himself. That's the kind of thing that gives a physics department a bad name.

But one of the elderly professors, Hugh Fowler, insisted that Melanie's life should be honoured by the department. Hugh was that peculiar creature of science departments, a doddering old guy who'd spent his life in academia, a kindly geriatric who never seemed to work but never retired either.

Hugh had contacted Hannah after a tutorial one day and asked if she would come into the office. He wanted a memorial for Mel, would she speak at it? So here she was the night before, staring at a blank screen. And it was worse because Mel's family was coming down to Kings Buildings tomorrow. Hannah didn't need that pressure on top of everything else.

Her phone rang. It was a mobile number, not in her contacts. No one ever called her except Mum and Gran. Probably just some marketing thing, but something made her curious and she pressed reply.

'Please don't hang up.'

Blood rushed to her face and she couldn't breathe. She struggled to swallow as panic snaked up her throat and into her mouth.

Indy frowned and gave her a look.

'I need to explain,' the man said. The man she'd known all her life, the man she'd last seen when she stood over him on Bruntsfield Links, as he bled out on the grass, admitted what he'd done, telling her he wanted to die. Her dad.

'How dare you,' Hannah said, her voice and hand shaking.

'I wasn't myself,' Craig said.

'You can't call me. You don't get to speak to me.'

She hung up. Tears in her eyes as she let out a shaky breath.

A look of realisation spread across Indy's face. 'No.'

Hannah looked wide-eyed.

'You're fucking kidding me,' Indy said. 'Babes.'

Hannah shook her head and tears dropped onto her laptop. She felt Indy embrace her, trying to comfort her.

'How can he just call you from prison?' she said.

Hannah couldn't speak, the sound of his voice in her head, the sight of him on his knees in the dark, blood pouring from his chin and chest. She wished he'd died, all of this would be easier.

'Why now?' Indy said.

Hannah extricated herself from the hug, wiped at her face. 'Maybe it's the plea thing.'

'Diminished responsibility is a joke.'

'I know.'

Indy nodded at the phone, like a radioactive source glowing on the desk. 'What did he say?'

'He wanted to explain.'

'What is there to explain?'

'He said he wasn't himself.'

Indy shook her head, angry now. 'You need to tell the police and the lawyers.'

Hannah looked at Indy, the intensity of her girlfriend's stare too much. She turned to look outside at all the people living their lives in the flats opposite, the crows in the trees, the vapour trail from a jet high in the darkening sky, a plane full of people escaping their lives for a moment.

'Tell them what?' she said.

7

DOROTHY

Dorothy sat behind the drum kit, her beautiful sunburst Gretsch, and tried to focus on the music through her headphones. It was early Biffy Clyro, full of sudden changes, dynamic bursts, odd time signatures. She wanted something to challenge her, something forceful too, nothing with too much feel. But it wasn't working. She kept thinking about that poor kid in the driver's seat, his cut forehead, blood, blank stare. No ID, few possessions, just a stolen car and a one-eyed dog.

She stumbled over a middle eight with lots of random stop-starts, her sticks clacking against each other. She never got back into the rhythm, unsure of herself. Behind the kit was usually a place she could be in control, but not today.

Where was Abi? She was already fifteen minutes late for her lesson. She loved drumming, never missed a lesson without sending a dozen WhatsApp messages of grovelling apology. Dorothy had fewer students since she'd taken over Jim's work at the funeral business, but she'd kept on a handful, all girls, and she loved that. In her own small way she was a role model – an old Californian woman bashing her way round the toms, back to the hi-hats, into syncopated snare trills.

The song settled into a groove and Dorothy with it. She thought about what Fiona said. Craig changing his plea was ridiculous, there was so much evidence against him. A court case was the last thing they needed, dredging it all back up. Dorothy had returned to yoga once her injuries healed but her muscles still nagged across her shoulders and back from where he'd slammed her against the wall.

She didn't believe in evil, but her former son-in-law had put that to the test. Dorothy had the least emotional attachment to him, and she keenly felt her inability to help Jenny and Hannah. Just be there, that's what she'd learned from her years in the death business. Same as being a mother or grandmother.

The song finished and Dorothy slouched and removed the headphones. Her arms were tired, her back grumbling. She checked her watch. Where was Abi? She picked up her phone, no messages. She called, got voicemail. No surprise, kids never used their phones to speak. She sent a message. Checked her watch again.

In the silence, her ears adjusted. Birdsong outside in the park, traffic on Bruntsfield Road. She heard someone coming up the stairs, then there was Einstein, ears pinned back, body low to the ground, tail wagging.

'Hey boy,' Dorothy said, putting her hand out.

Einstein scooted over and licked her hand, let himself be stroked behind the ears. Dorothy stared at the scar tissue around the dog's eye socket. It was well healed, must've been long ago.

'How did that happen, eh?' she said, holding the dog's face in her hands.

She thought about the guy in the car, everything she didn't know about him.

Then she had an idea.

'Let's go for a walk,' she said.

The dog was nervous off the lead, staying close to Dorothy across Bruntsfield Links and the Meadows. She got caught out when he went for a crap, didn't have bags. She wrapped the shit in several tissues and binned it.

Middle Meadow Walk was one of her favourite streets in Edinburgh, a pedestrian artery linking the centre with the south, cyclists and students, young mums and the elderly. She had Einstein on the lead as they went past the museum on Chambers Street, down Infirmary Street to the City Mortuary on Cowgate.

It was an unremarkable dark-brick building, boxy seventies design, built on a slope, surrounded by trees in an attempt to hide its purpose from the public. This was where any suspicious deaths came for post-mortems. If you died normally, a doctor signed it off and that was that. This place was for suicides, murder victims and anything else unexplained. Of course it was obvious how the joyrider died, but because the police were involved they needed the post-mortem.

Dorothy went into reception, past the small brass council sign. She pressed the buzzer at reception and waited. Looked at the posters on the wall, mental health, Samaritans, alcohol awareness, drug dangers, trying to keep people from ending up here.

Graham Chapel came through in his white overalls, peeling plastic gloves off. He was a professor of forensics but wore that lightly, seemed more like a friendly plumber or electrician. Greying hair neatly combed back, a barrel chest and wisps of hair poking from the shirt under his scrubs.

'Dorothy,' he said with a smile.

'Graham.'

He nodded at the dog. 'Who's this wee guy?'

'Einstein.'

Graham gave her a look. 'This about the car crash?'

Dorothy nodded.

'Are you OK?' Graham said. 'I heard all about it.'

'Bad news travels fast.'

Graham shook his head. 'There's nothing but bad news here, you know that.' He held the door open. 'Come through. You'll need to tie Einstein up.'

The post-mortem suite was similar to the embalming room back home only bigger. Three metal tables for bodies, a larger bank of fridges, and a viewing area behind glass. Graham opened one of the steel fridge doors and hauled a body tray out. Pulled the cover from his face.

'Did him first thing this morning,' he said. 'No surprises.'

The sheet was far enough down that Dorothy could see the start of the chest incision. Checking the organs and brain was standard post-mortem procedure.

'Died from the blow to the head on impact, severe cranial hae-morrhaging. Would've been pretty much instantaneous.'

Dorothy saw the cut across the boy's forehead, a cut that would never heal now. If the Skelfs did the funeral, Archie would be able to deal with that easily, patch him up and conceal it. She suddenly realised that she really wanted to do this funeral, whether they discovered his identity or not. It was unbearable to think someone else would deal with him. She was frustrated they didn't have a name, she couldn't keep referring to him as the joyrider or, even worse, the homeless guy.

'What's your interest?' Graham said. 'Apart from the fact he gate-crashed your funeral, I mean.'

'The police don't have an ID.' Her hand went out and hovered over the cut on the man's head.

'Join the club,' Graham said. He waved at the fridge bank and over to the lift in the corner which led to a much larger cold storage underground. 'We have an army of the unknown dead here.'

'But I need to find out about this one.'

'Is that his dog out front?'

Dorothy nodded, her hand still near the man's face.

'Well, good luck,' Graham said. He lifted the cover over the man and pushed the tray back into the fridge.

Dorothy's hand remained where it was, like she was blessing empty space.

Sylvan Place was a narrow lane off the south side of the Meadows, Victorian terraces and tenements up one side, the Royal Sick Kids hospital on the other. An ambulance was parked further up outside the entrance to A&E. Dorothy remembered having Jenny in there a couple of times as a kid, once with constant vomiting, another time when she split her forehead open on a skirting board as a toddler. They never got to the bottom of the vomiting, just rehydrated her and sent her home when it stopped. For the head knock, Dorothy got thin stares from the staff, on the look-out for abuse.

She reached number seven in the street, the sliver of garden scruffier than its neighbours, cracks in the paving stones. She looked at the digit painted on the door, the florid font making it look like an upside-down two, like they did in the old days. One of the millions of quirky things about moving to Edinburgh and building her life here, these beautiful old buildings everywhere she turned.

Einstein snuffled around the plants at the front door, chasing a scent. Dorothy wondered what the world looked like to a dog. A dog who'd just lost his owner. Another one of us building a new life.

She rang the bell, a brass button set into the brickwork, and heard the old fashioned ding-dong. There was a shuffle behind the door then it opened.

Abi's mum was short and thin, a little bird of a thing, so unlike her daughter who was already taller. She had sharp features, black hair in a bun, a twitch where she rubbed at her left wrist. Dorothy had met her a couple of times before, once at a school gig where Abi played drums for a covers band. Abi was far too good for the band but no one realised, including Abi and her mum.

Dorothy dredged the name from somewhere, Sandra Livingstone.

'Hi, Sandra.'

The look on her face suggested she didn't recognise Dorothy. Maybe out of context she was hard to place.

'Dorothy Skelf, I teach Abi drums.'

Sandra's eyes went wide. 'Of course, we met at that school thing.'

Dorothy nodded at Einstein. 'I was just walking this guy and remembered where Abi lived. I wanted to check she's OK?'

Sandra stroked at her wrist. 'Yes. Why do you ask?'

'She didn't turn up for her lesson earlier, that's all.'

Sandra looked confused, something about her seemed off. 'Did she have a lesson today?'

More touching of her wrist.

Dorothy remembered when Jenny was Abi's age. Once teenage girls gained that bit of independence they were untraceable for swathes of the day. In Jenny's case it was before mobile phones, of course. A flutter of panic came back to Dorothy from those days.

'She did,' she said. 'I left a message. Is she OK?'

'She's fine,' Sandra said. 'She must've forgotten, you know teenagers.'

'Of course,' Dorothy said. But it was not what Abi was like, not at all. 'Is she in?'

Sandra shook her head. 'Out with friends.'

'Where did they go?'

'Cinema, I think.'

'You don't know?'

'They went to the cinema.'

The door opened wider and a man stood behind Sandra. This was the stepdad, Dorothy remembered. Mike?

'Hi,' he said.

'This is Abi's drum teacher,' Sandra said. 'We met her at that concert.'

Mike nodded.

Sandra went on. 'Abi had a lesson today, she must've forgot.'

Mike nodded again.

Silence while they both looked at each other, then at Dorothy. Einstein gave a whimper at something in a hedge then came to rub against Dorothy's leg.

'When she gets in,' Dorothy said, 'can you tell her to message me? We can reschedule.'

'Sure,' Sandra said.

Mike smiled as he closed the door.

The last thing Dorothy saw was Sandra rubbing at her wrist, looking at her husband. One thing was sure, she was lying through her teeth.

8

HANNAH

She couldn't breathe, tried the relaxation exercises she'd learned when anxiety first bubbled up years ago. Closed her eyes, imagined her lungs as a mechanical pump, a perpetual-motion machine, oxygenating the blood that ran through her body, her brain, her heart.

That heart was thumping as she stood outside the lecture theatre and listened to the chatter inside. Two students from the year below went in and noise spilled out. She looked in. It was almost full, a couple of hundred people. She didn't think Mel was that popular, she was quiet, studious, not exactly a party animal. Or so Hannah thought until she went missing and another side of her emerged. Hannah tracked down affairs and more, painting a picture of a flatmate she hadn't known.

So here she was, expected to say something meaningful to a room of strangers about a woman she thought she knew, a woman she missed more than she would admit. A woman killed by Hannah's dad. What the hell were you supposed to say about that?

She felt a touch on her shoulder and turned. It was Xander, Mel's boyfriend. He had just as much reason to hate all this. Hannah had suspected him at first, accused him, said terrible things.

'Hey,' Xander said. He was tall and lean, still not used to his own physical space in the world. But then the women she knew her age were the same, her and Indy, still discovering their own bodies, each other's. When do you start to feel at home in your own skin?

'Hi.'

Xander nodded at the door. 'This is something, eh?'

'I guess.'

Xander examined her. She saw something in his eyes, the shared loss.

'Let's get it over with,' he said.

Hannah had sweaty palms, rubbed her hands on her jeans.

'It's good that we're honouring her,' Hannah said.

'You think?'

Hannah frowned.

Xander chewed his lip. 'I miss her like crazy. And I'm angry as fuck that she's gone. But all this...' He waved at the door in disgust then looked at Hannah's empty hands. 'What are you going to say?'

'No idea.'

Xander pulled on the door and held it open for her.

She walked past the rows of benches to the bottom. It was too bright in here, too loud. There was a large picture of Mel projected onto the whiteboard screen, her name underneath, 2000–2020. Hannah felt sick. Just two decades, it didn't make sense. She knew about the randomness of life from her studies. But the physical world obeyed rules, at least on a macroscopic level, there were consequences for actions, one thing led to another. But they shouldn't lead to a strangled body found by a dog walker in the bushes on the edge of a golf course five minutes from here.

She looked along the front row but couldn't see Mel's family. Maybe this was too much, still, after six months. Hannah understood that.

Hugh Fowler shuffled towards her. He was short and round, hands thrust in his tatty cardigan pockets, glasses sliding down his nose.

'Hannah,' he said. 'So glad you're here.'

Hannah nodded at the seats. 'No Chengs?'

Hugh dropped his head, looked away. 'They decided not to come.'

Then why the hell am I here? Hannah thought. She looked at the photograph of Mel, it was a snapshot of her in a physics society hoodie and leggings. She would've hated it, she had no make-up on, her hair in a messy pony. She thought about the pictures of Mel she'd discovered in a drawer, naked in a hotel, or on a date with a lecturer, signs of a different life. She thought about the baby Mel was carrying, if she had been far enough along for a scan photo.

She looked round the room. The rows seemed steep from down here, looming over her. The people and the noise, lights overhead buzzing a secret message, the clack of a fold-down seat as someone got up to let another along the line, people wandering in as if this was a lecture on some obscure physics concept, the whole room ready to fall on top of her as she tried to breathe and couldn't, found her hands shaking and felt Hugh's touch on her shoulder, saying something she couldn't hear, his lips moving, then the light at the edges of her vision was fading and she realised she was having an attack but couldn't stop it, then she was on the floor, cheap carpet rough against her knees and her lungs filled with concrete and her vision went black and she was lost.

She heard noises, people talking, moving, the clunk of hinged seats flipping up, the swish of doors. She liked that this was all happening around her and she didn't have to engage with it. She waited as the sounds faded until it was just silence.

'Drink this.'

She caught the oily stink of whisky, felt the glass against her lips. Opened her mouth and drank. Alcohol was always the solution for old people. Have a shock, take a drink, feeling stressed, take a drink, passed out at a memorial, take a drink. She felt the burn, like acid killing her insides.

She opened her eyes. She was still in the lecture hall, but it was empty. The electronic hum of the AV set-up, the buzz of the overhead lights, the taste of whisky.

She lay along seats in the front row, Hugh next to her. A young guy, one of the building's support staff, was sitting on the other side. He was doughy and pale, spots on his forehead. He had a first-aid kit open but looked like he didn't have a clue what to do with it.

She swung her legs round and sat up.

'I'm fine,' she said, though no one had asked.

The young guy looked from Hannah to Hugh, but didn't speak. Hugh gave him a nod and he swallowed and packed away the kit, left without speaking. This was obviously too much for him.

Hugh held out a plastic cup of whisky. She noticed a hip flask and a bottle of water on the floor next to him.

'Another sip?'

She shook her head.

He drank the whisky himself and refilled it from the flask.

'Some water, please,' Hannah said.

He passed the bottle and she drank, looked around. The picture of Mel was still on the screen.

'What about the memorial?'

'Postponed,' Hugh said. 'We were all very worried.'

'I'm so sorry.'

He waved that away, then stared at her. 'How do you feel?'

Anxious, depressed, confused, overwhelmed.

'Fine,' she said.

Hugh smiled. 'Well you look terrible.'

Hannah laughed. 'Thanks.'

She examined him as he took another sip. He was like a friendly wizard, hair a mess, buttons done up wrong, bare patches at his elbows and knees. She wondered if he had someone looking after him, someone to share old age. She was vaguely aware he had a reputation for a significant discovery or theory, something quantum that nudged physics forward. Not quite up there with Professor Higgs, who still sometimes wandered the halls even though he was almost ninety. But something worthwhile all the same. Must feel good.

'Why did you arrange all this?' Hannah said.

Hugh looked uncomfortable. 'That poor girl. What she must've gone through.'

'But you weren't one of her tutors.'

Hugh shrugged. 'No one else was doing anything. I thought her life should be celebrated.'

'That's very kind.'

Hugh looked at her. 'I'm not sure if it was a good idea after all.'

'Why?'

He waved a hand around the lecture theatre. 'This was too much for you.'

Hannah felt her chest tighten, tried to remember how to breathe. 'Everything is too much for me.'

Hugh smiled. 'I feel like that too.'

'Really?' Hannah took a drink of water. 'Don't you have life sorted by your age?'

He let out a loud laugh and sipped whisky. 'If only. The one thing I guarantee, young lady, is that life makes less sense as you get older.'

'Wow, that's really cheered me up.'

'It should,' Hugh said. 'Once you accept that, you can get on with living.'

'You're like a wise little Yoda, aren't you?'

'I prefer to think of myself as a mature Robert Redford.' He smiled at his own joke.

'And I'm Jennifer Lawrence.'

'I don't know who that is.'

Hannah eased off the bench and stood up. Hugh's hand wavered behind her, as if she might fall. Then he let out a breath and stood up too, with some effort.

'I'm sorry about the memorial,' Hannah said, looking at the picture of Mel. There was a smudge on the whiteboard by her head, and she thought about her dad's hands on that neck, squeezing.

'Do you think Mel's in a better place?' she said.

'Heaven?' He seriously considered it. 'Maybe. People think that science and religion are incompatible, but plenty of my colleagues still believe.'

'Do you?'

Hugh pressed his dry lips together. 'I believe there's still a huge amount we don't know.'

'That's not an answer.'

'It's not.'

Hannah filled her chest with air. 'I'm going to counselling.'

'Is it helping?'

'I don't know yet.'

'I did the same when my daughter died.'

Hannah paused, took him in. Imagined the quantum field between them, changed by their presence. 'I'm sorry. Did it help?'

'No.'

Hannah laughed. 'You're really encouraging.'

'Is it better if I lie?'

Hannah looked at him. 'No, it's not.'

He fished something out of his pocket. 'I've enjoyed speaking with you, Hannah.'

He handed her his card, a bunch of letters after his name.

'If you ever want to talk, please call.'

Hannah touched the edge of the card, thought about Mel alive in a parallel universe. 'I will.'

9

Jenny

She put her phone and bag in a locker then went through the metal detector. Signs everywhere saying no electronic devices, metals, liquids or gases. A sniffer dog nudged against her leg. The prison guard with the dog smiled like this was routine, which it was.

HMP Edinburgh had a new brick frontage with the name emblazoned along the top, but everyone still called it Saughton Prison. She'd gazed at the high concrete walls and cameras on poles as she approached, but now inside, the waiting room was like any office, posters on the walls, beige and cream furniture.

She was led through corridors and heavy metal doors by a different guard, a guy Hannah's age, brown shirt and trousers too loose, so that he kept hitching up his waistband. He looked like he was playing dress up. Jenny didn't fancy his chances if a riot broke out.

She followed him down more corridors, back outside through an exercise square, along a covered walkway. They passed two guards with an inmate, no handcuffs, happy and joking, just people going about their business.

She saw a block of cells in the distance, but they turned away to a newer building, through another giant steel door into an open-plan visiting room. Cheap metal tables, arranged four by four across the room, seats either side of each. Most were occupied, prisoners in different coloured sweatshirts, all with the prison crest. She wondered what the different colours meant.

The guard nodded at the far corner. There was Craig staring at the posters on the wall, warnings about drug smuggling, others trying to be motivational. Jenny imagined getting motivated in here.

She stood still, not wanting to go to him. But he sensed her, turned and smiled apologetically, like he was late for a date or something.

She rubbed at her stomach through her T-shirt, touching the scar he'd made there. She stopped, then didn't know what to do with her hands, so just stood there like a robot on standby.

He eased his chair back and stood, pointed at the seat across from him. She didn't move. She'd known him for more than half her life, fallen in love with him, had Hannah with him. This was the man who'd killed a young pregnant woman. Smiling at her like old times, as if they were flirting in the pub, it was always the pub, their relationship steeped in booze.

She unclenched her fists and walked to the table.

'Hi,' Craig said.

She soaked him in. He looked good, had grown a beard that suited him, lost a little weight, maybe.

She sat down and he eased into the seat opposite.

'It's good to see you,' he said.

She shook her head, jaw clenched.

'You look well,' he said.

She couldn't stop swallowing, suddenly too much saliva in her mouth.

He nodded at the door. 'You got through security all right?'

'Yeah.'

She wasn't sure if she'd be allowed to see him given the case, and Skelf was a memorable name, so she booked the visit through her old married name and brought her out-of-date driver's licence. The guards didn't bat an eye. The irony of presenting herself as Jenny McNamara was not lost on her.

He smiled. 'Why did you come?'

He was playing dumb. They knew each other so well, all that shared experience and memory and history. He wasn't dumb, had never been dumb.

'You know why.'

He leaned forward. 'I can't imagine what you must think of me. It can never be enough, but I'm so sorry for what happened.'

Fucking sly, 'for what happened', taking himself out of it, as if he didn't lie and cheat and hurt and kill.

'You did it,' she said through her teeth.

'What?'

'It didn't just happen,' Jenny said slowly. 'You did it. You killed Mel, you stabbed me, you strangled my fucking mum and you would've killed us both.'

He ran a hand through his hair then touched his beard. Shook his head, a tiny movement, almost a shudder. 'I wasn't myself.'

She had to fight the acid rising in her stomach. 'Don't do this.'

He put his hands out to placate her, as if this was an argument about putting the bins out or emptying the dishwasher. 'Don't do what?'

She bit her tongue to distract herself. She leaned in so that their faces were close. Lines across his forehead that she hadn't noticed earlier, but his eyes were still sharp.

'You were absolutely yourself,' she said. 'When we stood in my kitchen and you stabbed me in the stomach.'

She lifted her T-shirt and showed him the scar. Ran her finger along the rubbery flesh, felt the knitted-together muscles underneath and the wire mesh they'd put inside to help her heal. She was unashamed of the extra few pounds she carried on her hips, fuck it, he'd seen it all anyway, and she wanted to shame him.

She tapped the scar. 'When you did this, you were the truest version of yourself I've ever seen. The look in your eyes, you knew what you were doing. And you loved it. You relished it.'

She lowered her T-shirt.

'I wasn't in my right mind,' he said.

'All bullshit was stripped away, all pretence gone, you were yourself, the disgusting animal you really are.'

'Not true.'

'I *know* you,' Jenny said. She waved around the room. 'The guys in here don't know you, the lawyers don't know you, Fiona doesn't know you, a jury won't know you. But I know you, Craig. I fucking see you.'

He nodded. 'You're the only one who gets me.'

She breathed deep, in and out. 'Then change your plea back.'

'I can't.'

'For Hannah's sake.'

Tears formed in his eyes and she felt fury rising. How fucking dare he?

'Plead guilty,' she said.

He put his hands on the table, offering them as if she might take them. Her skin buzzed at the idea.

'I was out of my mind,' he said. 'Diminished responsibility.'

She barked out a laugh. 'You've never taken responsibility for anything in your life. But I'm fucking begging you, please take responsibility for this.'

He went to take her hand and she balled her fingers into fists. She remembered holding his hand in The Pear Tree that night, kissing him against the wall of her mum's house like a teenager even though they were middle-aged and divorced, feeling his body pressed against hers, the familiarity of it, the alcohol making her long for something she used to have.

He'd always been a charmer, always used his smile and twinkling eyes to get what he wanted. From her, Fiona, Mel, everyone. He was repeating the same pattern, excuses, deflecting attention, evading the truth.

'You're the one,' he said.

'What?'

'You said earlier that you see me and that's true. You were always the one, Jenny, the love of my life.'

'Don't you fucking dare.'

'We'll always be linked, you and me, till death do us part.'

'You've got some fucking balls,' she said.

The worst thing was he was right, they would always be linked, by all the tiny gestures, in-jokes, common ground, shared breaths and touches and heartbeats. And always, always, they would be linked by Hannah.

'That wasn't me,' he said.

He was crying now. A tear dropped onto the table and her chest tightened. She dipped her finger in the teardrop and sucked it, hint of salt. She imagined the drop sliding down her throat into her belly, mixing with the acid, a chemical reaction producing an explosion that raged up her throat and out of her mouth, all over him and the table and the room until the whole prison was drowning in her vomited vitriol.

She squeezed her eyes shut, deafened by the roar of blood pounding in her ears. She looked at him, her sight blurry as she lunged across the table, grabbed him by his sweatshirt and hauled him towards her. He didn't resist, let himself be dragged like a cowering dog and she hated that even more, swung a fist into his face that connected with his cheek, then another punch caught his nose, blood spraying across the table, the colour shocking. He didn't put his hands up to defend himself, instead stuck his chin out. She took the invitation and punched, felt the jawbone rattle under his stupid beard. Her vision narrowed and the sound dialled down on the world, there was only the two of them, the purity of their relationship, he was right, they were linked forever, her next punch landed and pain shot from her knuckle up her arm, then there were hands pulling her away, but they couldn't break the connection, she would feel his pain combined with her own forever.

10

DOROTHY

Walter Veitch died with his trousers around his ankles. His wife Annabel got in from nine holes of golf at the Braids and shouted hello. No reply, so she presumed he was out. An hour later she went upstairs and realised the bathroom door was locked. Banged on it. Nothing. She got young Michael from next door to force the door open, and they found Walter face down on the floor in a puddle of his own urine, him and the piss both cold.

A long history of heart disease made it easy for the doctor to certify. He'd handed Annabel a card with the Skelfs' number on it, so here were Dorothy and Archie in the bathroom doorway, the smell in their nostrils. Dorothy had told Annabel there was no need to come upstairs, they could deal with things, but she was here, fascinated by her husband's undignified posture.

'Please, Mrs Veitch,' Dorothy said. 'It's best if you leave this to us.'

Rigor mortis would've begun, so there might be some corpse manipulation to get him into a body bag and downstairs. It wasn't the sort of thing loved ones needed to see.

Annabel stood with her arms folded as if exchanging gossip in the golf clubhouse. 'We knew this was coming. He wouldn't give up the Lorne sausage.'

Salty processed meat aside, Walter looked like a heart attack waiting to happen. Rotund belly, the red face of a heavy drinker, varicose veins in his legs, rolls of flab under his arms. He would be hard to get in the van. Dorothy was too old for this.

'I really think it's better if you leave us to it,' she said, guiding Annabel away from her husband. 'Maybe pop the kettle on?'

Annabel looked disappointed and headed downstairs.

Archie breathed deep. 'Christ, not a lot of dignity here.'

Dorothy remembered finding Jim in a similar situation, dragging his body to bed, putting new pyjama trousers on him, lying with him for hours before calling anyone, hoping to keep reality at bay. Annabel seemed to have no such qualms, but Dorothy was careful not to judge, everyone experienced grief in their own way.

She mopped up the piss with toilet roll, threw it into the bowl, clearing a space for the body bag which Archie unfolded and laid on the floor. They took Walter's arms and rolled him onto the plastic, then zipped up. The handles at the ends of the bag strained as they lifted, Archie reversing down the stairs, taking the majority of the weight, Dorothy trying to keep Walter's feet from clunking on the steps.

Annabel was there when they reached the bottom. 'He's a lump, eh?'

Archie threw Dorothy a look.

'Could you open the door please?' Dorothy said.

They shuffled out to the body van and wrestled Walter inside. It was unusual to collect bodies from people's homes these days, most of their collections were from hospices, hospitals and the mortuary.

They declined tea, despite Dorothy's decoy request earlier, then closed up the van and drove away. In the rearview mirror Dorothy saw Annabel standing at her front gate looking lost.

It didn't take long from the Braids to Greenhill Gardens, ten minutes down Morningside Road. Dorothy looked at the knick-knack shops and gift boutiques, the rich old folk wandering from one to the other. Did any of them suspect there was a dead man in the van?

'Are you OK?' Archie said from the driver's seat.

'I'm fine. Why?'

Dorothy examined him. Archie was a kind man but he had plenty of worries. There was the Cotard's syndrome, the psychological condition that meant he believed he was dead. That was under control, thanks to Dorothy's patience and a clued-up doctor. But the business from six months ago had seen him regress, become less engaged. In the wake of Jim's death, payments from the Skelf business account led Dorothy to discover that Archie had accidentally killed a colleague ten years before after finding him raping a dead woman in the embalming room. Jim covered it up, paying a fake pension to the dead guy's wife. Archie helped Dorothy dig up the necrophiliac's hidden body, to prove it was all true. She hadn't reported Archie to the police, but kept an eye on him. He'd slumped, reliving the guilt, and he looked gaunt these days, going through the motions.

'It's just,' he said now, 'this is the first pick up we've done since Edinburgh Eastern the other day.'

Dorothy looked out of the window, a woman with a tartan trolley bag, a man in red trousers and a tweed jacket entering a fishmonger's. Like a bygone age.

'You saved me,' Dorothy said.

'What?'

'I never thanked you. You pulled me out the way of that car.'

Archie laughed. 'I pulled us both out the way.'

'Thank you.'

'There's no need.'

'Yes, there is.'

They turned at Holy Corner, then a left into their street. Large trees in every garden, expensive family cars and sporty numbers, the families around here could afford both. The Skelfs were lucky they'd had number 0 Greenhill Gardens for a hundred years. People keep dying, there will always be business in helping the bereaved say goodbye.

There was a police car parked in the street outside their house. As they got closer, both of the back doors opened, Thomas climbing from one side, Jenny from the other. A uniformed cop stayed in the driver's seat.

Archie turned into the drive, manoeuvring the van so that the back doors opened to the service entrance.

Jenny lowered her head as she walked towards them, Thomas a step behind.

Dorothy got out of the van and Jenny shook her head as she approached.

'I'm sorry,' she said.

'For what?' Dorothy said.

Thomas caught up and Jenny looked to him, giving permission.

'Jenny was detained today at HMP Edinburgh,' he said, hands out.

'At the prison?' Dorothy said.

Jenny rubbed at the palm of her hand with her other thumb, raised her chin. 'I went to see Craig.'

'Oh, Jen.'

'I couldn't help it.'

Thomas looked from one woman to the other. 'She's been charged with assault.'

Jenny started to cry. 'He deserved it.'

Dorothy wrapped her arms around her daughter. Your child was never too old, you never stopped caring, the weight of it, the glorious, heart-swelling burden.

'I'm sure he did,' she said.

11

HANNAH

Hannah stared at the whiteboards. The funeral one was organised, a series of acronyms after each deceased's name, order in the chaos of grief, reassurance in the way things were done. There was a system, a procedure that people found comforting. It was after the funeral that the bereaved often felt their grief most keenly, once that scaffolding was taken away, nothing to focus on except the absence.

Indy was downstairs now, leading a bereaved woman through that journey, taking her father's details, his funeral preferences, any religion, how he lived his life.

Hannah touched the whiteboard and thought about the thousands of names that had been wiped from it. Schrödinger came in followed by Einstein. He'd been acting like the cat's shadow, despite Schrödinger treating him with disdain. The cat jumped onto the kitchen table and arched his back at Einstein, who stood wagging his tail.

Hannah turned back to the PI whiteboard. At the top was written 'Jimmy X' in Dorothy's handwriting. Below was some stuff about Edinburgh Eastern, the dog, the car number plate.

She heard voices then her mum came in followed by Dorothy. Jenny had been crying, puffy cheeks, wiping her fingers under her eyes.

'What's up?' Hannah said.

Jenny got a drink of water from the sink, Dorothy pursed her lips. Einstein went to her, tail thumping, and she stroked him.

Jenny drank deeply, looked out of the window. 'I went to see your dad.'

'What?'

'In Saughton.'

Hannah felt her cheeks flush. 'Because he called me?'

Jenny clutched her glass. 'He what?'

'I thought Indy told you.'

'She never said anything.'

Of course she hadn't, Indy was loyal and discreet, always had Hannah's back. It was Hannah's turn to stare out of the window. Cherry-blossom trees budding, a man shuffling with his old dog by his side, two cyclists zipping past.

'He called me the other day,' she said.

'From prison?'

'Of course from prison.'

'What did he want?' Dorothy's voice was calm.

'I don't know, I hung up.'

'I can't believe him,' Jenny said. 'What does he want from us?'

'You have to stay calm,' Dorothy said.

'Fuck staying calm,' Jenny said. 'That bastard is playing with his own daughter's emotions.'

'It's OK, Mum,' Hannah said. 'I can handle it.'

'You shouldn't have to.'

'You don't have to protect me, I'm a grown-up.'

Silence for a moment as they all caught a breath.

Hannah looked at her mum. 'So what happened at the prison?'

Schrödinger jumped from the table to the floor, making Hannah start.

'I hit him,' Jenny said.

'Mum.'

'Don't,' Jenny said. 'Just don't.'

Dorothy walked to the table, Einstein tagging along. 'He's pressing charges for assault.'

Hannah's chest tightened. She imagined air bubbles trapped in her blood, giving her the bends, unable to decompress.

'Are you OK?' Jenny said.

She held the back of a chair and slid into it, legs wobbly, arms weak. Einstein came to her and she stroked him, felt his fur between her fingers. 'I'm fine.'

'How did the memorial go?' Dorothy asked.

She thought about not mentioning it. But word would get back one way or the other. 'It didn't happen.'

'Why not?' Jenny said.

She felt like a schoolgirl again, grilled by her mum after coming in late from a party. Jenny always expected Hannah to be blind drunk, but she didn't like to lose control, didn't use alcohol or drugs that way, that was more her mum's deal. And anyway, she'd learned the hard way they triggered her anxiety and depression, threw her into a hole.

'I passed out,' she said, head down.

'What?' Jenny was standing over her now.

'Jenny, sit down,' Dorothy said. 'Let's all just take a moment.'

Hannah sensed her mum hesitating, reaching out a hand, but then the hand dropped and Hannah heard chairs scraping against floorboards.

'I love sitting here with you girls,' Dorothy said.

Hannah looked up. Dorothy was smiling, Jenny worried.

'It reminds me of the day we buried Jim,' Dorothy said. She turned to Jenny. 'The day you moved back here. All three of us around the kitchen table, here for each other.'

'You need to tell us what happened,' Jenny said to Hannah.

'She'll tell us when she's ready,' Dorothy said.

Hannah shook her head. Einstein was still at her feet, the smell of him in her nostrils. 'A panic attack, I think. All those people.'

'You should never have agreed to it,' Jenny said.

Dorothy put a hand out to her daughter. 'Jenny, I know you're worried but you need to stop being so angry.'

Jenny wiped at her face as if there was a mark on it. 'I don't know what to do.'

Dorothy frowned. 'About what?'

Jenny waved a hand uselessly. 'Everything. Craig has changed his plea, he's hassling Hannah on the phone, she's passing out from anxiety, and Mum, you almost got killed the other day and you don't seem bothered.'

'I wasn't almost killed,' Dorothy said, voice level.

'The universe is fucking with us.'

Hannah found her voice. 'The universe couldn't care less about us.'

Dorothy placed her hands on the table. 'Look, I'll speak to Thomas about Craig, see if there's anything we can do.'

Jenny shook her head.

Hannah watched Schrödinger strut past Einstein with his tail in the air. Einstein padded after him, provoking Schrödinger to hiss and arch his back. A stupid game, get attention then turn on someone.

'I think you need distance from it,' Hannah said. She was surprised to hear it from her own mouth.

Jenny slumped in her seat like a teen in a sulk. 'So what should we do?'

Dorothy went to the whiteboards. 'Well, I need help with a case.'

Hannah watched her gran, graceful movements belying her age.

'Jimmy X,' Hannah said.

Dorothy nodded. 'The driver in the cemetery the other day.'

Jenny looked confused. 'What about him?'

'I want to find out who he is.'

'Why?'

'Because no one seems to know.'

'It's not your problem,' Jenny said.

'I'm making it my problem,' Dorothy said.

Jenny went over to the board. 'You called him "Jimmy X"?'

Dorothy nodded.

'You named him after Dad.'

'It's just a name.'

'It's just the name of your recently dead husband.'

'It doesn't mean anything.'

Jenny stared at the board. 'Like fuck it doesn't.'

Einstein followed Schrödinger around the room. The cat climbed onto the back of an armchair at the window, the dog sniffed at the cushions.

Hannah stood up. 'I'd like to help.'

Jenny watched the cat and dog show across the room, then turned back. 'OK, what can we do?'

Dorothy smiled. 'I have the address of the car owner, that's a start.'

'I can speak to him,' Jenny said.

Dorothy went to the kitchen worktop and lifted an old notebook. 'This was in his belongings. Maybe you'd like to take a look, Hannah?'

Hannah took it and felt the dirt on the cover, smelled the damp pages, riffled through them.

'I'll talk to Thomas about Craig,' Dorothy said. Then a look came over her. 'And there's something else I need to look into.'

'Another case?' Hannah said.

'I'm not sure yet.'

Schrödinger slashed out a paw at Einstein, catching his snout, making him yelp and cower. Hannah watched and thought about her mum hitting her dad in a prison visiting room.

12

DOROTHY

James Gillespie's was only five minutes from the house along Warrender Park Road. Jenny went to the same school, long before this new building went up. Dorothy wondered how much physical environment affected learning. Back in Pismo Beach as a kid Dorothy went to a cinder-block public high, seats in rows, strict teachers who remembered the war, sixties rebellion in the air.

That all seemed like a different planet. The reception at Gillespie's was in the new Malala building, kids in black joggers or skirts throwing bags around outside as she approached at break time.

The woman behind the desk was middle-aged, short hair, stern. Maybe the same age as Jenny, but she seemed older. Dorothy wondered if she'd been hardened by this place over the years.

Dorothy put on her old-lady face, angled her head, demure posture.

'Hello, I'm supposed to be meeting Abi Livingstone, she's in S3.'

'And you are?'

'Her grandmother.'

The woman had deep furrows on her brow. 'What's it concerning?'

'She forgot her lunch.' Dorothy lifted the lunchbox to show the woman.

'I can get it to her.'

'I have a message for her too,' Dorothy said.

'Have you tried calling her?'

Dorothy tried to look stupid. 'Her ringer must be off. I suppose they have to do that in class.'

The woman waved at the chaos outside the front door. 'It's break time.'

Dorothy smiled. 'Can you please check what class she has after break? I'll try to catch her on the way in.'

The bell rang, not an old-school ding but an electronic beep like a truck reversing. Herds of kids drove through the doors and into the belly of the school.

'What was your name again?' the woman said.

'Dorothy ... Livingstone.'

The woman looked at the lunchbox in Dorothy's hands. A few teenage girls were hanging around behind Dorothy, waiting to speak to the receptionist. They had crumpled forms in their hands and were arguing about the colour of someone's nails. Two boys flopped in behind them, waiting to give the receptionist grief. That was good, she would want rid of Dorothy. The receptionist turned to her computer, typed briefly, then her frown deepened.

'Abi is absent today,' she said, narrowing her eyes. 'She wasn't in yesterday either. Who are you?'

Dorothy looked around as if she just realised where she was.

'I'm sorry,' she stuttered, a trembling hand raised to her forehead. 'I think I got confused.'

She looked around again for good measure, then turned and walked through the gaggle of girls, the smell of their perfume in her nose.

'Wait,' the receptionist said.

Dorothy reached the door and pressed the release then she was outside in the fresh air, walking in the opposite direction from the kids streaming the other way.

'Hey.'

She didn't look back, sensed kids staring at her. She kept walking at the same pace, clutching the empty lunchbox to her chest, then she went out the front gate and turned right, kept going until the sound of the school had disappeared.

She walked to Abi's house on Sylvan Place. As she passed Sick Kids a woman came out with a young boy, his arm in a cast.

She felt stupid holding the empty lunchbox. Felt her cheeks burn from the receptionist's shouts, wondered about CCTV in the playground.

She reached number seven and rang the doorbell. Didn't know what to do with the lunchbox. The door opened and there was the stepdad.

'I want to see Abi,' Dorothy said.

It took him a moment to place her, then his face fell. He looked behind her as if searching for a rescue party, then stared at his hands.

'She's at school,' he said.

Dorothy examined him. Thinning brown hair swept back, a slight paunch, hunched shoulders. He was tall, big hands, looked powerful despite the hangdog demeanour. She wondered how long he'd been with Sandra, how that transition was for Abi. Hard at the best of times, getting a new dad, never mind muddling it up with puberty and hormones.

'She's not at school,' Dorothy said, her voice firm. 'I just came from Gillespie's, she hasn't been in for days.'

He locked eyes with her. 'Who are you again?'

'Her drum teacher.'

'Why are you checking up on her?'

'I'm worried.'

He hesitated. He was wearing a zip-up fleece, saggy old jeans. He looked like nothing special, but everyone has secrets.

'You've lied to me twice now,' Dorothy said. 'Why don't you just tell me where she is?'

He looked back into the house as if a monster might leap from the hallway. Dorothy wondered about his relationship with his wife. With his stepdaughter.

'She's not here,' he said, pulling on his earlobe.

'Where is she?'

He looked around again, his eyes couldn't settle on her.

'Tell me,' Dorothy said.

'You'd better come in.' He walked towards the kitchen.

She followed, taking in the IKEA artworks, the photo of Abi with her mum in a forest somewhere, the pair of them smiling. Mike wasn't in the picture. He sat at the breakfast bar in front of an old MacBook.

'Where's Sandra?' Dorothy said.

'At work.' He nodded at his laptop. 'I work from home.'

'Doing what?'

He stared at the screen. 'Software.'

Dorothy took the stool opposite him. 'So tell me.'

He looked up. 'She's missing, we don't know where she is.'

'Since when?'

'She left for school two days ago but never arrived. We got the automated call saying she was absent.'

'You've told the police?'

'Sandra spoke to them, they said they'd look into it but don't have the resources.'

'She's fourteen, for God's sake.'

'I know,' Mike said.

'You don't sound too bothered.'

He ran his fingers along the edges of the laptop. 'I'm worried sick.'

Dorothy ran her hand along the worktop, collected a few crumbs and dropped them. 'Maybe I can find her.'

Mike frowned. 'You're her drum teacher.'

'I'm also a private detective.'

'Sandra said you were something to do with funerals.'

'That too.'

'I don't understand.'

The fridge made a clicking noise and Mike jumped.

'Do you want to find her or not?' Dorothy said.

'Sandra says she'll come back. She's done it before.'

'When?'

He shook his head. 'Before I was in the picture. Eighteen months ago.'

Dorothy thought about husbands and wives. She'd had a happy marriage for forty-five years, and when Jim died she discovered he'd been lying to her. Jenny and Craig divorced when he had an affair. Hannah was just starting out with Indy, but who knows?

'What's your relationship like with Abi?'

Mike held out his hands. 'Great. I know I'm the stepdad, there's supposed to be conflict, but we're good. I mean, we're not best friends but we get on fine.'

'What's she like with her mum?'

Mike shrugged. 'You know mothers and daughters. They rub each other the wrong way.'

'You think that's why she ran away?'

'I don't know.'

'What does Sandra think?'

'She says it's nothing to worry about.'

Dorothy sized him up. 'But you're worried.'

'Of course.'

'What have you done to find her?'

Mike waved a hand as if conjuring up a magic answer. 'Called and messaged, tried tracking her phone, nothing. Spoke to her friends, none of them know anything.'

'What exactly did the police say they would do?'

'Sandra dealt with that.'

Dorothy smiled. 'I have a friend in the force, maybe I can help.'

'That would be great, but we can't pay a private detective.'

'Don't worry about it,' Dorothy said. 'Give me her bank details if she's got an account, that's a start.'

He lifted his phone, took Dorothy's number and texted the info. He seemed genuinely concerned. She'd always thought of herself as a good judge of character but the business with Jim made her worry she didn't know people at all.

'What about her biological dad?'

Mike nodded. 'Sandra spoke to him, he hasn't heard from her.'

'What's his name?'

'Neil. Neil Williams.'

'Where does he live?'

'He travels a lot,' Mike said. 'Internationally. Sales.'

'What kind of sales?'

Mike shook his head. 'I'm not his best mate, obviously.'

'But he's based in Edinburgh?'

Mike seemed to wake up as if this had just occurred to him, which maybe it had. 'He has a flat in Leith.'

'Do you know the address?'

Mike shrugged. 'He's in Canada at the moment.'

'Do you have it?'

Mike thought again. Dorothy couldn't work out if it was an act. His eyes widened a little. 'Wait a minute.'

Checked his phone, a few button presses. Then Dorothy's phone pinged.

'I've dropped Abi off there a couple of times,' Mike said.

'Have you ever met him?'

'Just when he's picked her up from here. Like I say, we're not friends.'

'OK.' She had Abi's phone and bank, a name and address for the dad, that was enough for now. 'I'll see what I can do.'

'What will I tell Sandra?'

'Tell her I'm trying to find her daughter.'

13

JENNY

Jenny didn't know why she was supposed to care about Jimmy X. Even the name got her back up, what the fuck was her mum thinking, naming this homeless guy after Dad? Your past was always there, tugging at your sleeve. Your past was smiling across the prison table at you, dragging you and your family into court to testify.

Jenny followed the sat nav on the body van to Sighthill, which took her the back way through Longstone. When she crossed the A71 she realised she wasn't far from the prison. Craig would be in there now, charming some gullible guard into giving him extra privileges. Or maybe his shit didn't work in there.

She reached the address and got out. Broomhouse Road wasn't the worst street in the world, brown pebble-dashed semis, but it was flanked by the rough schemes of Sighthill and Saughton, so no wonder your car got nicked if you lived here.

She rang the doorbell and looked around. Sighthill Park across the way, kids on a scrambler bike, revving it and churning up grass. Next to that, more new-build homes, everywhere you looked in the city, constant regeneration whether folk wanted it or not.

The door opened. Noor Sarwar had a fried chicken drumstick in his hand, a grease stain on the T-shirt stretched over his hard belly. Head shaved, big hands, bouncer material. Jenny felt small.

'What do you want?' he said.

'My name is Jenny Skelf...'

'I'm not buying anything, I'm having my tea.'

He waved the drumstick in her face. She smelled barbecue sauce.

'It's about your car.'

That got his attention. 'What about it?'

'We believe it was involved in an incident.'

Noor's eyes narrowed. 'Who are you?'

'Jenny Skelf, I'm a private investigator.'

It felt crazy saying that, even though she'd been doing it for months. And this wasn't even a case, no one was paying. But in the last six months they'd all got up to speed with the ins and outs of PI work. Mostly it was just being nosy as fuck and using Dorothy's contact at the police. Much of it was boring, spying on people. They got a lot of matrimonial, husbands and wives cheating on each other, how she got to know Liam. She wondered about him now. It was going slow, both of them damaged, but at least it was going. What a life.

Noor's eyebrows had gone up at the mention of a private investigator, and hadn't gone down yet. 'You got a card or something?'

Jenny pulled one out and handed it over. The cards were Dorothy's idea, it was amazing how people took you seriously if you had your name and email printed on a card.

Noor nodded, held the card in his non-chicken hand.

'What sort of incident?'

'A car crash,' Jenny said. 'Fatal.'

Noor waved his drumstick like a baton. 'It was stolen.'

Jenny could hear the television inside the house, something bubbly like *The One Show*, full of good feeling and showbiz guests.

Jenny nodded. 'We think whoever stole your car might be the same person killed driving it.'

Noor shrugged. 'Good. Cunt deserved it.'

Jenny rubbed at her forehead. 'But here's what I don't understand. He had the key.'

'OK.'

'So he didn't hotwire it, he must've stolen the key.'

'Maybe I dropped it.'

'How would he know which car it fitted?'

'Maybe I dropped it next to the car.'

'That doesn't seem likely.'

'Or maybe I left it in the car by mistake.'

'Is that the sort of thing you do often?'

He sucked his belly in a little, squared his shoulders. 'Dunno.'

Jenny sighed and looked round. There was a shit-heap Ford Ka parked in the street. 'Is that yours?'

'What if it is?'

Jenny tried to work out possible angles. 'Is it locked? Insured?'

Noor took another bite of chicken and chewed. He stepped forward so that he was standing over Jenny. She could smell his sweat mingling with the chicken fat.

'You don't need to know how my car got nicked. Things just happen.'

Jenny moved back to get some space, pulled her phone from her pocket.

'Can you just take a look,' she said, flicking through her camera roll. 'Have you seen this guy?'

The picture was one Dorothy got from her friend at the mortuary, so Jimmy X was grey-skinned apart from the cut on his forehead, a red line of raised flesh, puckered like a kiss.

Noor glanced at it and paused. Maybe it was the sight of a dead body, or maybe something else. He swallowed the mouthful of chicken he'd been chewing.

'Don't know him.'

'Are you sure? Maybe a neighbour?'

'Why would a neighbour steal my car?'

'A homeless guy?'

Noor looked across at the park. The kids were still grinding up and down on the grass, skidding the motorbike in squealing turns.

'There's no homeless around here.' He waved the drumstick, mostly just bone now. 'There's no money to be made begging out here. Everyone is already poor as fuck. Better tapping up tourists in town.'

Jenny had never thought about it before but it made sense, although maybe someone down on their luck might expect more empathy out here. But that obviously wasn't the case with Mr Sarwar.

'Are we done?' he said.

Jenny put her phone away. 'Aren't you curious how your car came to be involved in a crash in a graveyard?'

'Wait,' Noor looked confused. 'What the fuck happened?'

Jenny stared at him, wondering about his life. Was there someone to share that KFC? 'He crashed your Nissan into an open grave, there was a funeral happening at the time.'

Noor laughed. 'Sorry, but that's fucked up.'

Jenny pictured the car careering across the cemetery, almost hitting her mum. She remembered attacking Craig and felt that energy in her fists again.

She turned to leave.

'Hey,' Noor said. 'How do I get my car back?'

Jenny didn't turn back. 'You don't, it's a fucking write-off.'

14

HANNAH

Her eyes stung with tiredness. She pinched the bridge of her nose and scrunched her eyes closed and open a few times, stared again at Jimmy X's notebook. She'd got used to the smell by now, musty paper and a hint of wet dog, possibly urine. Her fingers were claggy from turning the pages, her brain sore from trying to decipher his scrawl.

As far as she could tell it was straightforward stuff, a young disenfranchised guy, everyone else's fault. Hannah wondered about that. The few lines she could decode blamed landlords, the local council, the government, social services, school teachers, parents. He was bitter and lonely, alone in the world and looking to belong. Hannah had some sympathy, it was easy for any of us to fall through the cracks of society. She was lucky, she had a supportive girlfriend, Mum and Gran had grounded her when she went through years of teenage anxiety and depression.

Likewise, without that help all the shit over the last six months could've sent her over the edge. The more she dwelt on her dad, the more she felt herself sinking into a black fog. Only Indy, Jenny and Dorothy kept her going, along with the uni counselling. It was so easy to just give up trying to stay afloat. What if you skipped rent and got evicted? What if you couldn't get to work in clean clothes because you couldn't afford to wash them? What if you had nothing to eat and nowhere to live and it was raining hard and that stupid Edinburgh wind was blowing from the west and there was a car you could take and sleep in. Of course you would.

'Come to bed,' Indy said.

Hannah turned and saw her girlfriend in pyjama trousers and vest, brown skin against white cotton, framed in the doorway like a mirage. Her heart swelled as if she'd conjured Indy out of thin air. That would be a useful superpower.

'Just a few more minutes,' Hannah said.

Indy came over and looked at the notebook. 'Getting anywhere?'

Hannah massaged her brow. 'Not really. He was angry.'

'So would you be, in his position.' Indy rested a hand on Hannah's shoulder, rubbed her tight neck. 'We all like to think we'd behave morally if pushed into a corner, but most of us wouldn't.'

'You think?'

Indy shrugged. 'There's plenty of evidence. People stampeding over others to get to lifeboats. It's easy to be moral if those morals aren't tested.'

Hannah waved a hand at the book. 'But this guy was full of hatred.'

'And that would be comforting,' Indy said. 'If you think you've been hard done by, anger is an energy to keep you going. It's easier if your shit circumstances are someone else's fault rather than the alternative.'

'Which is what, that it's your own fault?'

Indy shook her head. 'Random bad luck. Come on, Han, you're always talking about the randomness of the universe, all that quantum stuff, how things can just happen. This is the same on a human scale.'

Hannah angled her head into the neck massage and thought about that. The randomness of the universe underpinned the way she looked at the world, but that was physics not everyday life. That's why people turned to religion or conspiracy theories, as a way to defend against that randomness, a way to impose order on their lives. But she'd never had religion, Indy was a lapsed Hindu, so where did that leave them?

She stood, took Indy's hands and kissed her. Pulled back to look in her eyes and felt guilt. Indy had been through so much, her parents dying in a car crash four years ago, and she was as much a friend of Mel's as Hannah was. And yet Hannah always made it about herself. She was ashamed that she had to make a conscious effort to see things from Indy's point of view, it was a failure of empathy. Indy had no such trouble, so good with the bereaved.

'How was your day?' Hannah said.

Indy nodded. 'Oh, you know, the usual death-infused laugh-fest.'

Hannah smiled. 'You're joking but you love it.'

'I helped Mr Wilson pick out flowers and music for his wife's service,' Indy said. 'He was only a teeny bit racist.'

She put her thumb and forefinger together to indicate something tiny. Hannah copied her. This was a running joke, a way of defusing the unthinking racism that Indy came across every day, especially from old people. You don't have a name like Indira Banerjee in Scotland and go uncommented on.

'He was stationed in Burma during the war, don't you know, has always really liked "my people".'

'Christ,' Hannah said. 'How far is Myanmar from West Bengal?'

Indy laughed. 'A thousand miles through Bangladesh.'

Hannah's smile faded as she put herself in Indy's shoes. Part of the Scottish-Asian community, Edinburgh accent, dead Indian parents, no longer practising Hindu, funeral director, empathetic voice of reason. But the casual racism was interlaced with mis-ogyny, amplified because the funeral game wasn't for women in some people's eyes. If anyone had a right to be losing her shit just now it was Indy. And yet here she was with neck massages when-ever Hannah needed them.

Hannah kissed her stronger than before, trying to make her love obvious.

Eventually Indy pulled away. 'Come to bed.'

Hannah closed the notebook then her phone rang. Her throat

tightened, remembering her dad last time. Checked the screen, Hugh Fowler.

Indy raised her eyebrows.

Hannah bit her lip. 'Two minutes.'

Indy left and Hannah answered. 'Professor Fowler.'

'Hugh, please.' His voice was soft and shaky, like he was apologising for making any sound at all. 'I hope I'm not disturbing you. It is rather late.'

'It's fine.' Hannah went to the window and looked at the neighbouring flats, their rooms lit up against the evening gloom.

'I wanted to check how you were, my dear,' Hugh said.

'OK, thanks.' Hannah realised it was still the same day she'd fainted.

'That's good.' There was a chewing down the line. 'I'm afraid I haven't worked out when to reschedule Mel's memorial.'

'Don't worry,' Hannah said. 'She's not going anywhere.'

'Oh.'

'Sorry, I didn't mean...' Hannah sighed at her own stupidity.

'That's quite all right.'

Hannah heard Indy brushing her teeth in the bathroom, remembered the conversation she had with her counsellor yesterday.

'Hugh, what do you think of quantum immortality?'

A brief silence. 'An interesting idea, but just that, really. That's the trouble with thought experiments, they don't take the real world into consideration.'

'But where do you stand?'

'I don't stand on either side, it's a paradox, that's rather the point.'

'So you're like Schrödinger's cat.'

'I'm not in that situation, thank goodness. I'm pretty sure I'm still alive.'

'But that is quantum immortality. You're alive because you're the observer, and you can only observe yourself if you're alive.'

A cough down the line. 'You're going round in semantic circles.

Your statement can be reduced to "I'm alive because I'm alive". No philosopher worth his or her salt would entertain such a notion.'

Hannah couldn't think what else to say.

'Are you sure you're all right?' Hugh said.

Hannah rubbed at her forehead. 'Just tired.'

'Perhaps you'd like to continue this in person? I do like discussing quantum theory with students.'

Hannah wanted to tell him this was just a way to think of Mel as still alive, but it seemed ludicrous out of context. But she liked the professor, and he was nicer to talk to than a counsellor.

'Sure,' she said. 'Maybe we can get to the bottom of quantum immortality.'

Hugh laughed, a soft sound. 'Well, the best physicists on the planet have failed so far, but yes, that would be lovely.'

15

DOROTHY

The address, Lochend Butterfly Way, couldn't have been less suited to the warren of new-built flats cluttering up a forgotten part of Leith. Each flat had a little balcony with pastel-coloured metalwork looking out over more flats and building work.

It was a quiet corner of the city between Meadowbank and Hibs' ground at Easter Road. Dorothy thought about the car crash two days ago round the other side of the stadium, wondered if the Blackie family were over the shock yet.

She tried to remember what this part of town was like before these flats, but nothing came to her. Bonded warehouses, maybe, or factories. In the distance were stainless-steel skeletons of more apartments, cranes swinging between them like dancing giants. Beyond was the tail end of Salisbury Crags, yellow gorse springing into bloom below clouds nudging each other to the Forth.

She found number five and checked the buzzers, no Neil Williams. Flats three and seven had no names, just numbers. She pressed both and waited. No answer. Pressed again and stepped away from the doorway to look up. She could make an educated guess which was which, but there was no movement at any window.

She pressed the services button, nothing. Then tried number ten and waited.

'Hello?'

'Sorry, delivery for number three.'

Buzzed in. This was a nicely kept place, flowers in plant pots outside the first door, carpeted hallways.

She got to the first floor and looked at number three. Adams and Yong on the door. She knocked, cocked her ear. Nothing. She went up two more flights to number seven. No name. She knocked, looked around. No flowerpots here, just a basic brown welcome mat. She listened. Opened the letterbox and looked inside. Couldn't make out much, a plain hallway, no pictures on the walls, no jackets hanging up, no boots by the door.

She stayed there soaking it in until her back began to ache, then straightened up and checked out the door across the way. Went and knocked there too. Nothing, everyone out at work, these were not flats that shirkers could afford.

She went up another flight and stopped outside number ten. Ferrier on the door. She knocked, waited. Heard a noise inside, young, male, talking to himself. She knocked louder. Eventually the door opened, a boy, early teens, wearing headphones with a mouthpiece and holding an Xbox controller.

'Yeah?'

He was good-looking and skinny, big brown eyes, spots and the start of a moustache. Wearing joggers and a hoodie.

Dorothy had been preparing an excuse for why she was here, why she didn't look like a delivery person with a package.

'I'm trying to find Neil Williams,' she said, nodding downstairs. 'Number seven.'

'Yeah.'

'Do you know if he lives there?'

Shrug. 'No idea.'

'Well, who does live there?'

'Dunno.'

'Is it a man? Woman? A couple?'

His shoulders went up. Dorothy could hear someone else's voice spilling from the headphones.

'Just a minute,' he said, and she didn't know if he was talking to her or the online person. He pressed a button on the cable to mute them. 'What do you want?'

Dorothy sighed. She remembered Hannah at that age, and Abi had a tendency for monosyllabic answers, so she was used to this.

'Number seven, downstairs,' she said slowly. 'Who lives there?'

'No idea.'

'Have you ever seen anyone going in or out?'

'Probably.'

'Who?'

'Don't know.'

She realised now she'd been stupid earlier, hadn't got a description of Neil Williams from the stepdad. She made a mental note to go back and ask. Then she remembered something and pulled out her phone, scrolled through the pictures.

'Ever seen this girl?'

Held up a picture of Abi behind a drum kit from the school show. It was a year old and she'd stretched in that time like teenagers do.

'Maybe,' the boy said.

Dorothy handed over her phone. 'Please take a look.'

He stuck out his lips in a pout, chewed the inside of his cheek, his fingers still twitching over the controller buttons as if playing the ghost of a game.

'Yeah, I think so,' he said.

'You think so.'

'Yeah.'

'Are you sure?'

The boy shook his head, shifting his weight from one foot to the other. Dorothy couldn't decide if it was nerves or just excess teenage energy. He sucked his teeth.

'A lot of folk come and go from that flat.'

'What?'

He shrugged, mumbled. 'What I said.'

'A lot of people? Like, how many?'

'Half a dozen.'

'What kinds of people?'

'All sorts.'

'Teenage girls?'

'Not especially. She's the only one, I think.'

'So who then?'

'Just people, OK?' He looked behind him to the living room. 'Look, I need to go.'

'Shouldn't you be at school?'

He deadpanned her. 'Shouldn't you mind your own business?'

'OK, I just need to know as much as I can about...'

But the door was closed.

She stood staring at the letterbox, the name on the door, then she went downstairs, stopped again at number seven, and wondered about the people coming and going.

Thomas was already at a table outside Soderberg when she got there, a couple of pastries and a pot of tea in front of him. He smiled and got out of his seat to kiss her cheek. He felt solid and she thought about the last time she touched a man in a way that wasn't innocent. Six months since Jim had gone and she hadn't had the urge, not in that way. But Thomas was good company and he was in good shape. Maybe.

He poured tea in an unhurried way, slid a cup over to her.

'Are you OK?' he said.

She was a little confused by the question. 'Sure.'

He frowned at her raised eyebrows. 'It's only been two days since the joyrider thing.'

'Oh, I'm fine.'

'And have you found out anything about him?'

'Jimmy X? I went to see him at the mortuary. Jenny is looking into the car and Hannah has the notebook. We're going to try homeless shelters.'

'You named him.'

'I couldn't keep calling him the joyrider or the homeless kid.'

'But Jimmy?'

'Why not?'

Thomas sipped his tea. 'So why did you want to meet?'

Dorothy smiled. 'Can't a woman sit and chat with her old friend?'

'You only want to chat when you're after police info.'

Dorothy clutched her chest. 'I'm genuinely hurt.'

'OK, so you don't want anything from me,' Thomas said. That Swedish accent, the thick T sound, enough to make him stand out around here, just like her Californian echoes.

Dorothy put on a coy face. 'Now, let's not be hasty.'

She slid a piece of paper across the table. It had everything she knew of Abi's life, her mum, stepdad and biological dad, the addresses of her home and Neil Williams' place.

'Can you check these guys for anything weird?'

'Like what?'

'Abi is missing,' Dorothy said. 'I think she's gone to her real dad, this guy.' She pointed at the name on the page. 'At this address. But something doesn't feel right. I haven't been able to find him and the flat seems off.'

'Off how?'

Dorothy smiled. 'That's what I'm hoping you'll tell me.'

'Is this an actual case or another crusade?'

Dorothy swallowed some tea and put her cup down. 'I teach her drums. She's a good kid and she's gone missing. The parents don't seem that bothered.'

'How old is she?'

'Fourteen.'

'Shit,' Thomas said.

Dorothy reached out and touched his hand on the paper. 'There's something weird about the whole set-up.'

'You're worried.'

'I am.'

'I'll find out what I can.'

'Thank you.'

Dorothy cricked her neck, feeling her bones ache from the thing at the cemetery. Didn't take much these days to wipe her out, a tiny fall, an innocent bug.

'I worry about you,' Thomas said.

'I worry about you.'

He looked confused. 'Why?'

Magpies in the tree above them were clacking to each other, one arriving with a branch in its mouth to add to a nest. New life everywhere at the moment, young parents pushing buggies down Middle Meadow Walk, fresh-faced students easy in their movements.

'You're alone, like me.'

He placed his hand palm up on the table. 'We have each other.'

She put her hand in his. 'Do we?'

'Of course.'

She was a little tired of being friends, if she was honest. Six months as a widow was enough, it wasn't as if she had endless time left. She wanted to suggest that she and Thomas could be more than friends, but, Jesus, she hadn't had to let a man know she was interested in fifty years. But the look in his eyes, maybe he knew already. Maybe he was interested. In a seventy-year-old husk of a woman whose bones ached when she breathed.

Eventually he took his hand away and folded the paper into his pocket.

'How's Jenny doing?' he said.

'She wants me to talk to you about Craig.'

Thomas shook his head. A busker strode past with his guitar on his back. Two businessmen in expensive suits argued as they walked.

'She shouldn't have gone to see him,' he said.

'I know but she's worried, we all are. How could he change his plea?'

Thomas sighed. 'He's got a good solicitor.'

'Could I talk to the solicitor?'

'That's not a good idea.'

'What about the psychiatrist?' Dorothy said. 'Presumably he got a diagnosis about his mental state.'

'I don't think that's a good idea either.'

Dorothy straightened in her seat. 'We can't just do nothing.'

'You need to stay away, all of you.'

Dorothy nodded. An old woman walked past with the help of two walking sticks, rubber bases on them, moving slow. That would be Dorothy soon, forced into a slow-motion world. She looked at Thomas and he raised his eyebrows. He knew what was coming, it was good to have someone who knew you like that.

'Maybe,' Dorothy said. 'You could find out the psychiatrist's name for me.'

Thomas moved his tongue around his teeth as if he was thinking about it, but she knew he wasn't.

'Just the name,' she said, innocent eyes.

'So this was just a little chat between friends,' he said. 'No ulterior motive at all.'

16

JENNY

She watched as Liam slid out of bed and pulled his shorts on. She reached out and ran a finger down his spine, across the muscles of his back.

He looked back and threw her a smile. 'I have to get back to work.'

He stood and put his shirt on, then the suit. He'd come over on his lunch break, although they didn't eat anything. One of the benefits of being self-employed for Jenny, and having your bedroom in the same building you worked in. She looked out of her window now, cherry trees, crows hopping from branch to branch, sun trying its best through the clouds.

She looked back at Liam. She didn't want to be the woman lying in bed, asking the man to stay, but she wanted him to hang around all the same. She didn't know what this was between them, but it was something. She cared about him, believed he cared about her too, and he made her come. Several times.

She got up and ran a hand across his bum as she went to her clothes on the floor. She dressed quickly so he didn't see how inelegant she was, the creases of her belly as she bent over. She straightened up and saw that he'd been watching the whole time.

She walked him downstairs, the vague smell of sex lingering.

Indy raised her eyebrows at reception. 'Nice lunch?'

Jenny smiled. 'Great, thanks.'

Indy widened her eyes at the lie. Liam seemed oblivious, either being discreet or he really didn't twig that Indy knew.

'Call me,' he said, kissing Jenny longer than necessary.

She'd wanted to use him as a sounding board for this shit with

Craig. But when he'd arrived she couldn't bring herself to go into all that. Talking was useless anyway, talking about the bad things in your life just made you focus on the bad things. And she didn't want Liam to think she was still hung up on Craig. But that was stupid, Liam had just divorced, he understood how an ex was still a big part of your life even if you fucking hated them.

Liam eventually pulled away, then he was gone.

'You look happy,' Indy said.

'Don't tell Hannah.'

'She'll be glad to know you're getting some.'

'It's more complicated than that.'

'I don't think it is,' Indy said. 'You don't give her enough credit sometimes.'

Jenny was glad she could talk to her daughter's girlfriend. She tried to imagine a similar conversation with a boyfriend if Hannah were straight.

'She's much smarter than me,' Jenny said. 'You both are.'

'That's right,' Indy laughed. 'Gen Z will save you all.'

The phone rang and Indy put a hand on the receiver.

'Oh,' she said. 'Archie wanted a word with you or Dorothy.'

'Where is he?'

Indy angled her head towards the embalming room as she answered the call.

Jenny walked along the corridor then stopped in the doorway.

'Christ, Archie,' she said quietly.

Archie had a young girl on the embalming table, maybe ten years old, and he was reconstructing her skull. The skin and scalp were pulled away from the head, the brain in a tray on the trolley next to the table. There was a lot of damage to one side of the brain, the same with the shattered skull bone. Dead bodies didn't faze Jenny but a ten-year-old girl was hard to take.

Archie looked up. He was trying to glue a piece of skull into place, holding it with gloved hands, his mouth a thin line.

'Evie Brockhurst,' he said. 'Hit by a bus crossing the road.'

Jenny walked in, could see flesh and bone, the empty eye sockets. The rest of the body seemed mostly unharmed, two arms, two legs, torso intact, just a long bruise along her shoulder.

'Fuck,' Jenny said. 'How are the parents coping?'

'Dorothy says they're not.'

Jenny thought of Hannah at that age. She remembered grabbing her arm as she stepped into the road on Portobello High Street, a white van speeding past. Remembered catching her as she stumbled on Arthur's Seat one time. If something had gone differently, a moment of imbalance, a gust of wind, Hannah could've been on this slab.

Jenny couldn't take her eyes from Evie's skull, Archie's delicate touch as he fitted another piece of skull into place. Jenny had watched him work like this before, this was above and beyond the usual embalming stuff, and there weren't many in the country who could do cranial reconstruction. What was missing from the skull could be replicated by plaster, various methods of keeping the skull's integrity, hopefully making her look in the coffin like the girl she was when alive. Their job was much harder now there were so many open caskets. That hardly ever happened when Jenny was growing up but the trend was growing all the time.

Jenny reached out and touched Evie's cold hand, the delicate fingers, chipped nail varnish, skin shrunk on the bone. Archie hadn't embalmed her yet, reconstruction work first. Eventually these hands would look more lifelike. Not that it would make any difference to Evie's parents.

Jenny rubbed the back of Evie's hand and swallowed. 'Indy said you wanted to speak about something.'

Archie nodded, didn't look up, concentrating on the work. 'That's right.'

Jenny wondered about Archie's Cotard's, if it was ever really under control. Working with dead bodies must be bad for him, but he said the opposite, that it helped him come to terms with the fact he wasn't dead himself.

'So what is it?' she said.

'I have another funeral to go on the books.'

'OK.'

They sometimes got referrals from friends, word spread in a small city like Edinburgh and if you did a good job on someone's funeral it led to more work.

'Who is it?' Jenny said.

Archie paused, still holding a piece of Evie's skull in place, his other hand cradling her head. He kept his eyes on what he was doing.

'My mum,' he said.

17

HANNAH

She was back in the lecture theatre she'd fainted in, this time in a cosmology class with Dr Harper, a grey middle-aged man with a paunch who thought a dreary monotone was the best way to convey the wonders of the universe. Having said that, Hannah also hated the Brian Cox approach, standing on a windswept mountain saying we're all made of stardust. That was true, of course, but so banal. We all come from the big bang, but where do we end up? Scientists used to think we'd collapse into nothing, a big crunch, but recent evidence suggested the universe might expand forever, constantly cooling until the massive expanse was too cold to support life. Matter would be so spread out and energy leaking into black holes that we would end in a meaningless no-thingness, a void of existence, a big chill. Physicists sometimes called that 'heat death' but Hannah preferred the big chill.

Dr Harper was talking about dark matter and dark energy. The start of this course was fun, finding out how galaxies were made, but as it had gone on it became clear how little we actually know. The fact that all we can detect of the known universe is less than five percent of it seemed like a massive cop out. Then again, with her many-worlds idea for Mel, maybe those other dimensions were the dark energy we couldn't detect.

Hannah had plenty of her own dark energy. She saw Xander across the room, head on the desk, eyes closed. She looked around and felt lonely. She'd thought she was part of a team in the physics department, but Mel had been her only real friend on the course. Now she was out in the cold. And she didn't mind, to be honest. She resented the other students, still alive and coming to boring lectures, still going out socialising and studying together and going to that stupid Quantum Club that she joined because of Mel but she'd never been back to because it seemed pointless.

Yeah, she had plenty of her own dark energy, thank you.

Dr Harper was droning on about quintessence theory, a theoretical model for dark energy, a scalar field that tied into observations about the universe's acceleration. Possibly a fifth fundamental force, but there was no evidence for it yet. Hannah had got excited about physics at school because it seemed to provide answers. The neatness of solving an equation, the perfect way classical mechanics could be applied to everyday problems and give elegant yet simple solutions. But this stuff was pie in the sky, the closer you looked at the fundamental nature of things, the fewer answers you got.

She could relate. More dark energy.

Dr Harper checked his watch and finished and everyone woke up, got their stuff together and left. She watched everyone go, daring them to make eye contact, but no one did. She was the woman who fainted, the woman whose dad killed their classmate, the woman who worked at a funeral director's and private investigator's. Weirdo.

She packed her bag and left. Checked her phone then decided to go and see Hugh Fowler, what the hell. He was easy to talk to, not like most people.

She pulled Jimmy X's notebook from her bag. She hadn't tried to get any more out of it last night but it had a hold over her, as if there were secrets inside. Maybe just more dark energy swirling around her head, penetrating her body millions of times a second like cosmic rays, the dark neutrinos stripping all hope from her quarks, her atoms, her soul.

Jeeze, she needed to lighten up.

She took the stairs up two flights to the top floor, looking for room 442. One side of the corridor was small offices, grad students sharing three or four to a room, members of staff in pairs, senior staff with rooms of their own. The other side was labs – optics, condensed matter, fluid dynamics. First years in protective glasses fiddling with light sources or clamps, computers in a row.

She walked through swing doors, found the room, knocked and waited. No answer.

Knocked again.

Waited.

She remembered being on this floor six months ago, walking into another lecturer's office and finding pictures of him with Mel. She'd exposed him, thinking he'd killed her, but he was only having sex with her. His wife threw him out, the university dropped him and he killed himself.

Dark energy.

She knocked a third time and listened.

Heard a gentle thud.

'Professor Fowler?' She swallowed. 'Hugh?'

She cleared her throat and looked up and down the corridor, then turned the handle and opened the door.

He looked asleep, head on the desk, but something about the way his arms were positioned made her step inside. She glanced round the room, shelves of textbooks, notepads, journals. A poster of the Milky Way on one wall.

She stepped up to the desk. 'Hugh?'

It was only then she noticed the froth at his mouth.

'Hugh.'

In one hand he held a gold medal with something engraved on it. In his other was a small vial.

No, no, no.

She touched his hand, still warm. Felt for a pulse, pushed hard with her fingertips, as if she could conjure it with force.

Nothing.

'What the hell,' she said.

She lifted the vial from his fingers and held it up. 'Hydrocyanic acid' written on it. She caught a whiff of almonds and felt dizzy, her head spinning, tongue sweating, bile rising in her throat. She dropped the vial and pulled her jumper over her nose and mouth, backed away from Hugh and the desk and the poison, bumped into the doorframe as she staggered, nauseous and disoriented, then out through the doorway until she hit the opposite wall and sank to her knees.

18

DOROTHY

The whiteboards were getting full. Dorothy stepped back holding the marker pen and stumbled over Einstein lurking behind her. She apologised to the dog and scritched under his chin. The funeral board had more names, Walter Veitch, Evie Brockhurst and now Archie's mum, Veronica Kidd. Dorothy felt awful that she hadn't seen Archie since the news. She was frustrated that Jenny hadn't got all the details of Veronica's death, just that it was cancer, they had to pick the body up from the Marie Curie hospice in Frogston. That made Dorothy even more annoyed, that Archie hadn't spoken about what was happening with his mum. It was up to him, of course, but after all they'd been through she was sad he hadn't confided in her. She wondered if he would do the embalming.

When Jim died he hadn't wanted embalming, eschewing all the funeral protocols to be cremated on a pyre in the back garden. Dorothy wondered about that, Jim spending his life caring for the bereaved, carrying out the traditions only to abandon them for himself. Christ, if anyone knew about grief it was Dorothy, and her heart ached right now for Jim, and for Archie, what he was going through.

'What are you thinking, Mum?'

Jenny sitting at the table brought Dorothy back to reality. She turned.

'There's so much death.'

Jenny laughed. 'We're a funeral director's.'

Dorothy smiled. 'I know, it's just...'

She sat down opposite and tapped the marker pen against the table.

'Who's Abi Livingstone?' Jenny said.

Dorothy followed her gaze to the PI board, where Dorothy had written Abi's name. She had the names of Abi's mum, stepdad and biological dad underneath.

'One of my drummer girls,' she said. 'She's missing. I think she's gone to find her biological dad. At least I hope she has.'

'The parents hired you?'

Dorothy shook her head. 'I just need to find out.'

Jenny frowned. 'Like your joyrider.'

Jenny had already got Dorothy up to speed on the car owner. She reached over and plucked a loose hair from Dorothy's cardigan, and they both watched it drift to the floor. Dorothy still thought of herself as blonde but she'd been grey for a long time. The evidence of her body contradicted her mental image of herself, her aches and pains doing their best to remind her exactly how old she was. Maybe it was time to give up on all this, the mysteries, the missing and unknown, the dead and grieving. But she couldn't give up, she would die if she retired, and that realisation came with its own deep melancholy.

'So what did Thomas say about Craig?'

'He's going to try to get us a meeting with Craig's psychiatrist.'

'Not the solicitor?'

Dorothy rolled the pen between her hands. 'He doesn't think that's possible.'

'And my assault charge?'

'I'm sorry,' Dorothy said.

She felt guilty, unable to protect her daughter. That never went away. She heard the front door slam then footsteps up the stairs. Hannah appeared in the doorway, eyes puffy, cheeks red.

'What's up?' Dorothy said, already dreading the answer, feeling it tighten her stomach.

Hannah walked over and took the marker pen from her hand, went to the PI board and wrote 'Prof Hugh Fowler' and underneath, 'hydrocyanic acid'.

Jenny stood up. 'What's that?'

Hannah burst into tears.

19

JENNY

Ann Street was tasteful, rich Edinburgh, two rows of neat Georgian terraces in Stockbridge, some running to three floors and a basement, costing a packet but not ostentatious. Tasteful shrubberies on the steps leading to front doors, the original setts on the road, top-of-the-range family cars parked in the street.

Jenny found number eleven and rang the doorbell. Fiona answered looking bedraggled but somehow still elegant. She was wearing a St Andrews Uni sweatshirt that was too big, denim shorts, bare feet.

'You came,' she said, voice flat.

She walked inside, which Jenny took as an invite. She glanced up the spiral staircase and followed Fiona's tight ass into the living room, where a huge glass of white wine was sitting on a teak coffee table, almost empty, ring marks on the wood.

It was 10.00 am.

'You want one?' Fiona said, lifting a bottle from the floor and topping up.

'No. Thanks.'

'The sun's past the yardarm somewhere, right?' Fiona said, swigging.

Jenny looked at the abstract art on the walls, the stylish open-plan kitchen.

Fiona flumped into a cream sofa. Wine spilled on her hand, which she sucked at. 'Sit.'

Jenny sat opposite, ran her tongue around her mouth.

'We're fucked,' Fiona said, and took another drink.

Jenny raised her eyebrows waiting for more.

Fiona waved the glass around the room. 'A PR company stands or falls on its reputation. Can you imagine what Craig's bullshit has done to the company?'

Jenny sat with her hands in her lap.

'But we deserve it,' Fiona said. 'I mean, what does fucking PR matter when that poor young woman is dead.' She drank again. 'We'll have to sell this place, of course. And I'll need to take Sophia out of Edinburgh Academy. She'll be heartbroken.'

She ran a hand through her hair, scratched behind her ear. 'I need this divorce to straighten things out but his solicitor is being a prick. And now the sudden court case coming up.'

Jenny frowned. 'Have they set a date?'

Fiona's eyes went wide. 'Didn't they tell you? They got a slot, rush job. After six months of fuck all he's in court for the first hearing or whatever it is in three days' time.'

Jenny shook her head. 'That can't be right.'

Fiona sucked her teeth. 'It's not like the trial proper, just a plea thing.'

'So we won't have to give evidence.'

Fiona drank. 'You really need to speak to your solicitor.'

Jenny didn't have a solicitor. Fiona meant the prosecution, but they were useless at getting in touch and Jenny had tried to forget about it. Until Fiona turned up with the news he was pleading not guilty.

'I assaulted him,' Jenny said.

Fiona froze with the glass at her lips.

Jenny swallowed. 'I went to see him in prison.'

Fiona lowered her glass and leaned forward. 'Holy shit. What was he like?'

Jenny looked at the painting behind Fiona's head, bright red with slashes of yellow. It looked angry.

'He played me,' she said. She hadn't admitted this to Dorothy or Hannah but if anyone understood Craig like Jenny did it was his current wife. 'He played innocent. Can you fucking imagine?'

'Oh, yes.' Fiona's eyes were alive for the first time since Jenny walked in.

'I fell for it, got angry. Next thing I knew my fist was in his face.'

Fiona raised her glass in a toast. 'Bravo.'

'He's pressing charges for assault.'

Fiona looked out of the window, eyes watery. 'He's always got what he wanted, hasn't he?'

'We let him.'

'We did,' Fiona said. 'I'm sorry I took him from you.'

Jenny laughed. 'I'm not.'

Fiona smiled, wiggled her nose. 'I was horrible. I didn't give a shit who I was hurting when I started things with him. He pursued me and I liked it, isn't that fucking awful?'

Jenny sat back in the seat, felt the expensive upholstery. 'You don't have to apologise.'

'Of course I do. He was married, had a daughter already, and I didn't give a fuck. Some member of the sisterhood.'

Jenny swallowed. 'I kissed him.'

Fiona frowned. 'How do you mean?'

'The night he stabbed me,' Jenny said. 'And one time before that. We got drunk and I kissed him. I was going to fuck him if Hannah hadn't got in touch about Mel.'

Fiona sat still. 'Shit.'

'It was partly revenge, I wanted to hurt you. I knew he had you and Sophia, I just didn't care.'

'It's not us,' Fiona said. 'Remember that, it's him.'

'He played me, just like he did in prison. He dialled up the charm, pretended to be interested again, we fell back into old patterns. It felt so comfortable, to be with someone who knew me.'

'He's a charming snake.'

'But he was only doing it to keep tabs on what we'd found out about Mel, what the police knew.'

Fiona finished her wine and topped up. Jenny looked at the glass with envy, that would make things easier.

'Stop it,' Fiona said. 'Listen to us. We're talking about him again, that's what he wants, that's why he's changing his plea. He can't stand the idea we might forget him.'

Jenny's eyes were wet now and she felt a tear drop onto her hand.

'But I can't forget,' she said, touching her stomach, feeling the scarred skin.

'Me neither. It's pathetic, isn't it?'

Jenny wiped the tears from her cheek. 'To us he's just a fucked-up ex, but he's Hannah and Sophia's dad.'

Fiona sighed, a sound from the bowels of the earth.

A delivery van rumbled along the setts outside, sparrows flitting between trees.

'What can we do?' Fiona said eventually.

Jenny shook her head. 'I have no idea. I tried to get a meeting with his solicitor but it's a non-starter. I have the name of the psychiatrist who gave him the diagnosis to change his plea.'

'He won't speak to you,' Fiona said.

Jenny rubbed her hands together in her lap, felt them wet from her tears.

'I'll make him talk to me,' she said, but her voice had no conviction.

20

DOROTHY

Dorothy dipped the last of her cabbage dumpling in the sharp sauce and popped it in her mouth as she looked out of the window across the road. She was in Tea House, a no-nonsense Chinese café on Clerk Street, and she was watching Warners Estate Agents on the corner of Patrick's Square, where Sandra Livingstone worked. She could see her now at a desk in the office, chatting to a prospective buyer or seller. Dorothy sipped green tea and looked around. Old plastic tables and chairs, peeling wallpaper, chatter from the kitchen mingling with the smell of ginger and garlic.

Outside the window buses queued at the stop, the pavement a throng of students and locals. She loved this part of town, upmarket cafes next to nail salons, scruffy old pubs cheek by jowl with fancy sweet shops, acupuncturists, a skate shop, vintage clothes, vaping joints, Drum Central, a circus equipment store with a unicycle in the window. A huge Chinese supermarket along from the old art deco Odeon, boarded up and waiting for a new life.

She checked her watch. A bus peeled away, unblocking the view, and Sandra's seat was empty. Dorothy watched a minute longer, finished her tea, put money down for the bill. Sandra left the office pulling a jacket on and headed up the street. Lunch break.

Dorothy followed at a distance, hidden in the crowd. Sandra dived into Tesco Metro and Dorothy followed, saw her choosing a sandwich from the refrigerated section. She didn't look like someone whose daughter was missing. But that was unfair, we all put on a front, we all have to get on with our lives. But if Jenny had gone missing when she was fourteen, Dorothy would've spent every waking moment on the streets trying to track her down.

Dorothy left as Sandra paid at the till, waited in the gloomy vennel round the side of the shop, then emerged as Sandra came out and walked into her.

'Sorry,' Sandra said, then realised who it was. Her face fell.

Dorothy didn't try to pretend it was coincidence, she just wanted an honest reaction from Sandra when she saw Dorothy. Now she knew she wasn't welcome.

'Oh, hi,' Dorothy said.

Sandra had the scowl in place. 'What do you want?'

Dorothy kept her face bright. 'Any news on Abi?'

Sandra moved her Tesco bag from one hand to the other, ran fingers through her hair. 'No.'

'I spoke to Mike about her.'

'He told me.'

'And I went to see Neil Williams.'

Sandra swallowed.

'Didn't Mike tell you?' Dorothy said. 'He gave me Neil's name and address.'

Sandra's teeth were gritted. 'Neil's out of the country.'

'So I gather.'

'He travels a lot.'

'Doing what exactly?'

'Sales.'

'That's quite vague.'

'He's my ex-husband, I don't keep tabs on him.'

'But you've spoken to him since Abi went missing.'

Sandra shook her head. 'What's the point, he's out of the country.'

'So you said.'

'What's that supposed to mean?'

Dorothy splayed her fingers out. 'Would you happen to have a phone number for him?'

Sandra narrowed her eyes. 'Why are you so interested in this?'

'Your daughter's missing, Sandra.'

'You think I don't know that? You think I'm not worried sick?' Her hand was at her temple, pressing hard. The vein under her fingertips throbbed. 'You seem to think you care more about my daughter than I do.'

'I don't think that.'

'Please,' Sandra said, voice shaky. 'Leave me alone.'

She started walking and it took Dorothy a while to catch up on the busy pavement.

'I was wondering,' she said. 'Even if Abi's biological father is away, maybe she's staying at his place?'

Sandra was outside a fabric shop, bright sari material shimmering in the window. She shook her head and stopped walking with a rustle of her shopping bag. 'She doesn't have keys.'

'Maybe Neil gave her a set.'

'He never did that.'

Dorothy saw something in Sandra's face, a flicker in the eyes. 'So you have spoken to him?'

This got a big sigh. People skirted past them as they stood like rocks in a stream, gradually worn down by the water, millennia of erosion, the degradation of the self. Dorothy felt suddenly tired and sensed the same deep-boned fatigue in Sandra.

'Not that it's any of your business, but yes, I have,' Sandra said.

Dorothy raised her eyebrows.

'He hasn't heard from her, hasn't given her keys and has no idea where she is.'

There was something rote in the way she delivered the line.

'And you trust him?' Dorothy said.

'Pardon me?'

Dorothy smiled. 'Well, he's your ex-husband for a reason. Do you trust him?'

Sandra frowned, almost puzzled. A young man bumped her with a backpack and apologised, but Sandra stared at him like she would swing her lunch at his head. She turned back to Dorothy but it felt like the thread of their conversation was broken.

'He wouldn't lie about this,' she said.

Dorothy thought about what the neighbour said in Leith, lots of people coming and going at that flat.

Sandra gathered herself and went past Dorothy. 'I have to get back to the office.'

Dorothy touched her arm and she shook it off. 'What about Mike?'

She stared at Dorothy. 'What about him?'

'Do you trust *him*?'

Sandra's jaw went tight. 'What are you implying?'

Dorothy breathed in and out. 'A stepdad-stepdaughter relationship isn't easy.'

Sandra pointed a finger and angled her head, trying to keep herself in check. 'This has nothing to do with you. Leave us alone.'

Dorothy held her hands up, two passing teenagers giving her a sideways glance. They were about Abi's age, and she wondered if they were on their lunch break or bunking off.

Sandra strode across the road, dodging a taxi and a van. Dorothy watched her all the way to the office then stood wondering about all those empty properties the estate agents were trying to sell. All those properties Sandra had keys for.

21

HANNAH

'So how have you been since last time?' Rita said.

Hannah looked around the bright counsellor's office and felt like her head was going to burst. A sick laugh escaped her mouth, shocking her, so cynical. She didn't want to be cynical, but what was the universe doing to her?

She looked out of the window and tried to breathe, imagining her lungs as a mechanical device, her heart just a pump doing its job, not trying to crawl out of her chest and strangle her. It was a stupidly bright day out there, pink and white explosions of cherry blossom along the Meadows' pathways.

Rita shuffled on her plastic seat in a leather skirt.

Hannah smiled. 'Let's see, since I spoke to you last my murderous dad called me from prison, my mum then visited him in prison and assaulted him and he's pressing charges. I passed out at Mel's memorial service, which was then cancelled, and a lovely old professor in the physics department has killed himself. And I found his body.'

She felt sorry for Rita, having to deal with this shit. Hannah would never make a good counsellor, the idea of separating yourself from the problems of others, she couldn't handle it. She didn't know how Indy coped with the funerals, the bereaved, all that emotional stuff. Didn't it grind you to dust?

Rita had a notepad open on her crossed knee, the pen wavering above it, but she didn't write anything, just stared at Hannah. 'Jesus Christ.'

'I know, right?'

'If I were you, I would be in bits.'

Hannah felt her fingertips tingle, flexed her hands in and out, swivelled her wrists. 'Yep.'

Rita looked like she'd been hit by a bus. 'I don't know what to say.'

Hannah bit her lip, harder than she meant to as tears formed behind her eyes.

'Hugh drank acid,' she said. 'That's the professor. The same acid Schrödinger mentioned in his cat experiment.'

Rita frowned. 'Does that mean something?'

Hannah went wide-eyed, held her arms out. 'I really wish I knew.'

'You spoke about Schrödinger last time,' Rita said, flicking through her notebook. 'The many-worlds theory?'

Hannah shook her head. 'Stupid wishful thinking. The idea that every moment splits, and somewhere there's a parallel universe where Mel and Hugh are alive. How is that any different from believing in heaven?'

Rita shrugged, left space for more comment.

'It isn't,' Hannah said. 'I used to love physics, the big ideas, the way equations flowed, the logical sequence of cause and effect, but it's all bullshit. We know nothing about the physical universe, even less about the emotional one.'

'You're understandably upset.'

Hannah sat forward. 'I'm understandable, that's good. At least something is.'

Rita nodded to herself, a non-committal, sounding-board gesture that was meant to convey she was really listening.

'Say something,' Hannah said.

'Remember the de-stressing techniques we talked about.' Rita put the notebook down. 'Breathing, calming.'

'Being calm is not an option here.'

Hannah's chest was tight, and she remembered standing in the lecture theatre for Mel's memorial as the world went black.

'Tell me about passing out,' Rita said, mind reader that she was.

'Stress.'

'Have you seen a doctor?'

Hannah sighed. 'The pills don't work, I did that before. I know my own body and mind better than any GP.'

'And yet you're passing out from stress.'

Hannah sat back, crossed her legs. 'I can't help it if my life is stressful.'

'I'm just trying to help.'

Lungs, heart, do your job, stop trying to choke and strangle me.

Rita smoothed her skirt, left her hands in her lap. 'Do you want to talk about your dad?'

Hannah remembered their conversation from last time, *Bladerunner* and replicants. The police interview at the start of the movie.

She formed her hands into a gun shape, pushed her index fingers into her own mouth, spoke through gritted teeth.

'Let me tell you about my father, right?'

She made the sound of a gun firing and jerked her head back, then smiled.

'So you found him.'

It was a statement not a question, but Hannah felt she had to answer.

'Yeah.'

'I'm so sorry you had to see that.'

Hannah frowned. She was in the gloomy front room of Hugh Fowler's house on Lygon Road, round the corner from King's Buildings. She'd walked past the street sign a hundred times leaving campus, always imagined it was called Polygon Road with a couple of letters fallen off. She'd never been down the street until today, when she got the call from Hugh's widow, now pouring tea into china cups.

Wendy Fowler was the female equivalent of Hugh, in her eighties, small and compact, cardigan with thinning elbows, the bulge of a tissue tucked into her sleeve. Her comfy slacks were pulled too high, the jumper underneath the cardigan making her body seem like a stuffed toy. She had wispy white hair and wore a pearl necklace. She added milk to the tea and passed it over with a steady hand. Offered a plate of biscuits, pink wafers.

Hannah shook her head. 'I'm sorry for your loss.'

Wendy pressed her lips together and poked the tip of her tongue between them. 'I don't know.'

That was such a general statement Hannah didn't know what to do with it.

On the walls were colossal, detailed maps of Greenland, Baffin Island and Svalbard. They were framed and hung as a triptych.

Wendy saw Hannah look at them.

'We used to love exploring,' she said. 'When we were younger and fitter.'

Hannah tried to imagine being with Indy until they were that age, sixty years of shared experience, thrown away with a single swallow of acid. She pictured herself and Indy in matching cardigans, tramping over Greenlandic glaciers, spotting a polar bear in the distance, gazing at the northern lights in the crystal night. She pictured finding Indy slumped over a desk with foam coming from her mouth.

Hannah tried to breathe. 'I don't know what to say.'

'You don't have to say anything.' Wendy sipped her tea.

'You don't seem very upset.'

Wendy waved a hand around the room. 'This is all so small, don't you think?'

'I don't understand.' Hannah drank her tea and wondered if it was laced with something. She was still getting olfactory flashbacks to the almond smell of Hugh's acid bottle. She smelled it wherever she went, imagined poison in her veins.

Wendy waved at the maps. 'Those great expanses, the ice sheets, the tundra. The scale of it.' She turned to Hannah. 'We both lived very long and full lives. Lives full of love, too.'

'So why end it?'

Wendy smiled. 'Why stick around? We have no children or grandchildren to hang on for.'

Hannah thought about what Hugh said on the phone about losing a child. She swallowed hard. 'But why would he leave you?'

Wendy placed her cup and saucer down carefully. 'That's the wrong way of looking at it.'

Hannah had never felt more out of step with the universe than right now, talking with an existential widow and drinking probably poisoned tea in a dead man's parlour.

Wendy got up slowly and went to the Svalbard map. 'Do you know about the Global Seed Vault?'

Hannah felt a shudder through her, she was losing her grip. 'Sorry?'

Wendy tapped the map. 'On Svalbard. The Norwegians built a giant bunker full of samples of all the world's seeds. In case of apocalypse. It's supposed to last thousands of years. One of the problems is how to communicate the vault's purpose to future generations. Who knows how humans will be communicating thousands of years from now?'

'Why are you telling me this?'

'Because it's interesting, don't you think?'

'So we're totally insignificant compared to the massive expanses of space and time? I already know that, I study physics.'

Wendy laughed. 'Well, it's good to have perspective.'

Hannah shook her head, anger rising. 'Don't you want to know why he did it?'

'Why do you think he chose you?'

'What?'

Wendy turned away from the map to a framed picture on the mantelpiece. It looked like her and Hugh on a glacier somewhere, enjoying their perfect existentially meaningless existence together. Wendy lifted the picture.

'He spoke about you recently.'

'He did?'

'Said he felt terrible about what happened to Melanie.'

'It had nothing to do with him.'

'Of course not,' Wendy said, putting the picture down. 'But he can still feel bad, can't he?'

Hannah stared at the old woman, hunched over. 'You said he chose me.'

'Do you think it was a coincidence you found him?'

Hannah stood up. 'I don't know, do I?' Her voice was louder than she intended. 'No one will ever know, that's the point of suicide.'

'Not all stories have a resolution.'

'Come on,' Hannah said. She dug into her bag on the floor, pulled out the medal. 'He was holding this, what does it mean?'

'Not everything means something.'

'That's not good enough,' Hannah said, the medal clenched in her fist. 'This is some Yoda bullshit.'

Wendy frowned. 'I'm sorry, I don't know what that means.'

Hannah sighed, held out the medal.

'You keep it, dear,' Wendy said.

Hannah stared at the medal. The truth was she didn't want to give it back, not to a widow who didn't seem to miss her husband of sixty-odd years the day after he killed himself.

'Isn't there anyone else who will miss him?' she said.

'Edward, of course.'

Hannah scratched her arm, imagined the hydrocyanic acid in her tea coursing through her bloodstream, killing her quickly and painlessly.

'You said you didn't have children,' she said.

'Edward is Hugh's lover,' Wendy said. 'We enjoyed an open marriage. Edward and Hugh were together for thirty years.'

Hannah felt the edge of the medal cutting into her hand as she squeezed.

Wendy collected the tea tray and spoke over her shoulder.

'I presume the Skelfs would like to conduct Hugh's funeral?'

22

JENNY

Archie had made a beautiful job of Evie's face. The girl was lying in the open casket in the viewing room, head nestled on a small pillow like she was sleeping. Jenny could see her cheeks flushed and rounded out, the ear in one piece, a perfect little daughter. Evie's dad gripped the coffin edge, tears dropping onto the sleeves of his ill-fitting suit. Jenny heard Evie's mum outside the room, making gulping sobbing sounds. Archie had taken her out a few minutes ago when she fell to her knees by the coffin. Kids were always the hardest. Kids and babies, because we're grieving for all the possible futures that have been snuffed out.

Evie's dad held his daughter's hand, shoulders shaking as he cried. Jenny thought of Hannah and felt sick. She wanted to say something but what was there to say? She just stood there. Maybe it was enough to be another human presence in the room.

Evie had been with her dad when she was hit by a bus on Chambers Street. They'd just visited the museum, off to get an ice cream, Evie darting into the road without looking, straight into a tourist coach. A simple, careless moment, all the waves rippling out across the universe. Evie's mum and dad, her friends and family, teachers and pupils at her school, the coach driver, the paramedics who put her in the ambulance, the tourists on the coach, thousands of pounds spent to visit Edinburgh, returning home under a cloud, the horror and sadness, Edinburgh forever associated in their minds with the death of a little girl.

Sadness and grief were energies and forces in their own right, Jenny had come to understand that since getting into the funeral life. Unpredictable, uncontrollable forces that could destroy worlds, change lives.

Evie's parents would carry this forever, drown in it. It wasn't ever a matter of escaping, it was a matter of managing it, making it bearable somewhere down the line, but what the fuck was bearable about any of this?

Evie's dad wiped at his eyes with his sleeves, sniffed, a guttural noise from the back of his throat. Jenny wanted to wrap her arms around him, just that basic feeling of connection and empathy. She remembered Hannah scraping her knee badly as a little girl, she'd come off her bike in the park, wound herself into a minor hysteric, no amount of logical persuasion could get her to calm down. Jenny just held her tight for two minutes, listened as the sobbing slowly reduced, felt her daughter's heart rate drop, air sucked into her lungs, time and physical contact bringing her back from the edge of something.

Evie's dad kissed his daughter's lips and raised his head.

'It's time,' he said.

Warriston Crematorium was half empty. Maybe the Brockhurst family had few connections in the city, maybe it was just too much for people to handle. Folk liked to turn out for funerals of the elderly, the sense of a life well lived, it was their time. But none of that applied to a ten-year-old. If she had been a few years older the place would likely be mobbed. Teenagers were mature enough to understand the tribute and ceremony, and they were at a stage where the dark seemed dangerous, where death was something to be explored.

But this was too much.

Two sets of grandparents sat broken in the front row, heads bowed. There were no children here, though Evie must've had friends, maybe siblings, cousins. But decisions had been made not to expose them to this. Jenny wondered about that. It was a difficult call. And it was hard for her to gauge the effect on others, since she'd grown up around death and other people's grief.

Dorothy stood with her at the doorway greeting the stragglers. Elderly funerals sometimes had the feel of social events, friends catching up after years apart. But this was brutal, no words exchanged, disgust that any of them had to be here for this.

'This is horrible,' Jenny said under her breath.

Dorothy nodded.

Jenny pulled at the cuffs of her jacket. 'Why do we need this?'

Dorothy pursed her lips. 'You know why.'

'It doesn't help.'

'We don't know what helps.'

Jenny stared at Evie's mother, her fists full of tissues in her lap. 'Nothing can help these people,' she said.

Archie and Evie's dad came in with the coffin, along with two other bearers, uncles. At the sight of the coffin, Evie's mum gave a yowl and buried her face in her hands.

Jenny pictured Hannah lying in a coffin and her throat tightened up so that she had to make an effort to swallow.

The coffin was slid onto the plinth then Evie's dad joined his wife, grabbing her hand but not looking at her. As if the acknowledgement of this was too much.

The minister began speaking, an old, sonorous voice with quiet authority, and Jenny tuned out, unable to take the details of Evie's short life. She imagined being at Craig's funeral, if he'd died on the Meadows that night. She imagined sitting with Hannah, with Fiona and Sophia, a little girl grieving for her daddy, no understanding of what he was.

She wondered how she would feel if Craig died, and she was shocked that it felt like sadness. Loss. Despite everything. She tried to remember sitting across from him in the prison visiting room but that encounter was blurred in fog. He always pushed her buttons, why couldn't she control herself around him? She turned into a different person, the worst version of herself. She was terrible at self-reflection at the best of times, it wasn't in her nature, and she tried to dig into why that was. She still had the lingering Generation X thing of internally shrugging her shoulders at the stupidity of the world, barrelling along with no deep thought or analysis. That was a terrible way to live but it was so ingrained she struggled to fight it. She knew she let people down, Hannah, Dorothy next to her now. She wasn't a great mum or daughter and she didn't feel great about herself as a woman, but she tried, damn it. She had to be better, have more control, be there for others as they were there for her. As the Skelfs were here for the Brockhurst family in the middle of this terrible shitstorm.

She swallowed hard and looked around the crematorium at the broken lives. She pulled at her blouse, felt the scar tissue underneath like a comfort blanket.

The minister finished and the coffin sank into the plinth and Evie's mum wailed.

When the coffin was gone the congregation left like zombies, the parents not standing for that awful line-up where people shake your hand and tell you they're sorry for your loss. Jenny could understand why they wouldn't.

Outside the sunlight was painful after the gloominess of the chapel. The hearse was already gone and the young lad Keiran they hired as a driver was waiting by the family car, holding the door open.

Jenny looked at the crematorium, a square early-1900s brick affair with a concrete sixties extension. Buildings never stay the same, just like their home back at Greenhill Gardens. Extensions and demolitions, upgrading and renovating, change was the only constant.

'Are you OK?'

Jenny felt Dorothy's hand on her back.

'That was hard,' Jenny said.

'It always is.'

'I couldn't help thinking of Hannah.'

'I know.' Dorothy breathed deeply. Over in the cemetery birds were building a nest in a sycamore, twigs dropping to the ground. Instinct made them keep going, building for the future, raising new chicks, doing whatever was needed to continue.

'I've told the police we'll do Jimmy's funeral,' Dorothy said.

Jenny couldn't pick up her mum's thread. 'Jimmy?'

'Jimmy X. My homeless friend.'

Jenny smelled blossom of some kind, the world renewing. 'The guy who almost killed you.'

'He needs a funeral.'

'OK.'

'But I need to know who he was first,' Dorothy said. 'So we can give him a proper send off.'

Jenny hadn't got anywhere with the car, Hannah the same with the notebook.

Dorothy turned to Jenny. 'I'll take social care, you do the homeless shelters.'

23

HANNAH

Judging by the décor in the waiting room, the psychiatry business was booming, at least for Stanford and Carver. Moray Place was an expensive place to have an office, and the woodland paintings, Danish furniture and pristine blonde receptionist all suggested money.

The receptionist, Imogen according to her name badge, was in a turquoise suit that managed to be simultaneously flashy and understated, and it fit perfectly. Hannah watched as she greeted clients with a sincere smile, answered the phone with the right amount of buzz in her voice, clacked away at her laptop. Hannah's attention picked up when Imogen sashayed over to two large filing cabinets behind the desk. All the information in there for Stanford and Carver's clients. The cabinets were locked but the key sat in the lock, and Imogen turned it, slid a drawer open, placed a brown file inside. Interesting.

The phone rang and Imogen glided back and picked it up, nodded, replaced the handset.

'Ms Anderson,' she said to Hannah. 'You can go in now.'

Hannah smiled and stood up, smoothed her skirt. The fake name was essential given how recognisable Skelf was and what she was here to do.

Sally Carver was younger than Hannah expected, early thirties, pretty in a non-confrontational way that made her seem like a long-lost friend. She was heavy around the hips but knew how to hide it. Chestnut hair and matching eyes. She came out from behind her desk and pointed at two comfy chairs that matched the ones in reception.

'Have a seat.'

Sally mapped out what they would cover in this initial assessment interview then Hannah laid out her mental-health history, anxiety, periods of depression, a short spell of self-medication with booze and skunk that ended badly, and so on.

'So what brings you here today,' Sally said. Her voice was like Nutella, smooth but sickly.

'Well.' Hannah breathed deeply. This was meant to be made up but she was feeling it, talking about her teenage issues had made those feelings creep up on her. 'There's been a fair bit of trauma in my life recently.'

Silence.

More silence.

Sally leaned forward. 'Go on.'

'My dad. He had an affair with one of my friends.'

'And how did that make you feel?'

Hannah had already explained about Craig and Jenny's divorce. 'He'd remarried. Had another daughter. And he started sleeping with my mate on the side.'

'That must've been hard.'

Hannah felt a lump in her throat despite herself. 'But that was only the start.'

Sally put on an empathetic face. She'd stopped taking notes to show how much she cared. Or maybe she really cared.

'My friend went missing.'

Sally's face moved to a frown. 'OK.' She dragged the word out.

'And I started looking for her.'

Sally ran her tongue around her teeth. 'I'm really more interested in your emotional state. Your mental state.'

Hannah nodded, innocent. 'Sure. I was crazy, frantic. I couldn't understand why she would just disappear. I didn't know about my dad and her at that point, he kept it a secret.'

Sally's frown deepened and the beginning of a realisation came over her.

'My friend had been seeing a few guys apart from her boyfriend, it turned out, including Dad. I thought it was one of the other guys, accused him, and he killed himself.'

Sally looked uncomfortable. 'Look, I'm not sure where this is going, exactly, but...'

'I'll tell you where it's going,' Hannah said. 'Just wait. This is the best bit. So I discovered my dad's affair with her, and at that exact moment he was with my mum, about to fuck her, and she challenged him about it so he stabbed her. Then he tried to kill my gran by strangling her, and he only stopped when I walked in the door, then my gran stabbed him and he ran away.'

Sally checked the name in her notepad. 'Ms Anderson...'

'I chased him,' Hannah said. 'He was wounded and I chased him across Bruntsfield Links and the Meadows. He collapsed and I caught him and he confessed to everything. I looked him in the eyes and he told me he'd done it.'

Hannah was gripping the arms of her seat so tight it felt like her fingers might rip the fabric.

'I looked him in the eye, he knew exactly what he was doing. He was one hundred percent in his right mind.'

Sally shook her head. 'This is not appropriate.'

'So what I want to know is,' Hannah was breathing shallow, hardly at all, 'how the hell you decided Craig McNamara was suffering from diminished responsibility on the grounds of his mental health?'

Sally stood up and went to her desk. 'Please leave.'

Hannah stood too, followed her. 'I just want it explained to me, that's all. You met him for half an hour? An hour? And you decided he was mentally ill?'

'Leave now,' Sally said. 'I can't discuss another client, this is completely inappropriate.'

'Did he charm you?' Hannah said. 'Is that it? Fluttered his eyelashes and you fell for it? He's very good at that. Very good at focusing his attention on you, making you think you mean something to him, that you're the only woman in the world.'

'I'm calling security.'

Hannah laughed. 'You don't have security.'

'Then I'm calling the police.'

Hannah placed her hands on the desk, leaned in.

'Just tell me how you came to that decision?'

'Get out.'

Hannah waved a hand around the office. 'You're doing pretty well here. You get a nice juicy fee from the defence solicitor, is that how it works? Do you do a lot of assessments for middle-class prisoners on remand?'

'I have the highest professional standards.'

'Then how come you got this wrong?'

Sally had the phone in her hand, looked at it pointedly. 'I really will phone the police if you don't leave.'

'Did you fancy him, is that it?'

Sally started pressing buttons on the phone.

Hannah held her hands up. 'OK, I'm going.' She inhaled, tried to stop her head from spinning. 'I just want you to realise your decision has consequences. There are real people out there suffering because of what my dad did. And we have to give evidence in court because of you.'

Sally was still holding the phone receiver like a poisonous snake.

Hannah turned and left, closing the door behind her.

She went left instead of right, into the gents' bathroom, closed the door in a stall and sat. Five minutes went past as her breathing returned to normal, her hands stopped shaking. She left the bathroom and strode into the corridor, took her keys out and punched them through the fire alarm, then went back into the toilet stall. Stood on the seat and left the door open, pulled it half over to hide herself.

The alarm blared through the building and she heard voices and feet in the corridor. The bathroom door opened, someone shouted hello, checked under the stalls then left. She waited five more minutes, the alarm drilling into her brain, then climbed down and left the bathroom, walked along the empty corridor into reception.

Through the blinds she saw a dozen people standing outside, hugging their arms at the breeze swirling round Moray Place. She ducked under the window and crept to the filing cabinets behind the desk, turned the key and opened the middle one. Flicked through the files to M, pulled out Craig McNamara's folder, opened it. She looked round, no sign of anyone. She snapped pics of each of the three pages with her phone, slid the file back and locked the cabinet.

'Hey.'

She turned to see two firemen in the doorway in full gear.

She strode past them, putting her phone away.

'Thanks for saving me,' she said, then she was out the door and along the street, ignoring the fire engines with their lights flashing, ignoring Imogen and Sally calling after her.

24

JENNY

It was depressing how many hits Jenny got on Google maps when she typed 'homeless services, Edinburgh'. Dozens of pins scattered across the city, some she recognised like Shelter and Bethany's, but loads more she wasn't aware of, The Rock Trust, Streetwork, Four Square. She felt overwhelmed by the idea of an interconnected web, people doing small things to make life bearable for others. She was reminded of the map upstairs in the ops room, all the cemeteries, crematoriums, hospices and hospitals. Maybe the Skelfs were making a difference, helping people through tough times, but Jenny struggled to see it sometimes.

She made a list and printed it off, putting the Leith shelters at the top, since that's where Jimmy X's car was first spotted by the young cop. She checked with Indy that the body van wasn't needed today then headed out into metallic grey light, low cloud smothering the city like a shroud.

Four hours later she was even more depressed. She'd noticed the recent rise of guys sleeping on the streets, but hadn't realised the extent of it. Each visit was the same. She had a quick chat with a harassed volunteer, got handed to the manager, equally desperate. No one recognised Jimmy X from the picture, but he'd grown a beard and lost a lot of weight since it was taken, and added a layer of grime, so maybe this was pointless.

Each manager told the same story, funding cuts, understaffed social care, massive problems with universal credit. All of it was throwing previously solid people out on their arses into a city that wasn't prepared. The vast majority of people they housed had mental-health issues, drug and alcohol addiction to deal with, and now found themselves homeless.

Jenny spoke to people in the lounge of the Bethany place off Great Junction Street, they all had similar stories. Lack of family support, no jobs, one missed rent payment and they were lost, through the cracks and into a subculture that existed as its own ecosystem beneath the tourist gleam of Edinburgh. Most were young men but by no means all, there were plenty of mothers with children, families waiting months or years to be housed.

Jenny couldn't stand it. She was such a hypocrite. She broadly thought of herself as socialist, believed in helping others, but it was all lip service, she never really did anything to help, and there were so many people who needed it. She hated herself and her privileged middle-class background, her solid family and the work she'd fallen into. When dad died and she lost her journalism job, she moved back to the big house without worrying. She felt a swell overcome her when she thought of her mum, taking a middle-aged daughter back into the house without blinking.

Worse than the charity places were the privately run hostels used by the council for overspill emergency housing. Conditions were rank, no security, no privacy, filthy beds. Each one Jenny visited made her feel dirty and guilty, and above all lucky that she didn't have to live there.

Then there were food banks. She visited all the Leith ones, showing Jimmy X's photograph to volunteers, nothing. At the Trussell Trust round the back of Aldi she saw a Middle Eastern woman with two young daughters weeping with relief as she rummaged through a carrier bag full of tins. Inside, an elderly helper managed two seconds between organising shelves to look at the picture. Maybe she'd seen him, maybe not, she saw hundreds of people a day, people who don't want to be noticed because they're ashamed.

Jenny headed out of Leith to Holyrood Road, first Streetwork then across to the Sally Army on the corner of the Pleasance. A handful of drunk guys sat along from the entrance, one trying to light a roll-up from his friend's fag. They raised cans of Special Brew to her as she went in.

Inside it was the same story, everyone had a browbeaten edge, no one recognised the picture. Jenny sighed and left.

One guy sitting on the ground waved at her. 'Fancy a can?'

She'd had this at several places, the misplaced generosity of the lifetime alcoholic. She'd waved it away before but it was late afternoon and she was shit-tired and depressed and thirsty so she stopped and looked at the guy.

'You sure?'

His hand was unwavering. 'Aye.'

She took the can and opened it, slugged a good bit. It was syrupy and strong as hell, metallic aftertaste like it was made of blood.

The guy and his two mates cheered, clinking cans together, and Jenny joined them.

The guy on the ground was in a filthy orange sleeping bag, and Jenny slumped down next to him.

'Tough day,' he said.

Jenny took him in. Maybe her age, grey hair receding at the front and long at the back, couple of teeth missing. He wore a North Face fleece. She wondered where he'd got it, then felt guilty for wondering.

'Yeah,' she said.

'Tell me about it,' said one of the standing guys. He was older, hunched over, red checked shirt. He had a cut on his forehead that looked dirty and infected, and there was a dark stain on his collar. The other guy was younger, tall and skinny, bony arms, in a T-shirt, with a Kangol trackie top around his waist. The older guy wobbled on his feet and Jenny wanted to ask him to sit down. The young guy was jittery, constantly touching his face and neck. Taken together, they were like the three stages of homeless manhood.

Jenny drank. Fuck, it tasted terrible but she could feel the kick already, understood the appeal.

The guy on the floor was giving her the once over.

'You don't belong here,' he said, not unkindly.

'I'm not so sure.'

He shook his head. 'Don't joke about it.'

'How long have you guys been on the street?'

Their chests went out, like war veterans asked about their service.

'Seven years,' Floor Guy said.

Twitcher stroked his cheek. 'Eighteen months.'

'All my life.' Old Timer seemed to be talking to someone in the distance.

Jenny wondered how old he was, how long he had left.

'Hard life,' said Floor Guy.

All three nodded.

Floor Guy turned to her again. 'So what are you doing, apart from drinking my last can?'

Jenny fished a twenty out of her pocket and handed it over. Floor Guy took it without fuss and folded it away.

Jenny took out the photograph, creased along the edges, handed it over. 'Looking for this guy.'

Floor Guy examined it. 'A relative?'

'No.'

'But you're not a cop.'

'No.'

'So?'

'He's dead,' Jenny said. 'We're giving him a funeral. It would be good to know who he is.'

This seemed to satisfy Floor Guy.

'Don't know him,' he said, passing it to Old Timer.

Old Timer tried to focus, narrowed his eyes, swigged his can. Gave a tiny head shake and passed it on.

Twitcher switched the picture from one hand to the other, rubbed at his neck. Crouched and picked up his can, swigged, put it down again, looked at the traffic crossing Cowgate into Holyrood Road. He stared at the photograph, closed one eye, then swapped to closing the other. His feet tapped on the pavement and Jenny wondered if it was a disorder of some kind, or drugs. Or both.

'The guy?'

'Yeah,' Jenny said.

The head twitch turned into a shake, too long and too hard, like he was trying to dislodge something from his brain.

'Don't know him,' he said, 'never seen him, don't know him.'

Jenny held out her hand for the picture.

Twitcher's head was still moving, his tongue sliding along his teeth, back and forth. 'I know her, though.'

'What?'

Twitcher tapped the picture, pointed at the woman with Jimmy X.

'I know her,' he said. 'Definitely. I saw her the other day.'

25

DOROTHY

She turned away from Hibs' stadium into Albion Gardens. The flats were yet more new-builds, striated wooden panelling and brickwork to make them look older. Dorothy wondered how that would play when they really got old and the wood had to be replaced. She walked to the end of the street and looked up. Five floors from an elevated pathway, a garage built underneath. Sunlight glinted off the windows making her shield her eyes. She searched for movement, a shimmer of blinds or curtains, but there was nothing.

She turned to her right. From here there was a view of number five Lochend Butterfly Way, Abi's dad's flat. She looked up at the Albion Gardens block, the view would be even better from the small balconies on the tenement end. At the top was a Warners Estate Agents sign, matching the one at the stairwell entrance.

She'd spent hours trawling through Warners' website, waiting for something to catch her eye. While you could search via location, it was broad, so she'd stuck in Leith. But there were dozens of entries and she had to check the map location for each one. So many places for sale, so many empty properties. She thought about Jenny crawling around the homeless shelters, Jimmy X living in his stolen car.

She wondered if this was all nothing. Maybe Abi was hiding at a friend's house, a boyfriend's. But surely any fourteen-year-old would still have parents around, and what parent would hide someone else's kid? Unless the friend or boyfriend was much older. Or unless it was something else entirely.

She walked to the entrance and found the buzzer for top floor right. Breathed in and out and pressed it firmly. Didn't step back and look up in case someone was checking out of the window. She buzzed again, more insistently. Of course, this wouldn't work.

'Hello?'

Christ, a teenage girl's voice.

'DHL,' Dorothy said. 'I have a package for number nine, they're not answering. Can you buzz me in.'

The crackle of the intercom, the buzz of the door lock and Dorothy was inside. She went up the stairs wondering how to play it. Reached the top floor and rang the doorbell. Thought she heard something inside, a scuffle of feet. She opened the letterbox, looked in. Bare flat, pastel walls, no signs of life.

'Abi,' she said. 'It's Dorothy. I know you're in there. Please open up.'

Another sound, maybe just her own breathing.

'Abi.'

She heard the chain slide across and the lock click, and there was Abi looking down at her feet, touching her hair with her hand. She was in joggers and a baggy Paramore sweatshirt, the strap of a black vest visible at her shoulder.

'Can I come in?' Dorothy said.

Abi walked away leaving the door open and Dorothy followed into the kitchen-diner.

The views were amazing to Holyrood Park and the back of Salisbury Crags, marred by the huge Sainsbury's in the foreground. Also in the foreground was Neil Williams' flat, a few yards over the road.

Abi slumped in a sofa. There was evidence of action in the kitchen behind her, empty ready-meal containers by the sink, bread by the toaster, a box of tea bags.

'Your mum and stepdad are worried sick,' Dorothy said.

Abi looked at her nails, chipped and nibbled. 'They hired you?'

Dorothy shook her head. 'What's this about, Abi?'

She chewed her lip. 'How do you mean?'

Dorothy stared at her for a long moment. She tried to remember being fourteen, the insecurity, hormones, self-consciousness. But it felt like a million years ago. She had a flash of Jenny at that age, screaming about something, slamming a door and stomping up-stairs to the second floor studio she used as a sulk room.

Dorothy pointed out of the window. 'Neil Williams. That's his place.'

Abi shrugged, it wasn't a denial.

'Your biological dad.'

Another shrug.

Dorothy pressed her lips together and headed to the kitchen. 'How about I make us a cup of tea.'

She filled the kettle at the sink, found two takeaway cups in a cupboard, threw tea bags in. Went to the fridge and took out a small milk carton. There were also cheese slices, ham, a bag of salad.

'Where did you get this stuff?'

Abi nodded out of the window. 'Sainsbury's.'

'You have money?'

A slight nod.

'But that won't last forever.' Dorothy poured the tea. 'So what's the plan here?'

Abi pulled at her earlobe.

Dorothy brought the tea over, sat down next to Abi and handed one over. 'Let's start at the beginning.'

Abi shook her head.

'OK, how about I throw together what I know?'

'Do what you like.' Abi sipped her tea.

'Well, this place is up for sale through Warners, so I presume either your mum knows you're here.' Dorothy stopped and angled her head.

Abi gave the tiniest shake.

'In that case, you managed to steal or copy the keys from the Warners office.'

Abi shrugged. 'It's not hard, Mum brings keys home all the time if she's got a viewing last thing in the evening or first thing the next morning.'

Dorothy smiled. Now they were getting somewhere. 'And you're here because you can see your dad's apartment. I'm guessing you went there and there was no sign of him. Your mum says he's in Canada at the moment. You would've called him. Either he never answered or he said something that made you wonder. Or were you just planning on staying here until he came back?'

Abi said nothing.

'Then what?' Dorothy said. 'Live happily ever after with him, is that it? Travel the world together having adventures? Life's not that easy, you must know that.'

'It's not like that,' Abi said.

Dorothy drank tea. The girl was like a skittish fox, and Dorothy had to speak softly and move carefully in case she got spooked and disappeared across the horizon.

'What about this place?' Dorothy said, waving a hand around. 'What about it?'

'It's up for sale, presumably people are viewing it.'

Abi sat up, wanting to show how smart she was. 'I tidy up and leave when the public viewings are on.'

Dorothy smiled. 'What about private viewings, they could happen any time.'

Abi lifted her phone with a smirk. 'I'm synched to Mum's calendar. I know all her appointments.'

'Can't they track you with that thing?'

Abi shook her head. 'This is a new phone, they don't know the number.'

Dorothy took in the girl. Smart in a lot of ways but still so young, open to getting hurt. Her emotions were written across her face, she hadn't learned to mask them yet.

'But why?' Dorothy said. 'Is it something at home?'

Abi closed down, her body shrinking.

'Is it Mike?'

Abi looked up and Dorothy searched for something in her eyes.

'Mike's cool.'

'Really?'

'Really.'

Dorothy examined Abi's body, didn't see any obvious tells. Maybe the stepdad was cool, maybe it was something else.

'Your mum then?'

Abi shook her head as if sending herself a cryptic message.

Dorothy touched the back of her hand. 'Mothers and daughters are tricky.'

'She thinks I'm a little kid.'

'It's hard accepting that your baby is growing up.'

'It's pathetic.'

'Come on,' Dorothy said. 'For years, you needed her for every single thing, you were completely dependent on her. It's hard to give that up, trust me.'

Abi pouted.

'How is she with your biological dad?' Dorothy said.

Abi's body tensed. This was something maybe.

'Does she try to turn you against him? That's pretty common.'

Abi coughed out a laugh. 'I think she's turning him against me.'

Dorothy stroked a finger along Abi's hand. 'I'm sure that's not true.'

'He doesn't answer my calls anymore,' Abi said. 'Or when he does, he's always away.'

'He travels, though, right? With his job.'

'Apparently,' Abi said. 'But he's totally ghosting me.'

'Ghosting?'

Abi gave her a look like she was a child. 'Not answering any messages or calls. Making me feel I don't exist.'

'It must be hard for him being away,' Dorothy said. 'I'm sure he cares.'

Abi pulled her hand away from Dorothy's, rubbed at her arm.

'So you want to confront him?' Dorothy said. 'That's why you're here?'

'I don't believe he's abroad,' Abi said. 'I want to see him, make him talk to me.'

Dorothy looked at her, just as messed up as any other fourteen-year-old, still trying to find out what sort of person she is, where she comes from.

'You don't need him,' Dorothy said. 'You're a smart, funny, passionate young woman.'

The words bounced off Abi into the ether.

'Go home, Abi, no good can come of this.'

Abi shook her head. 'Not until I see him.'

'Your mum and stepdad are worried.'

'If they were worried the police would've found me, not you. There's been nothing on the news about me missing.'

'They do care,' Dorothy said, but her voice was unconvincing.

'No.'

'I care,' Dorothy said. 'You can't stay here forever.'

'You can't make me leave.'

Dorothy sighed. 'How about I tell your folks where you are.'

She sat up, rubbed her hands on her joggers. 'Don't. Please.'

'At least let me tell them you're OK.'

Abi fidgeted with her hands in her lap. 'That won't work. You'd have to tell them how you know.'

'This isn't fair on them.'

'I'm not leaving here until I speak to my dad.'

Dorothy was impressed at Abi's ingenuity, getting the keys, checking the work calendar, feeding herself. But her voice was wavering, her conviction in her mission too, and they both knew it. Dorothy tried to think how to play it. She went to the window and looked across the road, wondered about Neil Williams, where he was now, if he knew how much his daughter cared. It's never easy to live up to a kid's expectations.

'How about this,' she said. 'If you let me take you home, I promise I'll find your dad for you.'

Abi swallowed hard, tried to hold her chin up. 'How?'

Dorothy held her arms out. 'I'm a private investigator, it's what I do.'

26

HANNAH

Hannah stared at the solicitor. 'Tomorrow? You are kidding.'

'I'm sorry.'

Mr Erickson – 'call me Lars' – didn't look sorry, he'd had the same smug face since they walked into his office. He sat behind his large walnut desk, leaned forward on his leather chair and shuffled papers from one pile to another. The shelves were full of law books and box files, none of which apparently contained any information that could stop this from going ahead.

Hannah turned to her mum and gran for support. They looked like she felt, a bomb had gone off in their hands and they hadn't worked out yet how injured they were.

'How can the case suddenly be going to trial tomorrow?'

Erickson wiggled his nose like something was irritating his nostrils, and Hannah wondered if he was coked up.

'The defence solicitor persuaded the judge that his client was suffering emotionally and mentally the longer the investigation took.'

'Good,' Hannah said. 'He deserves it.'

Dorothy put a hand on her arm. 'Hannah.'

Hannah snapped at her. 'What?'

'Try to stay calm.'

Hannah shook her head and turned back to Erickson. 'I sent you the psychiatrist's file, it's clearly rubbish.'

'As we have already discussed,' Erickson said, 'that was highly inappropriate. And illegal. It didn't help at all.'

'He harassed me on the phone,' Hannah said.

'There's no evidence of that.'

'He admitted he was guilty at the time, doesn't that mean anything?'

Erickson touched his shirt cuffs. 'Of course, and I'll be using that, but it won't convict on its own. But don't worry, there's plenty of evidence, lots of forensics. They've played into our hands by jumping the gun, to be honest.'

Jenny piped up. 'It just...' She looked at the others. 'None of us are prepared for this to happen now.'

Erickson spread his hands. It was supposed to be reassuring but just seemed arrogant. 'I completely understand.'

His look changed as he focused on Jenny.

'Of course your little altercation in prison didn't help.'

Hannah swallowed down bile. 'She had every right to do what she did.'

'No one has the right to assault anyone, no matter how provoked.'

'He's right,' Jenny said. 'It was stupid.'

Hannah stood up and breathed deeply. 'This is what he wants, for us to fall apart.'

Erickson did the hand thing again. 'Try to stay calm. We've been over your statements. Just tell the truth and leave the rest to me.'

Hannah wandered to the window. They were high up on George Street, terrific views over the Forth. The expanse of water, Fife in the distance, the three bridges to the left, as far as Berwick Law in the other direction. You had to pay for a view like this so maybe Erickson knew what he was doing.

'The worst thing you can do is get emotional in court,' Erickson said. 'If you lose control the jury will turn against you.'

'But you said there's loads of evidence,' Hannah said, turning back.

Erickson shook his head, put on a resigned face. 'Sadly, logic and evidence are not always king when it comes to juries. We need to get them onside, give them a story to believe in.'

'But he's so...' Jenny trailed off.

'He's manipulative,' Erickson said. 'But so am I. I'll play him and the jury just as much as he's playing us at the moment.'

'I don't share your confidence,' Hannah said through her teeth.

'I don't need you to share it, I just need you to trust me.'

Hannah looked over the dark water, grey sky leaning down to meet it. She pictured being out on the firth, wind in her hair, the sea beneath her, worries drifting away.

'Just don't mess this up,' she heard someone say, and was surprised to find it was her.

She looked at Erickson, the same implacable confidence on his face. She did not have a good feeling about this.

27
DOROTHY

She stood for a long time in the doorway watching Archie work, unsure if he was aware of her. She loved watching him prepare the deceased, it was a joy to see someone good at what they do, taking care and attention. Jim taught him well, and Archie had taken to embalming like a natural, a feel for just the right kind of work needed to make the body presentable.

Today's was a simple job in one sense, no reconstruction, no major bruising or other marks to cover. Archie dealt with everything from car crashes to suicide, jumping off bridges or in front of trains. Dorothy remembered once searching the railway track with Archie and Jim for pieces of corpse as transport police watched and tried not to be sick. That one was a closed casket.

Everyone from babies to great-grandparents, death visiting just the same. And people you were close to as well. Jim, of course, but his parents before that, friends, aunts, cousins. With Dorothy's family in California she hadn't been involved in any of their funerals, except for attending, her family giving her a wide berth, partly because of the trade she was in, partly because she'd become a stranger, bringing up her daughter in a wet, cold land across the Atlantic, choosing dour Scottish weather over golden sunshine.

And now Archie had his mum on the embalming table, brushing her hair, checking the flow of embalming fluid into her neck, patting her hand out of love, but also checking the elasticity was returning to the skin, the fluid making the veins expand and hold their shape. Her cheeks were filling out, her lips coming back down over the grimace of exposed gums.

Dorothy came into the room wondering if she should reach

out and touch Archie, comfort him. But sometimes there wasn't much comforting to be done.

Archie glanced up and smiled.

Dorothy looked at Veronica Kidd.

'We could've got a freelance to do this one,' she said.

Archie shook his head. 'I wanted to do it.'

Dorothy understood. When Jim died, she felt blessed to spend some final moments with him before he was gone forever.

'If you need to talk,' she said.

'I need to speak to you about the arrangements.'

'That's not what I meant.'

'I don't want anything too expensive.'

Dorothy pressed her lips together. 'My God, Archie, you don't have to pay. What kind of person do you think I am?'

Archie touched the back of his hand to his mum's cheek. The fluid was filling her out but there was only so much it could do. Veronica had died of cancer, eaten away piece by piece, so she was diminished anyway when she died.

'I didn't want to presume,' Archie said.

Dorothy put a hand on his shoulder. 'Anything you want, just ask.'

'Thanks.'

He checked the gauge on the embalming pump. It wasn't necessary, he'd used it as an excuse to step away from her touch. Dorothy lowered her hands to her side.

'How are you coping?' she said.

He didn't answer for a long time, and she started to wonder if he'd heard her over the buzz of the pump.

'As well as can be expected,' he said eventually, still looking away, running his hand along the tube from the pump to Veronica's carotid.

Dorothy was struck by how little language was able to communicate. Words have meaning, of course, but they're so inadequate, and we each have a lifetime of hang-ups and quirks that feed into how we speak. Archie had never been much of a talker, most Scottish men weren't, and she got used to it. But she missed the openness of California, where you could talk your way into a new way of feeling. That seemed absent in Scottish society, buttoned up, isolated. But maybe things were changing. Hannah was seeing a counsellor. She and Indy had a much healthier and open way of communicating, maybe future generations would sort themselves out.

Dorothy looked at Veronica's bare arm over the sheet. Small hairs on her forearm, the pores of the skin, liver spots on her hand, the veins beneath filling up with artificial life.

She thought about her own mother, dead for twenty years now, a severe stroke in her sleep. At least it was peaceful, that was the comfort she took, but what did she know, really? Maybe Mom woke up confused and panicking, maybe there were long moments of paralysis and pain before the end. None of us know what anyone else goes through, that was the truth.

When Mom died all her experience and memories died with her. Edith had been a child of the Great Depression, her family moving from the dust belt to the promise of the West Coast, only to find things just as hard there. She married young and her husband came back from the Second World War a changed man, closed off to his family. Only one child, life as a housewife in Pismo Beach while Eric went out selling insurance best he could. In later years, once Eric passed, Dorothy spoke to Edith about her dreams as a young woman. She was trying to get her to widen her horizons but her mom was nonplussed, content with the smallness of her life, and Dorothy couldn't think of a good reason to argue.

She wondered what kind of mother Veronica was to Archie. When he came into the Skelfs' lives a decade ago, it was Dorothy who helped him with his Cotard's, a mother figure. If she was honest, she'd never given much thought to his real mother and she was mortified by that.

Archie glanced up, held her gaze for a moment then went back to work on his mum.

We all just have to keep going.

Dorothy walked to the front of the house, surprised to see reception empty. She heard a noise from the contemplation room, where the bereaved could sit and compose themselves at viewings. Crying. They had no viewings just now, no arrangement meetings in the diary.

Dorothy opened the door.

Indy was in an armchair, face in her hands, gently sobbing. She wore a bottle-green blouse that matched her hair, dark skirt, black Filas. She didn't hear the door open. Dorothy watched her shoulders shake, thought about leaving.

'Indy,' she said softly.

Indy jumped, lifted her face, grabbed a tissue from the box on the coffee table. 'Shit, sorry.'

Dorothy shook her head. 'Do you mind if I come in?'

Indy fanned at her face then rubbed at her temples. She waved at the chair opposite and Dorothy closed the door and sat.

'You must think I'm stupid,' Indy said.

Dorothy wanted to hug her. 'Of course not.'

Indy swallowed, fanned her puffy eyes again, blew her nose. 'The funeral director who can't handle death.'

Dorothy reached her hand out.

Indy took it, put on a smile. 'I don't want you seeing me like this.'

'Come on.'

'I'm trying to be a funeral director, I can't just fall apart.'

Dorothy squeezed her hand. 'We're a family here. You're part of the family. Understand?'

'Sure.'

'I don't think you do.' Dorothy looked around the room, lilies on a table at the window, a Highland seascape on one wall. 'I know what it's like to be an outsider, to feel like you don't fit in, I've felt that most of my life.'

She waved a hand in the air. 'I didn't choose all this, you know.

I chose Jim and this came with the package. You do what you do for love, the rest takes care of itself.'

'I'm not sure I can cope.'

Dorothy stayed silent, waiting.

Indy swallowed, wiped away tears. She nodded towards the back of the house. 'It's Archie through there with his mum. It brought it all back, about Mum and Dad.'

'It must be so hard,' Dorothy said.

'Do you remember when I first came here?' Indy said, voice wavering. She laughed. 'It was in this room, wasn't it? Where you helped me arrange the funeral.'

Dorothy smiled.

Indy shook her head. 'If only we'd known. Four years later, so much has happened.'

'You've always been strong,' Dorothy said. 'That day, the strength it took as a teenager to talk about your own parents' funeral. I was impressed by your spirit.'

'I was a mess.'

'Of course you were,' Dorothy said. They were still holding hands, Dorothy's thumb rubbing Indy's knuckle. 'Anyone would be. But you made it through, you're still here.'

'Only because of you,' Indy said. She took her hand away and tucked hair behind her ear.

'No, it was because of you, what's inside you.'

'No.'

'I love you,' Dorothy said. 'I mean it. You're the most compassionate person I know, the most selfless and caring. It's very rare. You're always there for Hannah.'

Indy breathed loudly. 'But who's there for me?'

Dorothy stared at her. 'We all are. We're here for each other. That's what gets us through. I meant it when I said you're family. You're as important to me as Jenny or Hannah, Archie too. Even Schrödinger and Einstein.'

Indy laughed. 'Great, so I rank alongside a cat and dog.'

Dorothy sighed. 'Please don't ever think you have to hide your feelings. You never have to hide from me, Indy.'

Indy nodded but seemed unconvinced.

The door swished open and there was Hannah swinging the van keys on her finger. She looked from Dorothy to Indy.

'What's going on?'

Indy stood and put on a smile. 'Just a wee chat.'

She glanced at Dorothy then brushed past Hannah in the doorway, kissing her cheek. Hannah watched her go, admiring her bum in the skirt. She turned back to Dorothy.

'Are we going?' she said.

They headed round Marchmont and down the Pleasance to the mortuary. Dorothy had Einstein in the passenger seat footwell, felt his fur against her legs, stroked his snout as he panted and licked her hand.

Hannah was an angry driver, sitting too close behind the car in front, accelerating through an amber light. They reached the Pleasance and were stopped by students on the pedestrian crossing heading to the sports centre. Dorothy saw the Sally Army hostel, thought about what Jenny found out there. She scratched Einstein behind the ear, wondered what he knew about his dead owner. She thought about the homeless community, supportive in some ways, toxic in others. The temptation to fall back into problematic behaviour patterns was strong. But wasn't that the same for anyone? Hannah and her anxiety, Jenny falling for Craig's lies. She tried to think of her own problems – her grief, her obsession with Jimmy X.

They parked at the side entrance of the mortuary by the corrugated door. Went into reception, buzzed and waited. Graham came through from the back, smiled when he saw them.

'Well, this has brightened my day,' he said.

He lifted his glasses from his eyes and checked a piece of paper on the noticeboard, ran his gloved finger down. 'Here for Hugh Fowler?'

'That's right,' Dorothy said.

'Come through.'

Dorothy tied Einstein up, reassured him, and he sat down and closed his eyes.

She and Hannah followed Graham through to the post-mortem suite and the fridges. A body was on one of the tables, skin burnt black, peeling and flaky. It was so badly burnt Dorothy couldn't tell if it was a man or woman. The smell of cooked flesh was in the air. Hannah swallowed as she took it in.

The body had the top of its skull removed, the brain sitting on a tray. The inside of the skull was bright against the blackened outside. The body's chest was open, heart, lungs and other organs laid alongside.

'House fire,' Graham said. 'Drunk and smoking seems likely so far.'

He pulled out a fridge tray and there was Hannah's professor under a sheet. Dorothy watched her granddaughter closely.

'You OK?'

Hannah nodded.

Dorothy had said she could do this alone but Hannah insisted. Headstrong, like her mum. And Dorothy didn't argue, how do we know what works for other people?

Graham pulled the sheet back to reveal Hugh's face, blue around the lips, eyes closed, white hair sticking up.

Hannah nodded.

It always helped to get a visual ID, make sure you had the right body. They'd once spent a day removing and embalming John Williams, only to discover they'd taken the wrong John Williams from hospital. Turns out two John Williams had died within hours and no one at the hospital had noticed.

'Did the post-mortem throw up anything?' Hannah said.

Dorothy took her in. It seemed like only yesterday Hannah was in a diaper, running around the funeral home at weekends when Jenny visited, Dorothy following her, explaining that the embalming room was off limits, luring her away with a favourite toy. How did she have such a strong, grown-up granddaughter already? Time was a bitch.

Graham shook his head. 'Simple poisoning.'

'Any sign of coercion?'

'None.'

'Are you sure?'

Graham touched the rim of his glasses. 'If someone pointed a gun at his head and made him drink it, there's not a lot I can do. But in terms of physical force, there's no bruising or sign of struggle.'

Dorothy wondered what Hannah was thinking. Maybe for her this was like Jimmy X, an itch to scratch.

'Did you get anywhere with your joyrider?' Graham said, like he read her mind.

Dorothy pictured standing in the cemetery, waiting for that car to hit her. She imagined not moving, the crunch of metal into her legs, the rush of air as she's flung over the windscreen and roof, the pain as her bones shatter, landing in a heap, head bleeding, heart and lungs burst. She imagined lying in one of Graham's fridge trays, no more worries.

'We might have a lead,' she said.

Graham tapped one of the fridge doors. 'Well, let me know what you find out.'

Dorothy realised that Jimmy X was inside that fridge. Of course, no next of kin, no one had claimed him. So unless she discovered who he was, he would be stuck here until the council gave him a perfunctory funeral.

'Can I see him?' Dorothy said.

Graham slid the tray out and lifted the sheet. She looked at the cut on his head, the only outward sign that anything was wrong. She went to touch it but Graham stopped her.

'Not without gloves,' he said. 'You know the rules.'

She shook her head and stepped back. Graham gave her a look then pushed Jimmy X back in.

Hugh Fowler was still lying there waiting to go.

'OK,' Hannah said. 'Let's get the professor out of here.'

She dragged a gurney from the corner and placed it alongside the tray. Pulled a body bag from a holdall and spread it open on the gurney. Graham passed a box of blue latex gloves around and they snapped them on. Dorothy went to Hugh's feet, Hannah at his head, Graham taking the weight in the middle.

'On three,' Hannah said.

Dorothy felt the cold ankles through her gloves and wondered about the acid in Hugh's veins, if it was any different from what was coursing through her own body.

28

JENNY

Jenny had never been to Cheyne Street before, and Liam missed the turn-off from Raeburn Place the first time. It was a downmarket lane for Stockbridge, grey tenements on one side, an angular spread of functional pebble-dashed concrete buildings on the other. They found a space next to the bins and parked, a street cleaner munching from a Gregg's wrapper and watching them.

Jenny checked the map on her phone. Edinburgh Women's Aid was in the concrete block somewhere, alongside an old person's charity, a swing dance society, a fencing club and some weird church with a long name.

She looked at the photo printout in her hand. Now she was looking for the girl. Twitcher at the Sally Army said he'd met her but was vague on details. The two things he could remember were that she was called Rachel and she'd got a place in a Women's Aid refuge. Jenny didn't know where the refuges were, but this was the only Women's Aid office in town, so here she was.

'Want me to come with?' Liam said, cutting the engine.

'I think it's best if you and your penis stay here,' Jenny said. 'The whole point of Women's Aid is to get away from the likes of you.'

'I'll keep my penis here.'

She leaned across and kissed him, left the car and went inside. She was surprised there wasn't a buzzer system, wondered about security.

She thought about what Craig had done to her and Hannah, if she could've claimed refuge for that. Abusive, check. Violent, for sure. Dangerous, you bet.

She walked past a bright café full of old people and found the

Women's Aid office. She took in the cheap furniture in primary colours that had faded and frayed, info and warning posters blue-tacked to the textured walls, a blonde wood desk with piles of papers.

Behind the desk was a beautiful young woman in a bright-green hijab that matched her eyes. The nametag on her blouse said Elif. She scoped Jenny up and down, assessing if this was a woman in need of help. Jenny wondered what it was like working here all day, dealing with the stuff men dealt out, the women at the end of their ropes. But this was a charity office, maybe there was good stuff too, people offering money, time, assistance.

'Hi Elif, my name's Jenny Skelf, I hope you can help me.'

Elif clocked the use of her first name, was wise to that bullshit.

'If I can,' she said.

Jenny pulled the photo from her pocket, flattened it on the desk, slid it over.

'I'm trying to find this woman.'

'OK.' Very guarded.

'Her name's Rachel.'

Elif nodded in a way that suggested the opposite of a nod.

'I think she's in one of your refuges,' Jenny said.

'Why do you think that?'

'A friend of hers told me.'

Elif touched the edge of the photograph but didn't pick it up. She looked at it, then up at Jenny, held her eye.

'So can't this friend tell you where she is?'

'He didn't know.'

'He.'

Jenny shook her head. 'It isn't like that.'

Elif smiled an empty smile. 'We can't give out information about women in our refuges, for obvious reasons.'

'I appreciate that,' Jenny said. 'Let me explain.'

She pulled a business card out of her pocket, handed it over. Elif held it like it stank.

'This doesn't fill me with confidence,' she said.

'Please just listen.' She stabbed at the picture. 'I'm actually trying to find out who the guy is.' She pointed at Jimmy X. 'Or was. He's dead.'

Elif softened a little. 'I'm sorry.'

'He died in a car accident.'

Elif looked at the picture again, taking in both Jimmy X and Rachel.

Jenny felt like she knew this couple now, they had names, they were living on the streets of a city she thought she knew. They'd been up Arthur's Seat together and taken this picture in happier times. They had a future. Now he was dead and she was hiding.

Elif frowned. 'Did someone hire you?'

'Not exactly.'

'Then who's looking for him?'

Jenny scratched at her neck, touched her ear. 'My mum.'

Puzzle on Elif's face. 'I don't understand.'

Jenny sighed. 'Nor do I, really. He almost hit her with his car. When he died. And she feels, I don't know, some connection to him. Like she's responsible, maybe.'

'That's crazy.'

'Welcome to my life.'

Elif stood for a moment. 'I'm sorry, I can't help you.'

She slid the picture and card back across the desk.

Jenny looked around the office, at the door through to the back. 'No offence, but maybe I could speak to someone else, like your boss?'

Elif smiled. 'When people say "no offence", it's immediately followed by something offensive.'

'It's just...' Jenny touched the photo, remembered being up Arthur's Seat with Craig at the same age, before Hannah was born, their futures ahead of them. 'Anything you can tell me would be great.'

Elif pressed her lips together. 'I'm sorry.'

Jenny tapped at the picture. 'At least tell me if you recognise her.'

She held it up. Elif looked and Jenny thought she saw something, a giveaway. She'd seen Rachel, she was in a Women's Aid refuge right enough. Or maybe it was just wishful thinking.

'No,' Elif said.

Jenny held out the photo for a few seconds then put it away.

Elif picked up the business card and tried to hand it back.

Jenny refused. 'No, keep it. Give it to Rachel.'

'I don't know this woman.'

Jenny touched her wrist. 'Please, just give it to her. Then it's up to her if she contacts me or not.'

'I told you.'

'Tell her that he's dead. We're planning the funeral, she might want to come. Tell her to call. We want to know who he is before we bury him.'

Elif flicked the card between her fingers then put it in her pocket.

29

DOROTHY

Abi was silent as they walked down Sylvan Place. Dorothy walked next to her feeling sorry and awkward, picking up on the girl's tension, which radiated like a beacon. A few doors away from number seven Dorothy touched Abi's arm.

'Wait.'

Abi stopped, nonplussed. Her shoulders were slumped but Dorothy couldn't tell if it was a sign or just teenage ennui.

'Is there something you're not telling me?'

'Like what?'

'About home.'

Abi looked at the pavement. Chewing gum hardened in places, weeds between the cracks.

'It's fine.'

Dorothy sighed. 'I know I said you had to go home, but there are other ways. I want you to be safe.'

Abi nodded.

'Are you safe at home?'

Abi nodded again.

At the top of the road a young couple were standing outside the entrance to Sick Kids' A&E, smoking and pacing. Their body language was pure stress. How much easier it was to worry about physical harm, if your kid has broken her arm or caught a bad bug or fainted. It was so much harder with mental health. Dorothy wondered about Abi's mental state.

'I need to know we're doing the right thing,' she said.

'It's fine.'

'Sure?'

'Sure.'

Neither of them started walking again.

'What I said before is true,' Dorothy said. 'I'll find Neil Williams, I promise.'

She went into her handbag and pulled out the keys for the flat on Albion Gardens. 'I have these. I'll watch his place from there. And I'll do some detective work.'

'Like what?'

'I have a contact at the police. I've already put feelers out.'

Abi laughed. 'My God.'

It was good to see her smile. 'What?'

'"Feelers out", you sound ancient.'

Dorothy laughed. 'I am ancient.'

Abi chewed that over. 'You always seem young to me, Mrs S. For a granny.'

Dorothy laughed again. 'Well this granny is a private investigator, so I'm gonna private investigate.'

Abi sucked her teeth.

'So we're good?' Dorothy said.

'Sure.'

They walked to the house and Abi let herself in. At the sound of the door Sandra and Mike came running, him from his laptop in the kitchen, her from upstairs.

Dorothy studied their reactions, looking for anything off. But it seemed like genuine joy and relief from both of them. Sandra had tears in her eyes as she hugged her daughter, Mike hanging back slightly but still looking overjoyed. Sandra pulled back from the cuddle, pushed Abi's hair from her face, kissed her cheek. Abi flinched but it was a standard teenage reaction, nothing more.

'My God, where were you?' Sandra said.

Abi put her head down.

Sandra turned to Dorothy. 'Thank you so much. Where did you find her?'

Dorothy looked at the girl. They'd concocted a story that Abi had been hiding at the empty house of a friend on holiday, that way no one was blamed and the police didn't need to get involved. Abi didn't want them to know she was looking for Neil, so she would say she just needed space to herself, some random teenage crap like that. She would just button down, that was the plan.

'I'll let Abi explain,' Dorothy said.

She took Sandra to the front door, out of earshot, as Abi accepted a hug from Mike.

'Go easy on her,' Dorothy said. 'She's a good kid. And she's back, that's what matters, right?'

Sandra narrowed her eyes. 'She's OK, though? Nothing happened to her.'

'She's fine.'

Sandra nodded then came in for an unexpected embrace, and Dorothy put her arms around her.

'I better go,' she said, pulling back.

She shared a look with Abi across the hallway. 'Take it easy.'

Abi nodded and turned away.

⊏━━▶

Dorothy put on The Avalanches' first album, placed headphones on her ears and picked up the drumsticks. She needed something with a groove, not too technically taxing. The opening bars of 'Since I Left You' jostled into life and she joined in on the kit, a tom fill leading to a simple shuffle on hi-hat, snare and kick. The music was all samples, the Aussie band spending years unearthing cool beats from the furthest reaches of their vinyl collections. People her age were usually purists for 'real music' played on 'real instruments', whatever that meant, but she loved the sampling culture of dance and hip-hop, easily as creative as guitar, bass and drums.

She leaned into the beat, felt her head sway with the syncopation. Tried to let her mind run loose but it was hard to think of nothing. She'd always used drumming as a kind of mindfulness before that word existed, it made her feel part of something bigger, giving herself over to the music, allowing herself to be insignificant.

She broke round the kit to the crash cymbals and glanced about the studio. She was lucky to have this space. She'd fought hard to keep a corner of her life for herself in the early years of marriage to Jim. With the funeral business downstairs then Jenny coming along and demanding so much energy and attention, it was easy to get lost in the needs of others.

But drumming was just for her, a simple physical and emotional pleasure. And as time went on she began to love teaching too, passing on her skills to young people, especially girls. Which led her mind to Abi, back at home with her mum and stepdad, uncertain about her place in the world, no corner of the planet where she could feel at home. Dorothy wondered about Sandra and Mike, if they felt lost trying to communicate with her, trying to give her what all parents try to give their kids. Then she thought about Neil Williams, if he cared for his daughter, what kind of dad he was.

Her rhythm around the kit had stiffened, her shoulders knotted, her grip on the sticks too tight. The song finished and she shook her head as if trying to shake her mind empty.

Being a private investigator was boring. Dorothy had been sitting in the empty flat for five hours looking out of the window. She had her laptop with her, had tried lots of random Googling about Neil Williams, the address and so on, but she hadn't come up with anything. Spent a long time trawling through Neil Williamses on social media but came up blank. She had a picture Abi had sent on her phone and she turned to it now. It was maybe two years old judging by the change in Abi's appearance. She hadn't yet had her growth spurt, still looked more like a girl than a young woman, a slight chubbiness to her face, something that had disappeared, leaving sleek cheekbones.

Dorothy squinted and tried to see a resemblance between Abi and Neil. Of course it didn't always work like that, Jenny didn't look much like Dorothy or Jim, but Hannah had a definite likeness to Dorothy, something which grew as she matured. There was something melancholic about that, seeing your younger self in your granddaughter, making the same mistakes. But that was nonsense, Hannah was her own person making her own mistakes. Still, it gave Dorothy a gentle ache to be reminded of her youth.

Neil Williams was tall and thin, so maybe that was Abi's genetic inheritance. He was handsome, strong jaw, brown eyes, hint of grey in his swept-back dark hair. He wore a subtle stripy shirt, and he and Abi were in a Mexican restaurant, plates of tortillas, rice and beans on the table, a coke for her, Dos Equis for him. Abi was taking the selfie, pouting a little, and there was a sparkle in Neil's eyes, spending time with his daughter, simple joy.

There was little action across the road. An old couple left with shopping bags towards Sainsbury's walking slow along the pavement, returning an hour later with bulging bags. A young mother with a toddler left at one point, the kid refusing to go in his buggy, having a tantrum, pulling his shoe off and throwing it into the gutter. The mum kneeled down and spoke sternly, pointed at the shoe, but the boy just sat on the pavement and cried. Eventually the mum picked up the shoe and the boy and struggled down the road.

Just when Dorothy thought she was going to die from tedium a young man arrived at the tenement door. It wasn't Neil, years younger and stockier, but he was dressed smart, shirt but no tie, beige trousers, shiny brown shoes. He pulled his keys out, opened the door and went inside. Dorothy waited. She'd worked out which flat was Neil's and could see two of the windows from here, the living room and one of the bedrooms. Both were bland, cheap art on the walls, not much spice in the décor, muted colours.

She watched the windows for a few minutes then saw the young man appear in the living room. She lifted her binoculars. He took papers from a bag and went through them, walking around the room.

A young woman was at the door of the block, waiting for the buzzer to be answered. She had long chestnut hair, wearing a maroon blouse and black skirt, heels. Smart but not formal. She tucked hair behind her ear, looked nervous. She was buzzed in then two minutes later she appeared at the living-room window with the man. They were chatting. He pointed to something on the page he was holding, she nodded.

Dorothy looked at the whole tenement again and checked she had the correct flat. Definitely Neil's place. Maybe he'd sub-let it or loaned the keys to a friend.

The man left and returned with a glass of water for her, handed it over. She drank. He touched her arm and she smiled at the re-assurance.

They both turned away from the window, another sound.

Dorothy looked and an older couple were waiting downstairs. They were middle-aged, the woman fussing with the man's tie, straightening her skirt. They were a couple, the way they were with each other. They were buzzed in.

Dorothy waited, then saw them in the living room of the flat, with the young pair. The guy showed them the view from the window and Dorothy removed the binoculars for a moment, moved away from her window but kept watching at an angle. The young woman explained something to the couple, pointed at the view, the young guy nodding and smiling. This went on for a few minutes then they all left, came downstairs and got into the young guy's car. It was a new saloon, a black Hyundai.

Dorothy grabbed the binoculars and got the number plate,

wrote it down as the car drove off. She watched them disappear round the corner and wondered what she'd just seen. She touched the number she'd written down then picked up her phone.

30

HANNAH

Dr Gilchrist was animated for a physics lecturer, at least compared to some of the dullards Hannah had endured. He was talking about the solar atmosphere – the photosphere, chromosphere and corona – and the solar wind, the high energy, charged plasma that escaped the sun's gravity at hundreds of kilometres per second. Hannah roughly understood but this wasn't one of her courses, she was here because she wanted to see what kind of man he was.

Because this was Edward, Hugh Fowler's lover for three decades. He was in his later fifties, maybe, and Hannah did the maths in her head. He would've been late twenties when he first got together with Hugh, who would've been around fifty back then. And they'd stuck together all that time, according to Hugh's wife. Wendy said an open marriage, did that mean open to other people too? Would an old man with an old wife and a middle-aged boyfriend restrict himself to that? Wendy said they were beyond physical stuff these days, but maybe she was speaking for herself, maybe it wasn't the case for Hugh, and surely not for Edward.

He was tall and handsome, full head of brown hair, no sign of grey. He looked fit in his button-down blue shirt and jeans. He was enervated as he talked to second years about the solar wind interacting with planets. On Earth we're protected by the magnetic field, the charged particles are deflected leading to auroras and electrical storms. But on a planet with no magnetic field like Venus, the solar wind stripped the atmosphere away. So much about the universe seemed lucky. If certain physical constants had different values, Earth would be uninhabitable, or the whole universe wouldn't exist the way it does. That seemed arbitrary and unfair, we're all lucky to be here at all.

Why end it? That's what Hannah couldn't stand, that Hugh just killed himself for no reason. Of course there could be a hundred reasons. Depression, mental health, physical problems, emotional ones. Guilt, blackmail, self-loathing. We're all a mystery to others and ourselves.

Edward finished up and the students filtered out. This lecture theatre was two doors down from the one she fainted in, but the shimmer and buzz of the overhead lights and air conditioning were the same.

'Dr Gilchrist,' she said, standing up.

He looked up from his leather bag, pushed his glasses up his nose.

Hannah tried to imagine him and Hugh having sex, lying in bed gently stroking each other's cocks. Or maybe just holding hands.

'I'd like to talk to you about Hugh Fowler,' she said.

He came up the stairs, smiled when he reached her. Hannah saw deep-set lines around his brown eyes, across his forehead. He looked a little older up close.

'You're Hannah,' he said, putting out his hand. 'Hugh talked about you.'

Hugh's widow said the same thing. What was Hannah's role in this?

'Really?'

Edward was taken aback by her tone. 'He liked you very much. Said you were an intelligent young woman.'

'He hardly knew me. And I hardly knew him, apparently.'

Edward nodded. 'You've spoken to Wendy.'

'Can you explain your set-up to me?'

Edward's face fell. 'I miss him so much.'

Hannah shifted her weight. 'When I spoke to Wendy she didn't seem all that bothered that he'd committed suicide.'

Edward touched the frame of his glasses. '"Succumbed".'

'What?'

'I think it's more sensitive to say he "succumbed" to suicide, rather than "committed". We commit crimes but succumb to illness.'

Hannah was annoyed she'd been called out, even more annoyed he was right. She hadn't considered the terminology before and her cheeks flushed. 'Sorry.'

Edward shook his head. 'There's no need to be.'

'I just need to understand.'

Edward waved around the empty lecture theatre. 'There's so much we don't understand.'

'About the universe. But what about here?' Hannah tapped at her chest. 'Surely we need to understand each other?'

Tears formed in Edward's eyes. He reached for a handkerchief and dabbed, blew his nose. He gradually recovered, touched his glasses again, a nervous habit.

'I first met Hugh thirty-two years ago.' He gave Hannah a look. 'Before you were even born. Which makes me feel incredibly old.'

Hannah tried to imagine Edward and Hugh as younger men, flirting with each other at a faculty do, shy looks over warm wine in plastic cups.

Edward's eyes were still glassy with tears. 'We woke something in each other. It was remarkable. I'd always known I was gay on some level, but it was buried deep. I was married when we met.'

'Not anymore?'

Edward shook his head. 'I was so unfair to Helen. I mean, I loved her, I truly did, but not in the way she ever wanted. I thought if I just kept on something would change, but of course it didn't. None of it was her fault. That's my one regret, that I had to hurt her to be true to myself.'

'So your wife left you but Hugh's wife didn't leave him?'

Edward looked around the room as if the answer might appear on the whiteboard. 'Hugh's situation was different, he was bisexual. And his relationship with Wendy was very different to Helen's and mine.'

'So you were happy to share him?'

'To begin with, happy would be overstating it,' Edward said, running a hand through his hair. 'But Hugh made it very clear where he stood. I can't say he ever gave me the wrong idea.'

'You never wanted more, you never wanted him for yourself?'

Edward shook his head. 'That wasn't an option.'

'And that was enough for both of you?'

Edward looked confused. 'I don't know what you mean.'

'I just wonder how open Hugh's marriage was. If he had a relationship with you, maybe he had other relationships.'

Hannah felt a draught as the door to the lecture theatre opened. A student poked his head in, looked round, left. The interruption burst the bubble around them.

'Why do you need to know any of this?' Edward said.

Hannah went into her bag and pulled out the medal. It seemed to throb with brightness in her fist. She held it up.

'This has to mean something, he was holding it when he died.'

Edward frowned and took it. 'Why do you have it?'

'And the acid,' Hannah said, ignoring the question. 'It's a crazy way to kill yourself.'

'If you say so.'

'Where did he get it?'

'I have no idea.'

'And the whole Schrödinger's cat thing.'

'What?'

Hannah chewed her cheek. 'It's the same acid Schrödinger used in his thought experiment. That's not a coincidence.'

'It must be.'

Hannah was surprised to feel tears coming. She swallowed. 'We talked about quantum immortality, quantum suicide. I think he was trying to tell me he was going to do it.'

'Why would he tell you, not me or Wendy?'

'I don't know.'

Edward pushed his glasses up his nose again, and Hannah wanted to grab those glasses and crush them underfoot.

'We don't always get answers,' Edward said. 'The scientific life has taught me that.'

Hannah put her hand out and he gave her the medal.

'That's not good enough,' she said heading for the door. 'It's just not good enough.'

31

DOROTHY

Dorothy closed her eyes and lifted her face to the sun, felt the warmth. She thought about something Hannah told her about cosmic rays, how thousands of neutrinos passed through our bodies every second. She imagined those particles tearing through her bones and organs and into the earth.

She opened her eyes. Middle Meadow Walk was busy as always, cyclists and skateboarders, tourists and students, young mums and pensioners. She realised she fell into the latter category and was surprised all over again to be a seventy-year-old widow in Scotland. She pictured herself as a seventeen-year-old high school student in Pismo Beach, skipping classes to hang at the beach or grab a milk-shake in the diner. Those two people seemed completely unrelated.

'Always the sun worshipper.'

She smiled as Thomas leaned in for a hug then sat. She'd arrived first so tea and pastries were on her. She poured him a cup.

'I'm confused,' Thomas said, removing his sunglasses. 'I thought you found the girl.'

Dorothy smiled. 'I did.'

'That's some good detective work, by the way.'

She bowed her head at the compliment. 'But I told her I'd find her father.'

Thomas nodded and added milk to his tea. 'Are you sure that was the only reason she ran away?'

'You mean something at home?'

Thomas nodded.

'I think so. I know stepdads are supposed to be evil paedophiles, but he seemed genuine when I spoke to him.'

'Well, the police don't have anything on him.'

Dorothy nodded. 'That's good. And Sandra?'

'Nothing to report.'

'She did seem odd when I spoke to her,' Dorothy said.

'Odd how?'

'I don't think she was telling me the whole truth about Abi's dad.'

Thomas picked up a Danish pastry and pulled off a chunk. 'I might be able to help you on that front.'

Dorothy raised her eyebrows and Thomas smiled. She had a sudden urge to lean over the table and kiss him, just to feel a man's lips against hers for the first time in months. She imagined touching his arm, his chest under his shirt. But he was so much younger than her, still with a life ahead of him.

'Go on,' she said.

Thomas sipped tea and sat forward. A skateboarder rattled past heading uphill, pushing hard. Thomas waited until the noise died down.

'The flat doesn't belong to Neil Williams. In fact, I couldn't find anything on him.'

'How do you mean?'

'He's not on the police info network. But I dug a little deeper, he's not on the electoral roll for that area either.'

'So he hasn't been in trouble with the police, he doesn't own the flat or vote, that doesn't necessarily mean anything.'

'You said he travels a lot?'

'That's what Sandra told me.'

'I got one of our guys to check online, nothing.'

'So?'

Thomas ran his tongue around his teeth. 'That might not seem weird to people of our vintage, but it's strange for someone who works in sales.'

'OK.' Dorothy took a bite of a small, sweet thing she'd ordered at random. 'What else?'

'The car,' Thomas said. 'It's owned by a company called CTL, Creative Talent Limited.'

'What do they do?'

'All sorts of things. They're entertainment promoters, they run a bunch of things during the Fringe. Also corporate events. And provide "bespoke creative logistics".'

'What does that mean?'

Thomas shrugged and took a piece of paper from his jacket pocket, slid it across the table.

'The info is there, along with details on the flat.'

'What about it?'

'It's owned by a property company, rented out.'

'To who?'

'You'll need to ask the owners.' Thomas tapped the paper. 'It's all there.'

Dorothy touched his hand and took the paper.

'So I've got a dad who doesn't exist, a promotions company and a flat rental. Not exactly smashing the case, are we?'

'Sorry.'

Dorothy smiled. 'I suppose *I'm* the private investigator.'

'Indeed.'

They both drank tea, Thomas poured some more. Dorothy watched the steam rise from the cups.

'So,' Thomas said. 'I heard about Craig's case coming to court.'

Dorothy took a deep breath. This thing with Abi was a useful distraction from that, but she couldn't avoid it forever. 'First thing tomorrow in the High Court.'

'How do you feel about it?'

'Pretty sick, to be honest.'

Dorothy's hand went to her neck as she remembered Craig's hands on her throat. The bruising was long gone but she pictured her windpipe being squeezed and felt her breath catch. She reached for her tea but her trembling hand fumbled the cup and it clanked in the saucer, spilled onto the table. Thomas took her hands in his and squeezed. Dorothy felt a jolt of energy up her arms, was warmed by his smile as they locked eyes.

'You're strong,' he said.

'I don't feel it.'

'You are.'

It was like he made it true by saying it. She squeezed his hand and decided.

'I want to ask you something,' she said, eyes darting to their hands on the table.

Thomas didn't speak, waited.

'When this is all over, I wondered...'

She didn't know how to finish. He didn't interrupt.

She looked up again, held his gaze. 'I wondered if you'd like to go out with me. On a date.'

The kindness on his face, the smile in his eyes. She knew what he was going to say before he said it.

'I thought you'd never ask.'

32

JENNY

'Thanks for coming,' Jenny said.

Liam made a face like she'd insulted him. 'Don't be daft, I'm here for you.'

He reached over and touched her hand on the scuffed wooden table. Saint Giles Café was a narrow space, exposed brick and distressed wooden beams, mustard walls in between, a blackboard of expensive specials. Everything was expensive in the city centre, twenty yards from the Royal Mile, but tourists still paid. Jenny looked out of the window down the street, saw the terrorist prevention gates, curved concrete blocks across the road. Except the central swing-gate was open, so in you come, terrorists, blow up the cathedral across the road, plough into the spread of visitors staring in the whisky-shop window. Please run over the jugglers and buskers.

Jenny breathed deeply and felt Liam squeeze her hand.

'You didn't sign up for this,' she said.

'I did.'

Maybe he did. He asked her out in the aftermath of Craig's violence, so he knew what he was getting into. She hated the way Craig got under her skin when she had this handsome, considerate man who wanted to be with her, and who had his own fucked-up backstory to deal with.

'Where are Hannah and your mum?' Liam said.

She checked her phone. 'On their way.'

She'd wanted to get here early. She looked across the road at the High Court. The front entrance was round the corner on Lawnmarket, the famous David Hume statue outside, his toe rubbed smooth for luck. How did that get started? Same with Greyfriars Bobby's nose, that wasn't a thing when she was young, now tourists risked death under the forty-two bus by standing in the road to get a picture of their friends touching the statue.

From here she had a perfect view of the side entrance to the High Court. Thomas told her that was where the accused were brought under police guard. It was important to see Craig being delivered. She didn't want to think about the psychology behind that. She'd been drinking black coffee for an hour so she was jittery as she waited for him to appear in handcuffs with a distraught look on his face, full of remorse or anger or hatred or she wasn't sure what she wanted him to look like, just that she wanted to see him debased.

She was ashamed of that impulse. At least she recognised it was shameful, that was something, but she was still here. Her life was out of control, she needed someone to blame and Craig fit the bill. But she'd chosen him, fell in love with him back in the day, laughed with him and fucked him and made Hannah together, what did that say about her? The truth was her life had never felt under control. She scoffed at meditation and mindfulness, poured scorn on her daughter's generation for going to therapy and talking about their feelings, but deep down she knew she needed something like that. But she was petrified what a therapist might find in the darkness of her soul. She was terrified it was just ugliness all the way to her core, a mess of contradictory bullshit that somehow coalesced into a human being. She thought about her mum, with her yoga and meditation, decades before they were popular, so grounded because of it. She wondered how the hell she could get a piece of that.

She looked at Liam and wanted so bad for him to be the anchor to keep her steady, but then she thought of Craig with his hands around Mel's throat, pushing the knife into Jenny's belly, smiling at her from across the prison table.

What a fucking mess this was. It was worse for Hannah, which also filled Jenny with shame, she'd failed to protect her daughter from that evil bastard. She wondered how Hannah was coping. Her daughter didn't talk about the counselling sessions and Jenny was too afraid to ask. Now this business with the physics professor, Jenny couldn't get her head round it. They saw dead bodies at the funeral home every day, but discovering a suicide was different. That was personal, and it seemed like a message. Or maybe it was nothing. But Jenny understood Hannah's need to solve it. Resolution was missing from their lives at the moment. Another reason she was here with Liam, hammering espressos and waiting for the prison van.

A Japanese family in matching rain macs walked past heading to the Royal Mile. A Tesco delivery van stopped down the street. It seemed amazing that ordinary people still lived amongst the tartan tat of central Edinburgh. She presumed they'd owned the flat for generations, no ordinary people could afford to live here now.

Jenny turned to Liam and he smiled.

'This place used to be called Café Florentine,' he said. 'Did you ever come here?'

Jenny smiled. Liam was a few years younger than her but they kept discovering that they'd spent time in the same haunts, known the same people, gone to the same clubs and bars and gigs. As if the universe was trying to get them together for decades, finally hooking them up in middle age. There was something comforting about that but it was bittersweet too, time and energy wasted with the wrong people in the wrong situations.

She shook her head. 'Yes, don't tell me.'

'Late at night.'

'After the clubs shut.'

'It was one of the few places still open that had a licence.'

Jenny smiled. 'It was either this place or...'

'Don't say Negociants.'

Jenny laughed and shook her head. 'Negociants.'

Liam sat back and stared at her. 'Jesus.'

Jenny looked in those green eyes. 'Why didn't I meet you twenty-five years ago?'

'I was a baby,' Liam said, giving her a look. 'You would've been cradle-snatching.'

'Nobody says cradle-snatching these days,' Jenny said, sipping her coffee. 'It's just paedophilia.'

'Then you would've been a paedophile.'

Jenny laughed. 'I love you, too.'

'I do.' Liam gave her a look that made her chest tight.

'You do what?'

He deadpanned her. 'I love you.'

They hadn't said it to each other yet. Jenny swallowed hard. 'Fuck.'

Liam leaned back and snorted. 'That wasn't quite the response I was hoping for.'

'Oh, babes,' Jenny said, reaching for his hand. He wasn't offended and she loved him all the more for that.

'I just wanted you to know,' Liam said. 'No biggie.'

'Fuck off, no biggie,' Jenny said. 'Of course it's a biggie.'

Jenny wanted to jump over the table and snog his face off, grab his arse, fuck him right here on the floor.

'Forget it,' Liam said. He was still smiling.

'It's not that I don't,' Jenny said.

She saw something outside, two police cars speeding round the corner and jamming to a stop outside the court entrance. She waited. She'd been expecting a white van with GEOAmey on the side, had done her research about prison transport. But no van appeared. The police cars sat for a moment, engines toiling, then an officer jumped out of one and went to the other car, spoke to the driver. He was wearing a lot of chunky black gear, but Jenny couldn't see if it included a gun. Only a few special cops had guns.

The cop across the road stared up and down the street. He looked worried. No sign of a van. Jenny started to feel sick.

'What?' Liam said, sensing her panic.

'Something's wrong,' Jenny said, picking up her bag.

Liam followed her gaze. 'You don't know that.'

But Jenny was already out the door, stumbling into a tall Scandinavian man in shorts. She pushed past, across to the cop standing by the car. He was talking into the radio at his lapel and Jenny heard static between voices, the void between what he said and the response. But she already knew what the response was, she'd known this all along, this was her destiny, to stand outside court and feel a panic attack restricting her breath and her blood flow and her voice.

The cop was shorter than a cop should be.

'Negative,' he said. 'No sign here.'

Jenny sensed Liam behind her, but it was like he was a million miles away, she was alone in the universe. She looked at the cops in the car, worried faces, avoiding her gaze.

Static on the radio.

'What is it?' Jenny said. 'Where's Craig?'

The cop looked at her as if she'd grown a second head. 'Who are you?'

'I'm his ex-wife. I'm the one he stabbed. I'm here to testify. Where is he?'

The cop tried to usher her away. 'You can't be here.'

'Tell me where he is,' Jenny said.

She felt Liam touch her arm and she shook him off.

'Tell me,' she said to the cop.

He looked like he was having the shittiest day, Jenny could relate to that.

Then the voice over the radio, anxious even through the static.

'Fucking hell, we've lost the van.'

33

HANNAH

The whisky burnt her throat, made her feel alive, stopped her from jumping out of the window. The ops room was busy and she wasn't the only one drinking. Normally she wouldn't touch this stuff, but with what just happened, she needed it. They didn't know the details yet. Indy was at the table with her, along with Dorothy, the almost empty bottle of Highland Park between them. Einstein wagged his tail at Dorothy, not picking up on the vibe at all. Schrödinger kept his distance, over at a window seat, licking a paw and stretching. Mum and Liam were there too, staring out of the window, and Jenny looked like she was about to cry. She scanned the horizon as if the prison van might trundle across Bruntsfield Links any moment.

The tension in the room was painful. Indy smiled at Hannah, a look that said she knew everything was fucked but loved Hannah anyway. Hannah was getting used to that look. She wished she could see her girlfriend with just a simple smile, one that said the world was going to be OK.

Thomas came in from the hall where he'd been on the phone to the station. He ran a hand through his hair. His body language was not promising.

'They found the van,' he said.

'Thank fuck,' Jenny said.

Hannah sensed something was up.

'Where?' Dorothy said.

Hannah shook her head and laughed. 'He's not in it, is he?'

Thomas looked at her for a beat. 'No. He seems to have escaped.'

Einstein gave up on Dorothy and slumped to the floor at her feet.

'How the fuck?' Jenny said. She had her arms crossed, Liam hovering behind.

'The van was found in an industrial estate off Sir Harry Lauder Road in Portobello.'

Jenny stared like she might tear Thomas's head off.

'There's a bus park there, railway sidings, factories and offices.'

'Get to the point,' Jenny said.

'Jenny,' Dorothy said, and it carried a weight that Hannah recognised. 'Please. Thomas is trying to help.'

'He's police, isn't he? The police have lost a murderer.'

'In our defence,' Thomas said, 'prisoners are the responsibility of the prison service until they're in court. In transit that's down to GEOAmey.'

'Who the hell are they?'

'Contractors,' Thomas said. 'It's all privatised now.'

'Well that's worked out great,' Jenny said.

'We're lucky we found the van so quickly,' Thomas said. 'A guy from a nearby office got nosy, went out for a look. He heard banging from inside.'

'Who was it?' Hannah said. She took another hit of whisky, felt it going to her head already. She wasn't used to the alcohol.

'The driver and one of the guards,' Thomas said. 'Hands, feet and mouths taped.'

'And no Craig,' Jenny said.

Thomas looked around the room. 'The other guard is missing.'

Dorothy shifted in her seat. 'You think Craig did something to him?'

Thomas looked uneasy. 'Her. The guard is a woman.'

Hannah felt her stomach tighten, knew what was coming.

'Here we go,' Jenny said.

'The driver said that she helped Craig escape. She let him out of his handcuffs and he assaulted the other guard. She helped tape the guard up. Then the two of them assaulted the driver and took over the van.'

Hannah thought she might puke.

'We don't know where they are,' Thomas said.

'But you can find the woman,' Dorothy said. 'She has an address, family.'

Jenny rubbed at her arm, paced around the room. 'Christ almighty. So this woman has given up her job, her life, for him? Is she young and pretty? Pointy tits?'

Dorothy put a hand in the air. 'Let's stay focused.'

'I can't believe this,' Jenny said. 'I actually cannot fucking believe this is happening.'

Thomas nodded, stayed deferential. Hannah liked him, he wasn't a typical cop, she saw why Dorothy was friends with him.

'We're doing everything we can to find him,' Thomas said.

'Exactly what *are* you doing?' Hannah said.

She was surprised that she was so coherent. This was insane. She thought back to when he called her from prison. What had he said before she hung up? Maybe there was a sign. She felt the brush of Einstein's tail against her leg and jumped. Maybe she wasn't as together as she thought. She reached down and stroked behind his ear.

Thomas looked around the room. 'There are a large number of police units looking for him. We're following up the guard's family and friends. We have her address, car number plate.'

Jenny looked at the clock on the wall. 'But this all happened several hours ago? They could be in Ullapool by now or the Lake District. Or they could've got flights, does he have his passport?'

'We're checking with Fiona,' Thomas said. 'But we haven't managed to get in touch with her yet.'

'You don't think something's happened to her?' Dorothy said.

Thomas couldn't help a sigh. 'Not that we know of.'

'This is a total clusterfuck.' Jenny pointed out of the window. 'He's out there running around, laughing at us, at the cops, the prison, the court, everyone. He's out there fucking some young prison guard, free as a bird, and we're in here scared he might come for us.'

'That's unlikely,' Thomas said. 'We'll post an officer here if that'll make you feel safer.'

'Fuck safer,' Jenny said.

She looked out of the window and Hannah followed her gaze. Her dad was out there, no consequences, no remorse. All that diminished-responsibility shit was gone. He was his own pure self. She wondered about her genetic inheritance. She couldn't stand the idea that she was anything like him, but she couldn't deny they were made of the same stuff.

She stared at the trees twitching in the wind and hoped he was on a flight to Bangkok or Nairobi or Lima, never coming back.

'Shit,' Dorothy said, looking at her watch and standing up. 'We have a funeral to conduct.'

34

DOROTHY

Dorothy was wrong about Annabel Veitch. When they'd picked up Walter's body Dorothy had noted how flippant Annabel seemed about her husband's death. But what right did Dorothy have to judge? She thought about her own reaction to losing Jim. Maybe constantly self-analysing did you no favours and stopped you moving on. When you're seventy years old is there anywhere for you to move on to? She thought about asking Thomas out, holding his hand, touching his chest, feeling his warmth against her skin. She wasn't dead yet.

Annabel Veitch sat in the dark, wood-panelled space of Morningside Parish Church with a large congregation of mourners. Dorothy had to hand it to the Catholic Church, they knew about ceremony. She was a lifelong atheist but there was something about the swinging incense, the sprinkled holy water, the recitation and intonation and murmuration, the priest in his robes like a seventies prog-rock keyboard player.

And they got a good turnout. Well over a hundred here, Walter's coffin down the front, Annabel staring at it wondering where her life would go now. No one to talk to when she came in from the golf, no one to nag about eating too much sausage. No one to touch her hip in bed at night, just to let her know he was still there.

Dorothy and Archie stood at the back, hands clasped in front of them, discreet. The priest gave communion to those who wanted, many of them touching Walter's casket as they passed. The flesh and blood of Christ, what an idea. Let's eat the saviour so he can be a part of us. Dorothy remembered standing over the cremated ashes of her husband after they'd burnt him on a pyre in the back garden, dipping her finger into the dust and sucking it, his atoms becoming a part of her. Not so different.

The ceremony eventually finished, and Dorothy and Archie came forward and wheeled the gurney with Walter's coffin down the aisle and out to the waiting hearse. They were heading to Mortonhall Crem, Dorothy's least favourite funeral space in the city, a brutalist seventies concrete construction full of odd angles and corners. It felt like cremating someone on the set of a cheap sci-fi show.

Dorothy and Archie got in the hearse and waited for the family to exit the church. It took a long time, they were doing the line-up, but Walter wasn't going anywhere. Sitting in contemplation was one of the advantages of the funeral business, you got a chance to think about things.

'Are you OK?' Archie said.

She looked at him. Thought about his dead mother lying in the fridge at the house. 'Shouldn't I be?'

'Just the whole business with Craig.'

'It's Jenny and Hannah I feel sorry for.'

'But it affects you too. You always do that, look out for others before yourself.'

Dorothy was surprised, Archie didn't tend to talk so openly. 'Do I?'

'All the time.' Said with a smile.

Dorothy thought about that. 'Speaking of which, how are you coping? With everything.'

'I'm fine.'

Fine, the word covered so many sins, a universal signal of not wanting to talk. Scottish men were always 'fine', even when they were suicidal, struggling to cope, losing their will or their minds.

'You know I'm here for you,' Dorothy said.

Archie squirmed in his seat. That kind of open declaration was like poison to him. 'I know.'

Dorothy looked in the rearview mirror. Mourners were still trickling out of the church, mostly elderly, the young don't want to face mortality. They're invincible, of course.

She thought about Jimmy X. The girlfriend in a women's refuge. They could've had a life together if things worked out differently. Just bad luck, maybe, or self-destruction, or society crushing the life out of them.

She thought about Abi, back with her family, her biological dad dancing somewhere in the wind. She thought about Hannah's dead professor, a wife and a lover left behind, and who knew what else. She thought about her daughter's ex-husband, alive and free out there somewhere.

She felt scunnered, a good Scots word, sickened.

35

JENNY

A police car was parked outside Fiona's place on Ann Street. That would make the neighbours talk. They probably already knew everything, Craig's escape was headline news.

The cop in the car eyeballed Jenny as she rang Fiona's doorbell. A female officer opened the door, Fiona behind.

'Let her in,' Fiona said.

The cop stood aside and Jenny followed Fiona to the living room. A little girl was watching cartoons on television, engrossed.

'Sophia, this is Jenny,' Fiona said.

The girl glanced round. 'Hi.' Then back to cartoons.

Jenny had never seen Craig's other daughter face-to-face, but felt like she knew her. She'd seen pictures of the girl from birth onwards, stalking Craig and Fiona online after Craig left her. She was startled to see the girl now, an anxious knot in her throat as if Sophia embodied Craig's betrayal, which was fucking ridiculous.

Sophia was seven years old but looked older in her blue blazer and pleated skirt. She had a punnet of strawberries in front of her, discarded green stalks piled in the corner. She lifted a strawberry and took a bite, and Fiona nodded Jenny through to the kitchen.

Jenny saw the half-empty glass of white wine on the kitchen island, then the boarded-up window out to the back garden.

Fiona saw Jenny's gaze and shook her head. 'He broke in while I was at work. Clothes, money, electronics he could sell. He knew the alarm didn't work, knew when we'd be out. Bastard.'

'Passport?' Jenny said, staring at the broken glass swept into a corner.

Fiona nodded. 'He's probably on the other side of the world by now.'

She took a large drink then went to the fridge and pulled out a bottle of pinot grigio. 'Want some?'

Jenny swallowed and nodded.

Fiona poured a glass and handed it over. She stood in a trance, staring through at Sophia watching TV.

Jenny drank. 'He is such a cunt.'

Fiona nodded. 'Total cunt.'

Jenny exhaled. 'Last time I was here, all we did was talk about him. Maybe we'll spend our lives talking about him.'

'He's the one thing we have in common,' Fiona said, a laugh under her breath.

Jenny waved at the window. 'Do you really think he's going to disappear from our lives? That seems too easy for him.'

Fiona glugged wine. 'What about the prison guard? The cop here won't tell me anything.'

'She's married,' Jenny said. 'Her and her car are missing. The police are watching her flat and her parents' house. But I don't suppose she'll show up, not until Craig's done with her.'

'You think she's in danger?'

Jenny lifted a hand to heaven. 'No more than the rest of us.'

Fiona slumped onto a stool and clunked her wine glass on the marble surface. She placed her face in her hands and sobbed, gulping noises and tears on her fingers, her shoulders shaking.

Sophia turned at the noise and stared at her mum, then looked at Jenny as if she was to blame. She slowly got up and came through.

'What did you say to her?' she said to Jenny.

'Nothing.'

The sound of Sophia's voice made Fiona jump and she wiped at her cheeks with the heels of her hands. 'Jesus, I'm sorry. Come here.'

The girl had a smudge of strawberry juice on her chin, and

Jenny had a flash of all the blood in Dorothy's kitchen when Craig stabbed her.

Sophia gave her mum a hug then untangled herself.

'We had burglars,' she said, pointing at the broken window. 'They took my iPad.' Her delivery was deadpan. 'So I have to just watch television until the insurance get me a new one. Mum says it'll be a better one than before.'

'OK,' Jenny said. Her grip on her wine glass was too tight and she loosened it before it shattered and spilled all over the floor.

Sophia walked back to the other room and Fiona swallowed hard over and over again. 'Obviously I didn't tell her.'

'How is she coping?'

Fiona shook her head. 'She was already having nightmares about her dad being locked up, now she'll probably have nightmares about strangers coming into our home.'

'Are the police sure it was Craig?'

Fiona gave her a hard stare. 'Who else?'

'No CCTV in the street?'

'They're asking neighbours.'

'He's fucking shameless.'

'We both knew that, didn't we?'

Jenny nodded.

Fiona drank. 'At least you got to hit him.'

'It didn't do any good.'

'I bet it felt great.'

Jenny smiled. 'It did.'

She looked around the kitchen, full fruit bowl, lilies in a vase, knife block with half a dozen handles sticking from it. She imagined Craig climbing through the window, an invader in his own home, taking what he liked, doing what he liked. His escape was just another message from the universe that whatever he did was fine. She imagined grabbing one of those knives and plunging it into his heart.

'We're selling up,' Fiona said.

'What?'

'The house, the business. I don't have any choice.'

'Can't you hold on until things settle down?'

Fiona made a noise like she was being strangled. 'The company is dead. All our clients have left. Even I can't spin this shit. And we've already missed several mortgage payments. We're up to our eyes in debt.'

'Surely they could cut you some slack.'

'We're moving back in with my mum.' Her face made it clear this wasn't welcome. 'Imagine, in my forties and moving back to Mum's house.'

Jenny had done exactly the same, but she kept quiet.

'The worst thing is,' Fiona said, 'Mum always warned me about Craig. If he was willing to cheat on you, he would be willing to cheat on me.'

'I'm sure she didn't have this in mind.'

Jenny counted her blessings with Dorothy. Through all that had happened, Dorothy always loved her on her own terms.

Her phone pinged in her bag. She took it out, a number she didn't recognise.

I'm gone. Have a nice life. Cx

She stared at the screen until the words blurred, then looked up and realised the blurriness was because of her tears.

36

HANNAH

Hannah threw herself into the seat and thumped her bag on the floor. 'Thanks for fitting me in.'

Rita tried to keep her face calm but something under the surface hinted at fear. Hannah embraced the idea that someone was scared of her, felt herself grow stronger.

'How are you?' Rita said.

'Well.' Hannah looked around the room, imagined someone jumping out of a cupboard at her. 'My dad has escaped from prison.'

Rita laughed, presuming it was a joke. After a moment she covered her mouth in embarrassment. 'Shit. Seriously?'

Hannah nodded. 'Haven't you seen the news?'

She grabbed her phone from her bag and handed it over. The BBC page had Craig's prison mugshot and an unflattering photo of the missing guard, plus a blurry shot of the prison van in an industrial estate surrounded by police tape.

Rita scanned the story, hand still over her mouth.

'Jesus Christ.'

'Right?'

Hannah felt something inside her, then she heard her own laughter, felt it forcing out of her, couldn't stop it, her diaphragm expanding and contracting. She laughed as her body shook and wondered about losing control, peeing herself here on Rita's cheap seat, her eyes welling with tears so that she bolted from the seat and pretended to look out of the window as she wiped her face.

'Hannah.'

She looked at the Meadows for a long time then eventually turned. Rita was holding her phone out.

'Please sit,' she said.

Hannah stretched her neck, thought about her dad out there. She tried to think what she would do if she was on the run. She took her phone and sat down.

'I don't know what to say,' Rita said.

'Don't bother,' Hannah said. 'We're beyond words.'

'Hopefully we're never beyond words, my job is talking about things.'

Hannah shook her head. 'This is off somewhere else now.' She mimed birds flying with her hands. 'This is out in the ether, the fabric of the universe, the interconnected energy fields, it's Buddhist and quantum and relativistic and it's everywhere.'

'I'm detecting anxiety,' Rita said.

Hannah clapped sarcastically. 'Genius.' She couldn't stop herself, the clapping kept going as if someone else controlled her hands. 'Anxiety. What else?'

'A lot of anger.'

'What about neutrinos?'

Rita frowned. 'Sorry?'

Hannah lifted her hands above her head as if praising the sun. 'Can't you feel them?'

Rita shifted in her chair. 'I don't understand.'

Hannah hunched forward. 'Do you know how many neutrinos pass through your body every second?'

'I don't know what a neutrino is.'

'It's a fundamental particle, probably the least understood.'

'OK.'

'The sun throws them out, gazillions all the time.'

'And what do they do?'

Hannah smiled. 'That's just it, they barely interact. No one really understands them. They can pass right through the Earth and keep on going. They're streaming through you right now. A hundred trillion every second.'

Rita looked at her own body.

'Can you imagine that?' Hannah said.

A shake of the head. 'No.'

Hannah put her hands out as if checking for rain. 'Can you feel them?'

Rita didn't speak.

Hannah scratched at her scalp. So much of the universe didn't make a bit of sense and it was killing her.

'Imagine being so hard to detect,' Hannah said, moving her hands around like a hippy dancing. 'Nature's ghost.'

She pictured the particles tearing the skin from her hands, her body. She pictured her dad, impossible to detect. She rubbed the invisible neutrinos against her face until her skin was sore, until she felt pain.

She ran her fingers along the fridge doors until she came to Hugh's one. A blast of air-conditioned coolness hit her from the vent above, made her think of a spirit leaving the body. On cheap supernatural shows they always had someone being hit by a gust of air, hair billowing, ghosts mysteriously acting like hairdryers.

She opened the fridge and slid him out. According to the notes he'd been embalmed but not prepped yet. He was still in the white body bag, and she unzipped the top, struggling as it snagged at the corner, then peeling it away.

She stared at his dead face forever. Looked at the bags under his eyes, the deep lines across the forehead, the wispy hair raised as if by static from his head even now. It seemed weird seeing his bare shoulders, oddly pointy given that the rest of his body was so soft and round. He had a pronounced collarbone, and she put her hand out and held it over his neck. It seemed like an intrusion to touch him, but Archie did it all the time in his job, manhandling the bodies into position, injecting them, draining arteries, massaging muscle and skin.

She unzipped the bag further and stared at his liver-spotted hands. Those hands that had touched his wife, his lover, God knows who else. The hands that had held the acid bottle, the medal. She touched the back of his left hand, felt the loose skin, the embalmed vein underneath.

'What are you doing?'

She jumped and turned to Indy behind her. She bumped Hugh's hand as she turned and it fell from the tray and dangled down, like he was chilling on a sun lounger by the pool. She picked it up and placed it by his side.

'Just saying goodbye,' she said, patting his hand and feeling stupid.

Indy came into the room, arms folded. 'Hannah.'

'What?'

'Now you're messing with dead bodies?'

Blood rose to Hannah's cheeks. 'It's what you do for a living.'

Indy shook her head, leaned past and zipped up Hugh's bag.

'Exactly, it's my job. We can't have just anyone hanging out back here, talking to the dead whenever they like.'

'I'm not just anyone.'

Indy slid the tray away and locked the door. She leaned against the body fridge. 'You can't come in here and muck about.'

'I wasn't mucking about.'

Indy softened her look. 'I know you're going through some stuff.'

'You think?'

Indy folded her arms again. 'I take it counselling didn't go well.'

'He's out there, Indy.' Hannah felt her voice break in her throat. 'Laughing at me.'

Indy pursed her lips. 'Your dad is not laughing at you.'

'He is and you don't give a shit.'

Indy stared at her for a long time and Hannah fronted it out.

Indy pushed away from the fridge. 'Fuck you, Han, honestly.'

Hannah wanted to grab her, stop her walking away, but she

didn't. She wanted to hurt someone, she wanted to lash out, and Indy was here.

Indy shook her head. 'You don't get to treat me like this. It doesn't matter where your dad is, what he's done. You don't get to treat me like an emotional punch bag, like it's all my fault.'

'That's not fair—'

'No, it's you who's not fair,' Indy said. 'Acting like the universe is out to get you. I've got news for you, babes, the universe doesn't give a shit about you, the sooner you realise it the better.'

Hannah swallowed, thought about all the bodies in the fridges behind her, all the corpses in all the graves across the city, nothing more to worry about.

Indy walked away, chin up, hair bouncing.

Hannah wanted to shout after her but couldn't think what to say.

Indy had already left as Hannah's phone rang in her pocket. She took it out, Wendy. She leaned against Hugh's fridge door and took the call.

'Is that the young detective lady?' Wendy said.

'Hi.'

A pause down the line. 'I need your help.'

37

DOROTHY

The Alba Property office was shiny, neat and bland. Dorothy waited in the beige reception until her name was called by the sparkly receptionist, then walked into the fragrant office behind a property agent whose name she'd already forgotten.

When they sat, she saw the woman's nametag said Melanie.

'So, you're looking for a property to let?' Melanie said.

The tone of her voice suggested this was a waste of her time. They had web listings, for God's sake, why not do it online? But Dorothy played the old-lady card over the phone, insisted on an appointment. She looked around the office, corporate art on the walls, blonde shelves, a discreet digital clock.

'That's right,' she said, making her voice sound weak. She'd also walked in unsteadily, all part of the game.

'What sort of area did you have in mind?' Melanie said, typing on her computer.

Dorothy remembered the water cooler in reception, with those little paper cones stacked up.

'I'm actually looking for something quite specific,' she said.

A bus trundled past outside the window, down Dundas Street towards Stockbridge. The sound of thick tyres on the old setts rattled the window, so Alba couldn't afford double glazing. Maybe the successful corporate façade was just that.

'Oh yes?'

'Do you have properties on Lochend Butterfly Way?'

Melanie put on a puzzled smile. 'That is specific, let me look.'

She typed and Dorothy coughed loudly, made a show of swallowing, coughed again and raised a tissue to her mouth. Melanie glanced up and winced at the germs spreading across the desk towards her.

'I'm afraid we don't have anything in that street, but there are several interesting properties in that part of Leith.'

She turned the screen to show Dorothy the listings. Dorothy leaned forward, coughed again, didn't quite get the tissue up in time, Melanie recoiled. Dorothy dragged her finger down the screen. Took her time. Melanie was uncomfortable being this close to a sick old woman.

'Are you sure about that street? I'm positive I saw one of your signs there just the other day.'

'If it's not in the system, we don't have it,' Melanie said, folding her arms.

Dorothy tapped the screen. 'Could you please check?'

Melanie didn't hide her sigh, turned the screen back to face her, typed some more. Paused. More typing.

Dorothy raised the tissue to her face and coughed hard, prolonged, her shoulders shaking. Eventually she settled down, still holding the tissue, as Melanie gave her side eyes.

'Ah,' Melanie said, moving her mouse. 'We do own a property on Lochend Butterfly Way, but I'm afraid it's on a long-term lease.'

'But I saw a sign.'

Melanie shook her head. 'Not recently.'

Dorothy coughed again.

'OK,' she said, between gasps. 'Is there something else in the area...'

She coughed hard, forcing air out of her lungs, doubled over, kept coughing as if whatever it was would never shift, kept retching with her head near her knees, her skirt shaking with the force of it. She tried to come up for air but coughed again, put her hand on the edge of the desk to steady herself. She straightened up, tried to speak, but was overtaken by coughing again, Melanie looking worried.

'Are you OK?'

Dorothy tried to nod between convulsions. 'Fine.'

Coughed again and again until Melanie was out of her seat and at Dorothy's side, hovering a hand over her back.

'How can I help?' Melanie said.

Dorothy gasped, put her head up. 'Maybe a glass of water?'

Melanie nodded and left the office, out to the water cooler.

As soon as she was gone, Dorothy stopped the fake cough and turned the computer screen to face her. Checked the listings, 5 Lochend Butterfly Way was rented to a private company, one she recognised.

Creative Talent Limited.

She turned the screen away and began fake coughing again as Melanie came back in spilling water from a tiny paper cone.

Jason was a smarmy sod. His office had posters for sold-out Fringe shows framed on the walls, a couple of awards on the mantel above the fireplace, which contained a phallic sculpture presumably meant to be edgy. He had a standing desk he was standing at, glugging an enormous green drink from Starbucks. Behind him was a tiny high window that looked out at bins round the back of an adjacent venue. They were in Guthrie Street, a few minutes from the city mortuary, and Dorothy thought about Jimmy X in there. She could smell stale booze and chilli sauce from the bins over the way.

'I don't understand,' he said, in a tone that indicated he couldn't care less. 'What do you want?'

He wore huge round glasses, hair in a quiff, a polka-dot blouse, Capri pants and expensive sandals.

Dorothy held her phone out, recording. 'It's just background for a piece I'm writing on the festival.'

Jason rolled his eyes. 'We are craaazy busy at the mo. You're lucky you caught me.'

'Right.' Dorothy moved closer to his laptop, covered in stickers. There was a screensaver of somewhere in the Far East, a beach in Thailand maybe, somewhere he went on his gap year.

'If you could just explain what Creative Talent do.'

She listened as he talked for a few minutes, about the shows they promoted, the famous people they brought up every year, the other stuff they got up to, musicals and dance shows, comedy, theatre, standard arts promo shtick.

'Cool,' Dorothy said.

It clearly tickled Jason that an old lady said 'cool'. In fact it probably tickled him that this old lady even existed and was in front of him in his crappy office. He didn't give the impression he'd ever spoken to anyone over the age of forty.

'And is that it?' Dorothy said, her voice demure, respectful.

'How do you mean?' Jason took a long slurp of his drink. Plastic straw, the climate message clearly hadn't got to him yet.

'I heard something about property development?'

Jason frowned. 'Where did you hear that?'

Dorothy put on her dumb face. 'Must've read it somewhere.'

'I think you're getting us confused with someone else. We don't own any properties.'

'Not own, lease. Flats around town or something.'

Jason narrowed his eyes. 'At festival time, for sure.'

'How do you mean?'

Jason looked at her like she was stupid. 'Have you any idea how much it costs to put on a show here in August? The city is crazy.'

Dorothy wanted to say she'd lived here for five decades, she'd seen the festival go from nothing to everything, but she kept quiet.

'Yes?'

'So for hospitality,' Jason said, sipping his drink. 'It makes like a gazillion times more sense to rent flats and houses than put artists in hotels.'

'And you do that?'

'For sure.'

'I thought artists had to sort that stuff for themselves?'

Jason rolled his eyes again. Dorothy wanted to take those big glasses and crush them.

'Well yes, but they might as well rent a place from us as someone else. That way CTL make more money.'

Dorothy nodded, looked at her phone. 'But you don't do that the rest of the year?'

'Like I said, we don't own anywhere, we just rent then sublet to artists.'

'So if I told you CTL were renting a place in Leith right now, that wouldn't make any sense.'

'No,' Jason said. 'It wouldn't.'

Dorothy sighed and switched her phone off.

38

JENNY

Jenny got back in the van. She picked up the printout on the passenger seat and crossed the Sally Army off the list. That made eight homeless shelters she'd visited, but there were so many more. She put the car in gear and drove down Holyrood Road. She was heading from Cowgate to Leith, trying to skip the terrible traffic. She drove past parliament and Holyrood Palace, tourists wandering into the road to get pictures of Salisbury Crags, a taxi delivering men in suits to the parliament building, two armed guards at the entrance.

She knew this was pointless but she had to do something. The idea of Craig being free made her skin crawl. She'd given Thomas the number Craig used to text her, but it came back with nothing. A burner that hadn't been used again or switched on. The police checked Craig's bankcards, Shona's too, that was the guard's name. Shona Middleton, who'd left a husband in Gorgie to embark on this shitshow. Anyway, neither had used their cards so how were they living? Shona had withdrawn a few hundred pounds before the escape so that would keep them going for a while. Or maybe buy them tickets to fly somewhere, but there was no sign of their passports being used at any Scottish airport. They could get to England and fly from there, or maybe hide on a ferry. Jenny couldn't fathom it. What was the game plan?

She tried to think like Craig. She'd known him for years, but she hadn't really known him, the divorce and all the rest proved that. She hadn't known a thing about the real Craig, so maybe she couldn't get inside his head. So this is what she was doing, driving around homeless shelters she'd already visited looking for Jimmy

X, with pictures of Craig and Shona, showing them to anyone. It was a long shot but it was all she had.

She drove over Abbeyhill and down Easter Road, cut along Dalmeny Street onto Leith Walk. There was comfort in knowing a city, growing up in a place, accumulating information about how parts are linked. It gave Edinburgh a personality, made it her own. She knew this city better than the tourists traipsing up the Royal Mile, better than the rich or poor residents stuck in their ghettos. She imagined the van as a drop of blood in the city's arteries, journeying from the heart to the outer veins, the roads less travelled.

She drove past the old Leith Water World, now a grubby soft-play centre where she'd taken Hannah as a kid. Then Great Junction Street, where she went to a crazy house party with Craig back when they were almost kids themselves. A lot of amphetamines and a sleazy guy with a waterbed were all she could remember. Then she was on Bonnington Road driving past the medical practice where she got NHS acupuncture after Hannah was born, for a trapped nerve in her back. This wasn't even her part of town and it was embedded in her heart.

She was almost at the Bethany place. It was a Christian charity, not normally Craig's bag, but maybe he was trying to throw them off.

Her phone rang on the passenger seat. It was not a number in her contacts. Her chest tightened and she swerved into a parking space by a bin, hit the brakes. The fucking bastard. She wondered about tracing calls. She stared at the jumble of numbers like it was a code to be unscrambled. Then she picked up and answered.

'Hello?'

Silence on the other end. The sound of breathing.

'Hello?' Jenny said again. 'Is this you?'

The phone glowed against her ear, heated up her hand.

'Is this who?' A woman's voice, young.

Jenny blinked, breathed, stared out of the window at the industrial estate across the road.

'Who is this?' she said.

A long pause. 'Are you Jenny Skelf?'

'Yes.'

'I don't know if I should be doing this,' the woman said.

'Take your time.'

Jenny heard a baby in the background.

Eventually the woman spoke. 'This is Rachel.'

Jenny wracked her brains. 'Who?'

Another pause, the baby crying, hesitation down the line.

'You asked about me at Women's Aid?'

Rachel had lost a lot of weight since the picture was taken but Jenny still recognised her easily. For a start, she was the only person in Artisan Roast who looked poor. Everyone else wore hipster shabby chic or yummy-mummy designer stuff, while Rachel was in grubby white joggers, hi-tops and a charity-shop Bill Cosby jumper. She was struggling with a young baby, trying to get a bottle into her mouth. Two women at a nearby table tutted under their breath at her and Jenny gave them a hard glare, which they ignored.

'Rachel.'

She looked up from her grappling match and nodded at the chair. 'Sit.'

There was only a glass of water on the table. A waitress came over and smiled pointedly and Jenny ordered a coffee for herself and a salted caramel milkshake for Rachel.

'Thanks,' Rachel said.

Jenny studied her as she wrangled the baby. She was tall and skinny, drawn complexion, sunken eyes, distinctly skeletal. Her jumper was worn at the elbows, the joggers stained, something dark on one leg. Her trainers were worn at the heels and threadbare in the toes.

'So he's dead?' Rachel said, settling the baby in the crook of her arm. The kid's vest was covered in snot and dribble.

'Yes,' Jenny said. 'Who is he?'

'Why do you want to know?' She had a strong working-class Edinburgh accent.

Why *did* Jenny want to know? It had started as Dorothy's obsession but Jenny had somehow taken it over. On one level it was an obvious distraction from Craig. But there was something about this now, being a real private investigator, she needed to solve things, create order in a universe where there was so little of it. To prevent the slide into chaos.

'We're doing his funeral,' Jenny said.

Rachel frowned. 'I thought you were a detective?'

'We do funerals too.'

'That's weird.'

'It is.'

The drinks arrived and Rachel took a long pull on her milkshake straw. The baby was oblivious, sucking up her own drink greedily. Jenny played with the teaspoon on her saucer.

'So who is he?'

'How did he die?'

Jenny clattered the spoon against her cup. 'Can't you answer a simple question?'

'Can't you?'

Jenny raised a hand. 'Sorry, let's start over.'

Another slurp of milkshake. Jenny sipped her coffee, it was too hot and she burnt the roof of her mouth. She got the picture out of her pocket, placed it on the table. It was crumpled so she smoothed it out. Rachel eventually picked it up, holding the edges like it might explode.

'Christ, we were wasted.' She looked up. 'What happened?'

The baby spat out the bottle and fussed, and Rachel placed her on her shoulder, listened for a burp. Jenny remembered doing the same with Hannah at that age, telescoping back in time to yesterday, it felt like. God, where does it go?

'He was in a car accident,' she said. 'In a graveyard.'

'You're kidding.'

'He was being chased by a police car. He almost hit my mum.'

Rachel nodded. 'Was anyone else hurt?'

'No.'

'What about Buster?'

'Buster?'

'His one-eyed hound.'

Einstein.

'My mum is looking after him. She wants to do the funeral for your friend but the police can't release his body until they know who he is.'

Rachel swallowed and rubbed a finger across the photograph. 'James.'

Jenny's chest went tight. 'What?'

'James.'

Jenny laughed and shook her head.

'What's funny about that?' Rachel said.

'My mum didn't know what to call him, so she's been calling him Jimmy, after my dad.'

'Wow.'

'Yep.'

'How does your dad feel about it?'

'He's dead too.'

'Oh.'

Jenny took a sip of her coffee, drinkable now. 'So you were friends? Boyfriend and girlfriend?'

The baby burped and sicked on Rachel's shoulder. She wiped at it with a napkin and placed the girl in her lap, gave her a spoon to play with. She pushed her milkshake out of reach of grabbing hands. Jenny remembered that awareness, constantly on guard for danger. It never changed.

Rachel smiled. 'No, we were smack buddies.'

'How do you mean?'

'What it sounds like. We took heroin together. On the street.'

Jenny looked around Artisan Roast, people paying several quid for hot drinks, same again for muffins and brownies, Stockbridge disposable income.

Jenny nodded at the baby, who was sticking the spoon in her mouth. 'So this little one isn't his.'

Rachel laughed. 'James was gay.'

'Right.'

'He used to work, you know. Gay bars and clubs. Money for blowjobs and handjobs. I did the same on the street.'

There was a straightforwardness about Rachel that Jenny admired. She didn't dip her voice when talking about this, wasn't proud but wasn't ashamed either.

'Then I got pregnant with wee Zadie here,' she said. 'There was a guy. Not Zadie's dad, a minder.'

'A pimp.'

'No one says "pimp" anymore.'

'What about him?'

'He didn't like that I was pregnant. Some guys get off on that but not many. It meant less work. He wanted me to get rid of her.'

'But you wouldn't.'

'No way,' Rachel said. She jiggled Zadie on her knee and the girl giggled, grabbed at the neck of her mum's jumper and pulled. Rachel untangled her little fist and held it. 'Look at her.'

Jenny nodded, sipped coffee.

Rachel looked round, stared at the door as if her pimp would walk in. 'So I went to Women's Aid. Said I needed somewhere safe, and they set me up. I got straight. Had the baby. I've been so fucking lucky.'

Small acts of kindness, that's all it took sometimes. But the opposite too, small acts of aggression, the world working against you and it could all fall apart.

'What about James?'

Rachel shook her head. 'They discourage any contact with your old world. Women's Aid. Makes sense, whatever you're hiding from will find you. I couldn't stay around that life. Getting clean, fuck me, it's not easy. You ever been addicted?'

Jenny thought about the question. Alcohol was the obvious one, though she hesitated to use the word 'addict'. But the truth was she couldn't imagine a life without it, so maybe she was. 'No.'

'You're lucky.'

Jenny drank and so did Rachel, holding her milkshake high above Zadie's grasp.

'So what can you tell me about James?'

Rachel placed her drink down and thought about it. 'Not a lot, it wasn't like a real friendship. We made sure we were sorted for gear, hung out together, looked after each other if one of us was fucked.'

Jenny tapped the table with her finger. 'What about this picture?'

Rachel smiled. 'We were trying to get clean. Methadone. Not our own prescription, neither of us were registered, it's hard to get your shit together, you know? We used stolen prescription pads and a contact. I dunno. We were trying, right? Anyway, it was James's idea to get some fresh air.'

'On methadone?'

'He was strange like that. I've lived in this fucking city twenty-three years and never been to the castle or up Arthur's Seat. From Wester Hailes, why the fuck would I?'

'How did you end up on the street?'

Rachel drank through her straw, cheeks sucked in. Zadie made a play for the drink so Rachel gave her the straw. Zadie sucked at it and her eyes almost popped out of her head, grin on her face.

'Fuck it, eh? You only live once.' Rachel smiled at Zadie, then held Jenny's gaze. 'Perv stepdad. Oldest story in the world.'

She tapped the picture. 'So we walked up Crow Hill.'

'Crow Hill?'

'That's what he called it, the one next to Arthur's Seat. Said he went there all the time as a kid.'

Jenny had never heard that name before, her whole life in Edinburgh, with the hills looming over her. A secret in plain view, a name no one knows.

'What's James's surname?'

'I never knew it. Some guys called him Gentleman James, how he spoke.'

'How did he speak?'

'Posh Edinburgh. That's not common on the streets.'

Jenny bit her lip. 'Did he ever talk about family or friends?'

Rachel thought about the question. Zadie had gummed the straw to bits and Rachel had to extricate bits of it from her mouth while she struggled.

'Not that I can think of. Like I said, it wasn't that kind of friendship. You live in the moment, you're just surviving.'

'He must've said something.'

Rachel shook her head. 'Everyone on the street is there for a reason, not a good one. People don't want to talk about it.'

'Please,' Jenny said, her fingers drumming on the table. 'Anything you can think of might help.'

Rachel looked out of the window at a delivery van across the road, a taxi trundling past. Then she looked around the room at the strangers they were sitting amongst. She was alone wherever she was, and being in a refuge didn't change that.

'He did mention a school. Said he hated it.'

'You remember the name?'

Rachel chewed on her cheek, screwed up her eyes. 'I think it had "Craig" in the name.'

Jenny got her phone out and Googled. 'Craigmillar?'

That was one of the roughest parts of town, you wouldn't sound posh in Craigmillar, not if you wanted to stay alive.

'No, that wasn't it.'

Jenny scrolled down. 'Craighouse?'

Rachel's eyes lit up as Zadie tried to wriggle out of her grasp.

'That's it, Craighouse. Said it was a total shithouse.'

A private boys' school in the west of the city. How the hell does a Craighouse lad end up hooked on smack and living in a stolen car?

39

HANNAH

Hannah stood outside Hugh's house on Lygon Road and wondered which subject to raise first. She was here to arrange Hugh's funeral but Wendy also intimated on the phone that she might have some detective work for the Skelfs. She rang the bell and waited. Saw a shimmer behind the engraved glass then the door opened and there was Edward Gilchrist raising his eyebrows.

'Come in,' he said, waving her to the living room, where Wendy was in an armchair with a clear drink in a shallow cocktail glass. The drink appeared to have a pickled onion in it. Edward picked up a similar glass from the coffee table.

'A Gibson,' Wendy said. 'Fancy one?'

Hannah looked from her to Edward. Those three huge maps along the wall drew her attention again. She spotted an island off the west coast of Greenland called Disko Island, wondered about that. She remembered something from *The Hitchhiker's Guide to the Galaxy,* about the old guy who designed Norway when they built Earth, got an award for the lovely crinkly edges.

'Sure.'

She wouldn't normally but everything was piling on top of her and she couldn't work out how to get out from the rubble.

Edward fixed her a drink from an ornate wooden cabinet, dropped an onion in it and handed it over. It tasted like sour rocket fuel.

'To Hugh,' Wendy said.

Hannah and Edward raised glasses and Hannah took a tiny sip of hers. It made her tongue numb. She wondered how many Wendy and Edward had already polished off.

'You needed my help,' Hannah said.

Edward stood behind Wendy's chair with his hand resting on it, the two of them like an old married couple. Hannah thought about their relationship, the wife and lover brought together in grief, organising the funeral together. Whatever gets you through.

Wendy glanced at Edward, who gave her a pat on the shoulder.

'I think I'm being targeted,' she said.

Hannah pursed her lips. 'How do you mean?'

'Someone has been calling, asking for Hugh.'

'That doesn't sound unusual.'

Wendy nodded. 'A young man, by the sound of it. I didn't recognise his voice. When I asked what it was concerning, he refused to tell me.'

'Probably just trying to sell something.'

'I didn't get that impression,' Wendy said, sipping her drink.

'Did you tell him Hugh was...'

'You can say "dead", you know.'

Hannah nodded. 'Did you?'

'Do you know how tiresome it is to tell everyone your husband is dead? So repetitive and tedious. Then they treat you like a leper. And ask how it happened. That's not an easy conversation.'

Hannah drank and coughed at the blast of alcohol. 'You didn't seem so bothered last time I was here.'

Wendy's neck muscles tensed.

Edward cleared his throat. 'I don't think that's fair.'

He was right. It was no business of Hannah's how other people grieved. Dorothy told her often enough it was different for everyone, no right or wrong. But this business with Hugh had got to her.

'Sorry,' she said.

'No, you're right, up to a point,' Wendy said. 'The fact he's gone is awful, but it's more awful having to tell everyone over and over again, the neighbours, the newsagent, on the telephone. I'm so tired.'

She suddenly looked it too, small and frail, swamped by that red armchair, the lean figure of Edward hovering over her. She sensed Hannah examining her, and patted Edward's hand.

'Edward has been a godsend. He understands. I don't have to say anything.'

Hannah nodded again. 'So is that it, a weird phone call?'

Wendy shook her head. 'A young man came to the door yesterday asking for Hugh.'

'OK.'

'I didn't recognise him. I'm not sure if it was the same one from the telephone.'

'What exactly did he say?'

'Just that he wanted to speak to Hugh,' Wendy said. 'He checked it was the Fowler residence, then used Hugh's first name.'

'How old was he?'

Wendy looked at Edward, got another pat on the hand.

'Around your age,' she said.

'A student?' Hannah said.

'Possibly. But he didn't seem to know Hugh was dead.'

'You didn't tell him?'

Wendy drank. 'I told you, it's so wearing. I just said he wasn't in.'

'Would you recognise him again?'

'Yes.'

'Can you describe him?'

She did, but it was average height and weight, fair hair, half the young men in the city.

'Was he handsome?'

Edward's grip tensed on the chair back. 'I don't see why that's relevant.'

'No?'

'What you're suggesting is unsavoury,' he said.

Wendy shook her head. 'I don't think it's anything like that, Hugh was an old man.'

And old men never fancy young men, right. Hannah rolled the onion in her drink then popped it in her mouth. It was boozy and bitter. She looked around the room, which seemed brighter than the first time she was here. Maybe it was diminishing grief, or her own changing mental state.

'It could be anything,' she said.

Wendy frowned. 'Hugh didn't keep secrets from me.'

Hannah looked at Edward. 'Really?'

Wendy followed her gaze. 'He was always completely open about Edward.'

'What about the fact he was going to kill himself?'

There was something about Wendy's demeanour that really got to Hannah and she couldn't help herself. Wendy swallowed and looked at the fireplace. Edward squeezed her shoulder again.

'That's uncalled for,' he said.

Hannah put a hand out in supplication then realised it was the hand holding her Gibson so it looked like she was toasting something. She switched hands as Wendy drained her glass.

Hannah got herself together, sat upright. 'So what do you want me to do?'

'Find out who he is and what he wants.'

'You could've just asked him.'

'I did,' Wendy said. 'He refused to say.'

Hannah shook her head. 'I'm not sure how I can help unless he makes contact again.'

'He said he would come back, can you be here?'

'I have motion-activated cameras, I can fit one at the front door. Get a visual on him.'

'How will that help?'

'I'm hoping I'll recognise him. It's most likely he's a student.'

Edward shook his head. 'And if he's not?'

He had a point. Hannah wasn't thinking right, maybe it was the hundred-proof alcohol. 'When he arrives, confront him, tell him Hugh's dead. See what he says.'

'Then what?' Wendy said.

'Stall him and phone me.'

'How can I do that?'

Hannah waved her empty glass. 'Invite him in for one of these.'

Edward and Wendy frowned at each other.

'I don't want him in the house,' Wendy said.

Hannah nodded, thinking. 'I have these wee tracking devices.' She held her fingers apart. 'This big. I can give you one, stick it in his pocket or something.'

'Sounds dangerous,' Edward said. 'What if she gets caught?'

Wendy put a hand out. 'I don't mind.'

Edward shook his head. 'I still think you should call the police.'

Wendy looked at Hannah. 'Hugh trusted her, so I trust her too.'

Edward looked unconvinced as he finished his drink.

Hannah felt the buzz from her cocktail kicking in, the room fuzzy around the edges, those giant maps pulsing with energy.

Wendy got up unsteadily and walked to the Greenland map. Hannah felt something pulling her and went over to it too. She looked at the place names, long words with lots of 'q's, 'a's and 'u's.

'The Inuit have never really had much of a burial culture,' Wendy said. 'Before Christianity they would just wrap the body in caribou hide and leave it on the ice somewhere, weighed down by rocks.'

'OK.'

'With the permafrost, you see. Digging a hole in the ground is hard.'

Wendy turned to face Hannah. Edward was fixing himself and Wendy another drink, clink of bottle and glass. Hannah noticed he wasn't making her one.

'But we love a ritual here in the civilised west.' Wendy's tone made it clear she didn't regard us as civilised at all. 'Hugh wouldn't have wanted any fuss.'

'But it's good to say goodbye,' Hannah said.

'I suppose.'

'Closure.'

'If you say so.'

Wendy clearly didn't believe in closure and Hannah had a hard time with it herself, especially with suicide or whatever happened to Hugh. Without answers, how can we get closure?

Wendy accepted her Gibson from Edward who melted into the background. She drank then turned to Hannah. 'I want the smallest funeral possible. Cremation, no hole in the ground.'

So now they were arranging the funeral, apparently. Hannah nodded. 'OK.'

Wendy smiled. 'And of course we'll need some Inuit throat singers.'

Hannah sucked her teeth. 'Throat singers?'

40

DOROTHY

A sharp wind cut through the trees making Dorothy pull her collar up. The sky was gunmetal and the air was biting, what happened to spring? She'd read about false springs, the equivalent of Indian summers, a short period of warmth before things froze again, just in time for the Scottish summer. She longed for the Californian sun soaking into her bones, that beautiful sharpness, rather than this sludgy cold. Forecasters were warning about a big freeze from the north, maybe snow.

She looked around Binning Memorial Wood, it was beautiful despite the cold. One of a growing number of green burial sites, it was half an hour's drive from the house, Dorothy behind the wheel of the hearse, Archie in the passenger seat. Behind them in the van were Hannah, Indy and Jenny.

Archie had decided on a private service and ceremony, said his mum wanted it by the end. Veronica had outlived all her closest family except Archie, most of her old friends gone too. She didn't want a fuss, like mother, like son. So they had a simple ceremony in the chapel at home, Archie saying soft words, resting his hands on her willow coffin, voice shaky.

And now they were here, with a sturdy young man who worked for the site in attendance, but really Archie and the women were handling everything. They'd done plenty of burials here in the past, they knew the ropes. Literally, as Archie, the staff member, Hannah and Jenny lowered the coffin into the hole with the ropes, tucking them in alongside and stepping back.

Veronica Kidd wasn't religious, so no Bible reading, just a simple goodbye from her son. There was a shallow hole at the head of the grave, and Archie placed a sapling cedar there, filling the earth around it. Then they began on the grave, Indy, Hannah and Jenny grabbing shovels from a pile and helping.

Dorothy remembered digging up two graves six months ago, one with Jenny, the other with Archie. All to prove something to herself which she couldn't really understand now. Digging holes, filling in holes, none of it meant anything in the end. The ceremony mattered, the process of saying goodbye, maybe that was the only thing.

Rain began to fall and the canopy of trees shivered in gusts of wind. Dorothy loved the idea of green funerals and they were getting more popular as people became more aware of their connection to the environment. Indy's Hindu background meant she seemed to understand this more. It seemed like every religion except Christianity had a handle on the interconnectedness of things.

Dorothy lifted a shovel and began helping. Veronica's coffin was covered in earth now, the soil wet and claggy as they dumped clumps into the hole. Dorothy noticed a coldness between Indy and Hannah, they'd barely looked at each other through the ceremony. They were usually so close, unable to take their eyes off each other. Dorothy knew better than to interfere, Hannah was a grown woman, but it pained her to see her granddaughter unhappy. The same for Jenny. The business with Craig, my God, what must she be feeling. She was shovelling dirt like her life depended on it, sweat on her brow despite the weather.

The rain was heavier now, drilling tiny holes in the dirt. Dorothy saw a worm on her shovel, a pink squirm of life, as it was dumped into the grave.

Eventually they were done and placed the shovels in the back of the green van parked nearby. The site employee drove off, leaving them all standing in the wind and rain, the trees whispering and shushing around them, the air stinging their exposed faces.

Archie sank to his knees by the graveside. Hannah went to help him up but Jenny held her back. Archie thrust his fingers into the fresh earth, grabbed two handfuls and sat on his haunches looking at his fists, squeezing mud through his fingers. He lurched onto all fours and lowered his head, rain pattering on his back. He made a pitiful noise from deep inside his chest, his voice breaking as he opened his mouth and roared, eyes closed, tears down his cheeks, falling to the ground. He was like an ancient animal of the forest, mourning himself and all the other species that will never walk the Earth again. Dorothy had never seen him out of control before. She watched, feeling the sheer emptiness and exhaustion of it, and wished she had the freedom of spirit to join him.

41

JENNY

Jenny had been awake for a while before the sun began bleaching through the curtains. She wasn't used to having a man in her bed. Liam was a heavy sleeper but peaceful, as if the world didn't penetrate his subconscious. Lucky boy. She stared at him while he slept, felt pervy, too full on. His hair was a mess, chest rising and falling with his breath. She ran a finger along his shoulder and down his arm, and he snuffled and turned.

The radiator in her room rattled as the heating kicked in. This house had survived a hundred winters, would likely survive a hundred more, and Jenny thought about all the drama played out within the walls, teenage tantrums, some of them her own, midlife crises, accidents and arguments, quiet times and loud, the dead shuffling through on their way to the next world.

She thought about Archie, howling in the rain like a beast, so unlike him, but grief can make you lose yourself entirely. And she thought about James, driving his stolen car into a hole in the ground. Craighouse School for Boys. It was a long way from there to a homeless addict. She thought about Hannah chasing a professor's suicide for reasons she couldn't fathom. But reason was overrated, we do things because we're compelled. As Archie demonstrated, we're not so evolved from animals in the dirt, even if we like to think we are.

There was a gentle tap on the door and Liam woke up.

'Come in,' Jenny said.

Dorothy's head appeared round the door. Jenny had a flash of awkward guilt, like she'd done something wrong, zooming back to her teenage years, worried about getting caught with a boy in her room.

Liam pushed up on his elbows and rubbed at his eyes.

'Sorry,' Dorothy said. 'I thought you should know, Shona's turned up. The guard who helped Craig.'

Thomas made a face like he was explaining something to a toddler. 'Of course you can't speak to her.'

'Why not?' Jenny said.

She knew why but wanted to make him say it.

Dorothy leaned over and put a hand on Jenny's knee.

They were in Thomas's office, the view of the Crags grey and dismal today, trees in the park shaking nascent leaves, the skyline dark, the rock face damp with swirling rain.

'She's being interviewed downstairs right now,' Thomas said, looking to Dorothy for support. 'She has her lawyer. We're trying to get to the bottom of it.'

'Does she know where Craig is?'

Thomas shook his head. 'Says she has no idea.'

'Did she dump him or the other way round?'

Thomas sat forward and splayed his fingers. 'Please, we don't know yet.'

'Why the fuck not?'

Dorothy spoke up. 'I'm sure Thomas is doing everything he can.'

'Has he left the country?'

'I know as much as you do at the moment.'

'That's not exactly encouraging.'

Jenny got out of her seat then didn't know what to do. She went to a shelf of paperwork, box files with acronyms and dates on them. These couldn't be actual case files, not just sitting in an office.

'I told you there was no point in rushing here,' Dorothy said.

Jenny ran a finger along the shelf, it came away dusty. 'What was I supposed to do?' She scratched at her scalp, felt energy trying to escape her body. 'This is a lead.'

Thomas looked at his watch. 'It could be hours until the interview is finished. Then I don't know whether she'll be charged straight away.'

'Of course she'll be charged,' Jenny said. 'She helped a criminal escape.'

'Technically, Craig was on remand,' Thomas said. 'So he's not actually guilty of a crime yet.'

'Oh fuck off with that,' Jenny said.

'Jenny.' The tone of her mum's voice took her back to being a teenager, reprimanded for stumbling in drunk from the hotel bar along the road.

'I promise to let you know anything as soon as I know,' Thomas said.

Jenny stared at him and wondered. He was so buttoned down, held together, how did he cope with his wife's death? How did a black guy from Gothenburg end up in the Scottish police? How did any of us end up here dealing with this shit?

'Please sit,' Dorothy said, her tone mellowed.

Jenny breathed through gritted teeth then sat down.

Thomas leaned back in his chair and spoke to Dorothy.

'Have you got anywhere with drummer girl's dad?'

Dorothy shook her head. She explained about some promotions company, a flat rental, Jenny didn't follow, she was picturing Shona downstairs spinning lies to the cops, wriggling out of their net.

'And what about your homeless person?'

Dorothy smiled. 'Jenny got a lead. He really is called James and he went to Craighouse School.'

Thomas's eyebrows went up. 'Really?'

'So we'll go there, find out a surname, track down the family.'

'They must have money,' Thomas said.

'Exactly,' Dorothy said.

Jenny sat with her face like fizz, unwilling to take part in this happy banter when the lead to find her ex-husband was sitting downstairs.

'Are we done?' she said, standing up again.

She sat in the body van and waited. Students in Lycra and joggers streamed up and down from the uni sports centre along the road. She stared at the police station and chewed her cheek. Cops came and went carrying coffee cups or Gregg's bags, such a cliché. Sometimes they had someone with them, a civilian making a statement or a suspect, but Jenny never saw handcuffs.

She'd dropped Dorothy at home, making an excuse that she had to catch up with Liam, then headed straight back here and waited. Three hours. An hour ago she was bursting to piss so nipped into The High Dive bar to use the toilet, and she worried ever since that she'd missed Shona coming out. Or maybe she was being held overnight, or taken out the back door. There were a million ways it could go wrong, but this was all she had.

Another hour and it paid off. She recognised Shona as she came out the revolving door followed by a glistening, fat man in a grey suit, her solicitor. They shook hands and she flagged a cab in the street. Jenny fired up the engine and followed. Round the Meadows, Marchmont, Bruntsfield, they skirted close to the Skelf house and Jenny wondered what was happening inside. Then they were at Ritchie Place, a quiet street of Victorian tenements, double-parked cars making it a slalom. Jenny pulled the van alongside a Skoda and jumped out as Shona paid the taxi driver.

'Hey.'

Shona turned. She was early thirties, black hair in a fringe, dark eyes. Nothing special to look at just young, no bags under her eyes, no baggage. And she was tall, which wasn't Craig's type, he liked to look down on his women if Jenny and Fiona were anything to go by.

'Where is he?'

Jenny strode towards her as she reached into her bag and pulled out keys. Shona looked at the door to number nine then turned back and made her hand into a fist, the point of a key shoved between her knuckles as a weapon. But she looked scared, more than scared, downtrodden, wiped out. Jenny tried to shake the twinge of sympathy from her mind.

Shona nodded in recognition. 'You're Jenny, he talked about you.'

That put Jenny on the back foot. She stood a few feet away, felt the bitterness in the air, brooding clouds overhead, the taste of rain. Shona looked defeated.

'Really?' Jenny said.

Shona swallowed. 'Not at the start, obviously. At the start he was all charming and attentive. I guess you know what I'm talking about.'

Jenny nodded.

Shona shook her head. 'You've no idea what it's like in that place. It wears you down being around all that bitterness and aggression, it grinds you to dust. When someone comes along and notices that you're a woman under that hideous uniform, it's something.'

Jenny didn't want to interrupt, the more Shona talked, the more she might say something useful.

'It's not hard to find time alone together and we couldn't help ourselves. But he was playing me the whole time, obviously. Using me to get out. I was pathetic.'

'You said he mentioned me,' Jenny said.

Shona stared at her. 'He changed, just like that.' She clicked her fingers. 'As soon as we were away from the van. Then he couldn't stop talking about you.'

'I don't get it.'

Shona gave her the once over, looked hard. 'I don't either, but you've got some kind of hold over him.'

Jenny pushed that to the back of her mind. 'What happened?'

'I told the police everything.'

'Tell me.'

Shona chewed her lip, looked at the ground. 'I woke up and he was gone.'

'Where?'

Shona shook her head.

Jenny sighed. 'Was he worth it?'

'Fuck no.' But something in her voice said she wasn't so sure. She still had a thing for Craig, and Jenny wanted to shake it out of her.

'I could've told you, saved you a lot of grief.'

'I wish you had.'

Jenny nodded at the door behind Shona. 'Is he taking you back?'

Shona looked at the door as if it was the saddest thing she'd ever seen. 'It's over. It's been over for a while to be honest.'

Jenny squared her feet, hardened her heart. 'Are they charging you?'

'I think so.' She swallowed. 'If I end up in prison, holy fuck.'

'What were you thinking?'

Shona waved her hands around, the fist still with the key between her fingers. 'What do you want me to say? Clearly, I wasn't thinking. My first bit of male attention in years and I lost my mind.' She glanced up at a window. 'The idea of running away from everything, I was drunk on that. Haven't you ever wanted to run away?'

Jenny didn't want to think about that. 'Please tell me something that'll help find him.'

Shona looked at the door of the tenement again then back at Jenny.

'He's still in the city,' she said. 'I don't know where but he's still here.'

'Why?'

Shona smiled. 'Unfinished business.'

Jenny shook her head.

Shona pointed with the key-fist at her.

'With you,' she said.

42

DOROTHY

Another day, another boring stakeout. Dorothy sat at the dining table in the flat on Albion Gardens, looking across at Neil Williams' place. If it was his place. She still couldn't understand what was going on here, and was frustrated at the dead ends with the landlord and the promo company. Something to do with the festival? But how did that tie in with Abi's dad? Who was he and where the hell was he?

She used the silence to think, hoping something would bubble to the surface. She was a little surprised she'd been able to get in here, the keys were still presumably missing from the Warners office, had they even noticed? Dorothy wondered if they would arrive unannounced to show a young couple around the place. She had no excuse for why she was sitting here with a pair of binoculars, sipping green tea and spying on people across the road.

This was nothing like *Rear Window*. She loved that movie, Jimmy Stewart and Grace Kelly were so beautiful and classy. But they had murders to witness, killers to catch, nail-biting intrigue. She'd sat here for five hours and all she'd seen was a couple of couriers, an old man on a mobility scooter and two teenage lads sharing a joint. Not a glamorous murder in sight.

She had the laptop open in front of her, sifting online for anything about Neil, but she'd drawn a blank. Really, she didn't have a hope of finding anything, she didn't know how to do this kind of stuff, she was old school, like James Stewart.

She imagined sitting here with her own James and felt a pang of longing. The stabs of grief came at unpredictable times and her eyes grew wet as she remembered a day out on Salisbury Crags with him and Jenny, she must've been about ten. Dorothy could see the Crags now looming over the city, one of the few things that stayed the same no matter what changed. They'd walked along the cliff, a tremor of anxiety at the sheer drop, especially with Jenny there. Dorothy was more anxious than James, who trusted his daughter, she was a sensible kid who wouldn't do anything stupid.

Was Jenny still that kid? Do we inhabit the same personalities we grow up with? All our cells are replaced, but somehow our essence remains, or does it? Dorothy wondered if she knew Jenny these days. She thought about her shouting at Thomas, chasing Craig's shadow across the city. But they were all chasing shadows. Jenny had found a name for Jimmy X, but no resolution. Hannah had no solution to Hugh's death. And Dorothy had no answer for Abi, no reason why her father had disappeared. Maybe life is just chasing shadows, following leads, trying to find answers. Maybe if you found the answer, that was the end, no distance left to run.

She spotted something across the road, picked up the binoculars. It took her a second to find the right flat.

Then she saw him.

Neil Williams.

She swallowed, felt her heart thump against her ribs. Kept the binoculars on him for half a minute, then lowered them, checked she had the right place. She picked up her phone and found the picture Abi sent her. Soaked it in then looked across the road again.

It was him. In a smart suit, standing and smiling at the window. He stepped out of view and she lowered the binoculars, stared at her phone screen, then back at the flat.

She picked up her stuff and headed out the door. She emerged at the bottom of the stairwell moments later, pulling on her jacket, closing the door. She gazed at the window on Lochend Butterfly Way, nothing. Then the door to that block opened and there he was, fifty yards away. Coned-off roadworks stood between them, so she went the long way round, up a few steps. She lost him for a few seconds then saw him again, about to get into a car.

'Neil,' she shouted over a workman's drill.

He got a key out and the lights on one of the cars blipped.

'Neil Williams,' she said.

He turned. He was more handsome than in the photograph. More confident, stronger presence, upright stance. He looked blankly at her.

She walked towards him, putting on a smile. 'Neil Williams.'

He frowned, car key swinging on his finger.

As Dorothy got closer she noticed his suit wasn't as expensive as it first seemed.

'Who are you?' he said.

She was ten yards away, the drill noise enveloping them, bringing them together.

'My name is Dorothy Skelf. And you're Neil Williams.'

He shook his head but he'd lost confidence. 'You've got the wrong person.'

'I don't think so,' Dorothy said. 'Your daughter Abi asked me to find you.'

A flicker of panic at the mention of Abi. He bolted off the kerb to the driver's side of a black car.

'Hey,' Dorothy said, following him onto the road.

She reached for his sleeve but he shook her off.

'You've got the wrong man,' he said.

'No I don't.'

He opened the door and tried to get in. Dorothy held the edge of the door and pulled it wide. He slapped her hand away, hard, a jolt of pain up her arm.

'Your daughter is worried,' Dorothy said. 'Don't you want to speak to her?'

He squeezed past her and threw himself into the driver's seat.

'Her mother, Sandra,' Dorothy said. 'You have a kid together?'

Neil tried to get his key in the ignition. 'You're confused.'

Dorothy held the door open, pulled out her phone, got the picture and shoved it in his face. 'Look.'

The engine started and he tried to pull the door closed but Dorothy had wedged herself into the space.

'Get out the way,' he said.

'Not until you tell the truth.'

'I am telling the truth,' he said, pushing her arm.

'She ran away from home.'

He hesitated then accidentally revved the engine as he leaned forward and pulled at the door again, which smacked Dorothy on the hip. She would have a big bruise tomorrow.

'She ran away to find you, doesn't that mean anything?'

There was a moment of weakness in Neil's face, then his look hardened. 'I can't help you.'

He shoved at her hips and she staggered into the road, lost her balance and fell. Neil looked panicked. The workmen across the road had stopped to watch. Neil slammed the door and swerved out into the road. Dorothy breathed hard, her hip throbbing, fingers tingling. She watched the car disappear and realised it was a black Hyundai, the same car she'd seen here before, driven by someone else and owned by CTL.

43

HANNAH

Hannah sat in Mel's old room, the sun dappling through the oak trees outside. She looked across the Meadows, joggers and students, life going on under a cold, sharp sky. The forecast was for snow but skies were clear for now.

She turned to the room. They'd eventually cleared Mel's stuff into boxes and her brother Vic took them away. Her whole life packed and forgotten. Six months after her murder and Mel had begun fading in Hannah's memory, the horror of that time receding. It was part of being human, a way to cope with trauma. Moving on and all that. But how can you move on when the past is still gnawing at your heart?

She thought about Wendy and Edward moving on past Hugh. She'd been rude to the pair of them, their reserved demeanours had raised her hackles, but it was really frustration over the chaos in her own life that she'd directed at them.

She wondered if punishing her dad would make a difference to her behaviour. If Craig had gone to trial, if the dirt of his crimes was exposed, would Hannah feel any better? Nothing compensated for a friend being killed, her father would always be a murderer, a liar, the only dad she would ever have.

The room was bare except for a few photos pinned to the noticeboard, Vic said it was fine to keep them. One of Mel, Hannah and Indy in the Pleasance beer garden at festival time, flyers for comedy shows strewn across the table, plastic pint glasses in hand. Another of Mel with Xander, dressed up for a ball. Hannah thought about Xander, how she'd suspected him. She'd gone mad when Mel's body was found, and she'd never got back on an even keel since.

Indy came into the room and leaned against the desk. 'You OK?'

They hadn't spoken much since the embalming room.

'I'm so sorry about the other day,' Hannah said, chewing her lip.

She glanced at Indy then turned her face to the floor, couldn't stand what she saw there.

'Are you?' Indy said.

'Of course.'

Silence for a long time.

'Of course,' Indy said under her breath. 'Of course you're sorry, of course I'm worried about you, of course I'm always here asking if you're OK because that's what I do, right? I'm the one who has to be the rock for all your insanity.'

Hannah's cheeks flushed with shame, Indy was right, Hannah took her for granted.

'What if I wasn't here, Han?' Indy said. 'What if I left?'

Hannah looked up. 'You're not serious.'

Indy raised her chin. 'Why the hell not? I love you, Han, but sometimes I don't think you notice I'm even here except when it suits you.'

'That's not true.'

'Isn't it?'

Hannah swallowed. It stung that Indy was right, that Hannah was so self-centred in all that was going on, so single-minded she never stopped to think about her girlfriend's point of view.

'I'm so sorry,' she said. 'I mean it.'

Indy shook her head. 'Your gran said something recently. We're a family. We need to be here for each other, support one another. It can't be one way. If things go on like this, I don't know, honestly.'

Hannah imagined Indy walking out the door, bag packed, off to find a girlfriend who appreciated her, who treated her right. She felt her throat close, tears behind her eyes. Her breath shook in her mouth.

Indy shook her head. 'Wake up, Han, that's all I'm saying. Wake up to what you have in front of you.'

Indy opened her arms and Hannah went to her, wrapped herself into a hug, buried her face in Indy's hair. She let herself be held for a long time, felt Indy's hesitant hands on her back and hip, tried to remember what it was like the first time they met, the electricity between them. But after a moment her mind flitted to an image of her being held by her dad as a kid. Then suddenly she was thinking of Craig kneeling on Bruntsfield Links that night, blood dripping onto the grass.

Her phone went in her pocket.

When she pulled away from Indy her eyes were wet, and she wiped them with the back of her hand. The call was from Wendy.

'He's been again,' she said. 'I planted your gizmo on him.'

The throbbing dot on her phone screen moved up Clerk Street onto Nicolson Street at walking speed. Hannah jogged through the Meadows, past the tennis courts and play park. Wendy said she'd thrown the tracker in the guy's hood as he walked away from her house. Hannah had a decision to make, head to Greenhill Gardens and get the van or follow on foot. But the dot was moving slowly, about ten minutes' walk away, so she left Indy and here she was, heading to the corner of Buccleuch Street. The dot jerked left at the Mosque Kitchen on the corner of Nicolson Square then along the lane towards Potterrow. The same way she was headed, too easy.

Hannah remembered watching *Alien* as a teenager with Mum, where the characters spent half the film tracking a dot on a screen, a dot that killed everyone except Sigourney Weaver. Jenny was trying to bond with her but Hannah was in a bout of depression, so the whole thing washed over her. She didn't care about the deaths of fictional characters, just like she didn't care about real people, including herself.

But that was in the past, she was more together these days, at least she had been until recently. The counselling wasn't helping, or maybe it was just too raw. The counsellor mentioned displacement theory, she was compensating for lack of control with her dad, trying to impose control on Hugh's suicide. That's why she was here, striding past Appleton Tower as a squall of icy rain hit her in the face.

The dot on the screen throbbed into Bristo Square then stopped. Hannah kept walking, glancing up. She was only a few minutes away. She looked at the screen. The dot jerked, maybe just the GPS catching up, and she sped past Teviot House into Bristo Square, three hardy skateboarders rattling around the space as the rain got heavier and the wind stung her cheeks.

She strode through the skaters, closing in on the dot, which had stopped again. She looked up at the skaters then went to the north end of the square, buses grinding past on Lothian Street. Her phone said she was right on it. She looked around, no one nearby, two benches on the edge of the square, a couple of trees that had survived recent renovations. She went to the benches, looked around, shielding her face from the rain, the wind snagging her hair, the skaters moving like fish in a stream, bus engines rattling and chugging.

It was here somewhere. She went to the nearest tree and spotted something at the roots. The tracker, sitting in a patch of exposed dirt. It wasn't clear if it'd been placed there or just fallen from the guy's hoodie.

She looked around the square, up at the black clouds, over to McEwan Hall. This was the heart of student territory, did that mean anything? One of Hugh's students?

She remembered the camera she'd set up at Wendy's front door.

She sighed, picked up the tracker and trudged away in the rain.

44
DOROTHY

Craighouse School for Boys was more like a stately home than a place to send your kids. The long sweeping driveway from Glen-lockhart Road cut a swathe through manicured lawns and groomed woods, cricket and rugby pitches in the distance. Two packs of teens were huffing in a scrum over there, steam rising from them like something primal, as a bitter wind cut across the space, stinging Dorothy's face.

She reached the front entrance, tasteful topiary shuddering in the wind, Greek columns flanking oak doors. This was all designed to impress the right kind of people and intimidate the rest. Dorothy felt intimidated. There was a superior British feel to the place, though Lord knows the Ivy League could give this bullcrap a run for its money.

Dorothy went to reception, guarded by an impeccable middle-aged woman with glasses on a silver chain around her neck. She gave her name and waited, watching as uniformed boys loped past, energy outstripping their self-awareness, plenty of confidence. This place cost thousands, having that money to burn was bound to instil confidence.

'Mr Grisham will see you now.'

Deborah behind reception gestured at a large door and Dorothy stood, straightened her dress, knocked and went in.

More oak panelling, a Greek bust on the desk, views of the playing fields and woods. Dorothy could see the remains of a castle, vines and bushes sprawling amongst the tumbledown stonework. They had an actual ruined castle on their grounds.

Daniel Grisham was more like middle management than old-school headmaster, doughy around the middle, bland smile, perfect side parting.

He stood up and held out a hand.

'Mrs Skelf, please sit.'

'Dorothy.'

He nodded, but didn't offer his own first name.

He made a cathedral of his fingertips. 'How can I help?'

Straight to the point, that's how you ended up in charge of a place like this.

'As I explained to your secretary,' Dorothy said, 'I'm a private investigator, trying to find someone's identity.'

That raised his eyebrows. Dorothy wondered how she came across, a seventy-year-old woman, traces of an American accent, simple dress and comfy shoes. Not exactly gumshoe material.

'Really,' Grisham said.

She pulled the picture from her pocket and placed it on the desk. He didn't pick it up.

'I believe he went to this school.'

Grisham nodded but still didn't pick up the photograph.

'His first name is James, but I don't have a surname. Early to mid-twenties, so he would've been here six or seven years ago.'

Grisham touched the edges of the picture like it was fragile and lifted it. He folded his lips in and out of his mouth then ran his tongue around his gums. It made his face seem fat.

'Where did you get this picture?' he said.

'Why?'

'Just wondering.'

'It was in his possessions when he died.'

That made him pause. 'I'm sorry to hear that.'

'We're trying to find living relatives,' Dorothy said.

He looked up. 'Is there money involved?'

'Why would you ask that?'

Grisham shrugged. 'Why else would you be trying to find relatives?'

'To inform them of his death.'

'Who's paying you?'

'That's none of your concern.'

Grisham tapped a finger to the photo. 'Who's the young lady?'

That phrase sounded creepy in his mouth.

'I'm not at liberty to say.'

Grisham looked put out by that.

'I've been here twelve years,' he said, placing the picture on his desk. 'And I've never seen this young man before.'

Dorothy stared at him and he looked down at his hands. Maybe he was lying, maybe it was the truth, maybe he didn't like assertive women, there were plenty who didn't.

She slid the picture closer to him. 'Can you please look again?'

He glanced down, perfunctory. 'I'm sure.'

'There must've been thousands of boys through here in your charge,' Dorothy said. 'You can't remember all of them.'

He stuck his chest out. 'Here at Craighouse we pride ourselves on the very best. Academic, sporting, pastoral care too. If this boy went here, I would know him.'

Dorothy tried to keep her voice level. 'Maybe you could ask the staff, see if anyone recognises him?'

'We're all very busy as I'm sure you understand.'

'Please take one last look.'

He tapped the picture. 'Where did you get the idea he's a Craig-house boy, from this woman?'

She took the picture and looked at James and Rachel. Trying to get straight, sort their lives out. Now one of them was dead and the other in hiding. It had started here for James, she was sure of it. But how did he go from here to the streets?

Dorothy shook her head.

'Deborah will show you out,' Grisham said, standing and holding his hand out.

Dorothy stared at his hand but didn't take it, then left.

She nodded to Deborah as she passed, too quick to let the

secretary get up, then she was outside. She took the PDF map she'd printed of the school grounds from her pocket and checked it, then turned left towards the staffroom at the back of the main building. She'd checked this before coming, made her appointment during lunch break so the staffroom would be busy. Two middle-aged women were smoking outside a fire exit propped open with a plastic chair. She nodded like she knew them and squeezed past into the bustling room packed with teachers.

She brass-necked it, going around older staff first because they had more chance of being here when James attended. She played the helpless old lady, that always helped with gallant guys, saying she was a friend of Daniel Grisham, he'd said to come and ask. She hoped Grisham wasn't the kind of headmaster to socialise with minions.

She was getting nowhere. Surely someone must remember this kid, it wasn't that long ago. But all she got were shaking heads and a number of odd looks. What was this interloper doing invading their precious downtime?

The two smoking women came inside, nicotine lingering on their clothes, and Dorothy approached them. One wore a pearl necklace, the other had slouched shoulders under her cardigan. They were in their forties, still attractive but playing down their looks for work. Dealing with hundreds of hormonal boys every day must be wearing.

'Excuse me.' Dorothy handed over the picture. 'Do either of you recognise this man? His name is James, he went to Craighouse about seven years ago.'

Pearls narrowed her eyes at the photo, shook her head. 'Who are you?'

'Friend of a friend,' Dorothy said. The less you say, the less chance of getting caught in a lie.

Pearls handed the picture to Cardigan, who examined it. She looked at Pearls, then Dorothy, then back at the photo. There was something in her eyes.

'Do you know him?' Dorothy said. She couldn't keep excitement from her voice.

'James, you say?' Cardigan's face lit up at the idea she could be useful.

'That's right.' Dorothy thought of mentioning what Rachel said, that James was gay. But it seemed unlikely he came out here, you'd have to be ballsy to do that in a place like this.

'He's a lot older here,' Cardigan said, tapping the photo. 'But I think it's the Dundas boy.'

Pearls blanched and took another look.

'Dundas?' Dorothy said.

Cardigan nodded and looked around, as if including them in a conspiracy. 'It was just after I started here, he left under a cloud. Had a thing with his housemaster who discreetly resigned. All hush-hush.'

Dorothy pointed at the photo. 'You're sure it's him?'

Cardigan shrugged. 'Not a hundred percent but I think so.'

Dorothy smiled and took the photograph back, staring at James Dundas as if she'd known him for years.

45

JENNY

Jenny reached down and stroked Einstein's fur, smiled as his tail thumped against her leg. She stared out of the window across Bruntsfield Links. Such an incredible view of the castle, a crazily beautiful city, teeming with tourists all year round. She saw a family in matching rain macs, the dad checking his phone then looking around, the rest in his slipstream. The pavements were slick with rain, welcome to Scotland.

Einstein nudged her with his nose and she jumped. She hadn't relaxed since Craig escaped, knowing he was out there. She felt sick all the time, a rock of anxiety lodged in her stomach. She thought about Fiona at home, her window boarded up, Sophia oblivious to what a shit her dad was. She wondered if there was still a police officer out front. Maybe Fiona had moved back in with her mum already.

Her phone rang on the table and she jumped again. Maybe she needed to visit the doctor, get something for her nerves. But then she would have to explain everything and she wasn't that kind of person, couldn't stand the idea of talking about her life like that.

She went over and picked up her phone, saw it was Thomas.

'Hi,' she said.

'We got a ping,' Thomas said.

'A ping?'

'From Craig's phone. The number he texted you with. We got a ping from it.'

'Where?'

Jenny stood on The Shore looking around, waiting for Craig to pounce from the shadows. Daft but she couldn't help it. This part of Leith waterfront was busy, buses chundering across the Commercial Street bridge, the Water of Leith shimmering below, barges and boats clanking alongside. A patrol car crawled across the cobbles heading for the police van outside the Malmaison Hotel. Officers traipsed in and out of bars and cafes along the shore, starting at the hotel and working south. The ping from Craig's burner phone only gave a rough location, he wasn't on for long enough to get better triangulation. He'd called Fiona's number and Jenny wondered what the fuck she said to him. She'd kept him on the line as long as possible, had been told to by the cops if he got in touch.

Thomas walked towards her from the car parked up the way. She didn't want to be too close to the police, felt like she had her own thing with Craig, didn't want him scared off. If she had her way she would be here alone, one-on-one, a fistfight to the death. She pictured them brawling, pulling each other's hair, tripping over the low, metal-chain fence and into the water, splashing amongst the ducks and junk, pushing each other's heads below the surface, her hands forcing him down, holding on until his lungs filled with water and he sank to the mud at the bottom.

'You don't need to be here,' Thomas said.

'You knew I would come.'

Thomas smiled. 'I did.'

'So?' Jenny waved at two cops entering Fishers.

She had a meal there with Craig years ago, before they were married, they joked about the aphrodisiac properties of the oysters they were downing, sharp with lemon and Tabasco, a shiver of cold down the throat. Maybe he was sending her a message, making the call from somewhere that meant something to her. He must have known his phone was monitored since he texted Jenny, he wasn't stupid, he knew they could get a location.

She knew he wouldn't be here anymore, he sent this message then headed elsewhere. But there must be sightings, waitresses, passers-by, taxi drivers at the rank across the water, someone must've seen something. And CCTV of course. She realised suddenly that Malmaison was where he took Melanie for their liaisons, where Hannah had found out about him. Maybe that was the message. But what did it mean?

Thomas followed her gaze. 'No sign in Malmaison.'

The cops coming out of Fishers shook their heads and headed into The Shore gastropub next door.

'What is Craig doing?' Thomas said.

'You're asking me?'

'You know him.'

Jenny nodded. 'This isn't a random location, right?'

'Right.'

Jenny looked around, seeing Craig's face everywhere in the rush-hour workers heading along Commercial Street. 'What did he say to Fiona?'

'I haven't heard the recording yet,' Thomas said. He pushed his glasses up his nose. 'But I gather he apologised for breaking into their home. Said he had to do it.'

'He's lost his mind.'

She looked up the road at The King's Wark pub, remembered being there with Liam. Not just the recent time but earlier, when she followed him as a PI. Liam, why didn't she realise before, maybe that was the message.

'Shit.'

She ran across the cobbles, darted between cars on the road and into the pub. She recognised the barmaid from the other week, young and tall, tight T-shirt and leggings.

'Excuse me, have you seen this guy recently?'

If the barmaid recognised Jenny she didn't show it.

Jenny found a picture of Craig from Facebook and held her phone up.

The barmaid nodded. She had a piercing through the bridge of her nose that wasn't doing her face any favours. 'He was in a while ago.'

'What did he do?'

The barmaid's shoulders went up and down. 'Bought a lager, drank it, left.'

Jenny heard the door open behind her, Thomas and a uniformed officer in the doorway. 'When?'

'Dunno, not long ago.'

'Can you check the till receipt?'

She looked at the police now standing behind Jenny. 'Really?'

Thomas smiled, placid. 'It would help.'

She went to the till and scanned through. 'He paid cash, pint of Stella.' Ran her finger along the screen. 'Here it is, ninety minutes ago.'

'You don't remember anything else?' Jenny said.

The barmaid turned. 'Middle-aged bloke, ten a penny.'

The most anonymous disguise, ordinary guy.

'Anything at all?'

The barmaid touched a finger to the bolt in her nose, something came to her.

'He had a bag with him, a small rucksack. Looked heavy, clanked when he put it down, like it might have tools in it.'

Jenny couldn't work out what it meant.

Thomas spoke up. 'Anything else?'

The barmaid's eyes widened as she remembered something. 'He smelled of paint.'

Thomas looked confused. 'Paint?'

Jenny was already heading for the door. She pelted along Bernard Street into Maritime Street, cobbles underfoot and old bond warehouses either side. She knew what this meant, but didn't want to believe it. She pulled out her phone as she ran, found Liam's number and called, listened as the ring bounced in her brain, praying he would answer, tricking herself into thinking she didn't know exactly what was going on. Liam's voice came on and for a microsecond her heart relaxed, but it was just his voicemail, chilled, happy Liam, leave a message and he'll try to get back to you as soon as possible.

She hung up as she reached the vennel, went through. This tiny cul-de-sac was so familiar from when she was hired to follow him by his ex. She bolted to the artist studios on the left, turned inside to Liam's studio and stopped dead when she saw the open door. She had a flashback to kicking that door in herself, faking a break-in to find out what he was doing inside, discovering his weird paintings, pictures she loved straight away.

She stared along the corridor, heard noises from one of the other studios, drilling or welding, something industrial. She turned back to Liam's studio, pushed the door and went in.

'Liam?'

The place was turned over. Liam kept it organised, paints put away at the end of each visit, canvases neatly stacked. But it looked like an elephant had been through it now. Canvases were scattered all over, torn and ripped. The tray of paints was upturned, brushes strewn across the floor, paint tins opened and emptied over everything. The easel was smashed, legs in the air like a rigor-mortised corpse. The place stank of paint and turps so Jenny pulled her T-shirt over her nose. She picked her way through the debris, avoiding the paint splatters and broken canvases.

Thomas and the cop appeared at the doorway taking it in.

She called Liam again, phone pressed to her ear. Voicemail. She tried to keep her voice steady.

'Hey babes, give me a call when you get this.'

Thomas and the cop looked confused as they stepped into the room.

'What is this?' Thomas said, lifting the corner of a canvas and staring at the hole in it.

Jenny thought back to what Shona said outside her flat.

'Unfinished business,' she said.

46

DOROTHY

The hearse was parked next to the bins on Guthrie Street, and the stench of stale booze and kebab leftovers was strong. The road was backed up, a delivery van bumped up on the pavement with hazards on, queues of cars both ways. Guthrie Street was technically two-way, but like a lot of Edinburgh's Old Town it was cramped and crowded. Eventually the DHL guys left and traffic began to ease.

She didn't want to bring the hearse but Archie was on a pickup with the body van, so she had no choice. She glanced across the road at the Creative Talent office, then at her watch. It was six in the evening and she wondered how long they worked into the night. She'd wait as long as it took.

She picked up her tablet and checked through the online phone directory for Edinburgh. Might as well deal with one case while working on another. She had a list of Dundases in Edinburgh and had started going through, narrowing it down. She recognised a lot of street names but checked on Google Maps just in case, she was prone to the odd senior moment.

She discarded addresses in poor areas, no one in Dumbiedykes or Wester Hailes would be sending their kid to Craighouse. There were some medium-priced houses that she put in a 'possibles' list. That left a handful of Dundases in rich areas, Morningside, Trinity, Comely Bank. She ranked these in order of location, the west of the city at the top. Not that it always worked like that with private schools. So she had eight Dundases arranged in order, this private-investigator malarkey was easy, really, just be organised and persistent.

She pictured James Dundas lying in the mortuary fridge. She remembered him in that Nissan, blood oozing from his ear, Einstein whimpering in the back, her own body beginning to tremble with shock. The chirp of birds in the trees, the car's wheels spinning, the look on the Blackie family's faces.

She thought about why she needed closure on this. Everyone has a story but so many go untold, ordinary people surviving another day. James was no different from anyone else, that was the point, his story needed telling the same as Dorothy's or Abi's or Hugh's. What the Skelfs did with funerals and cases was precisely that, try to tell people's stories, join the dots in their lives, make some sense of the mayhem.

She saw movement across the road. It was Jason from CTL shutting the office door and locking up. He crossed the road and walked downhill towards where the hearse was parked. Dorothy threw her iPad on the passenger seat and breathed deeply. She tried to be mindful, imagined herself ready as she opened the door and stood on the pavement in front of him. He clocked her getting out, gave the hearse a second glance, then began to walk round her. Old people weren't on his radar, he didn't remember her.

'Jason.'

He stopped and took her in. Arrogance and irony in his body movements, as if the world was a joke only he got, and everyone else was a sucker.

'Sorry, do I know you?'

'Dorothy Skelf, I interviewed you recently about CTL.'

A light of recognition, a nod.

'Sweet ride,' he said, looking at the hearse.

Dorothy got her phone out and found the picture Abi had sent her.

'I need to find Neil Williams,' she said.

'I'm sorry, what's this about?'

'I'm a private investigator.'

He laughed. After a moment, her manner made him shut up. 'Seriously?'

She nodded.

He looked her up and down. 'An old dear private eye driving a hearse. Honey, someone should write your story.'

The rank smell of the bins was overpowering as Dorothy breathed, tried to stay calm. She handed her phone over, the picture of Abi's dad.

'Neil Williams, I need to find him.'

He held the phone but didn't look at it, just stared at her. 'I don't know any Neil Williams, love, you've made a mistake.'

Dorothy nodded at her phone. 'Just look.'

He stared at her for a few more seconds then turned to the picture. He couldn't hide it, he recognised him. His demeanour went from cocky bullshit to nervous kid in a moment, as if he'd had the air let out of him.

'You know him,' Dorothy said.

'No.' He handed the phone back.

'Don't lie.'

'Look lady, I don't know why you're hassling me but you're wrong.'

'He's been staying in a flat you sublet, and I saw him earlier today driving a car registered to CTL.'

'He's nothing to do with us.'

He went to walk around but Dorothy blocked him.

A bin lorry drove down the street, straight past the bins, the waft of rubbish trailing behind.

'Just tell me,' she said.

'Fuck you.'

He tried to walk away but she held his arm. She lowered her voice and spoke in his ear.

'I just want to find this guy, nothing else. It's obvious CTL are up to dodgy shit but I don't care about that.'

'We're not.' His confidence was ebbing away.

'I have a very close friend, Detective Inspector Thomas Olsson, based at the Pleasance. I'm sure he'd be very interested in what CTL are up to.'

She was betting he had crooked secrets, most people have stuff they want to hide.

'You're bluffing.'

Dorothy shrugged. 'I'm actually a terrible bluffer, no poker face at all. What you see is what you get.'

Jason looked at Dorothy's hand on his arm, and she removed it, brushed the material of his lurid jacket. He thought it over then nodded at her phone. 'What he's doing is not illegal.'

The implication being something else at CTL *was* illegal.

'So tell me.'

She could smell his breath, a day's worth of coffee, fear too.

'The police don't need to get involved,' he said.

Dorothy smiled. 'Not if he's not doing anything wrong.'

Jason stepped back and got his phone out, scrolled down. He showed Dorothy the screen:

Stephen Marks, 42 East Crosscauseway.

He had a hangdog face. 'Remember, he's not doing anything wrong.'

'Who's this?' she said.

'This is Neil Williams.'

47

HANNAH

Hannah leaned back in her chair and pinched the bridge of her nose. She rubbed at her eyes, gritty and sore, she'd been staring at her laptop for too long. She scrunched her eyes then opened them, took in the grainy picture on screen.

It was the guy who'd been pestering Hugh's widow. Who had ditched the tracker, knowingly or by accident. Hannah had returned to Wendy's house and removed the SD card from the camera, and here was the guy. He was about Hannah's age, tall and skinny, dark bags under his eyes, nondescript hoodie and black jeans, white trainers. Could be any of thousands of young men kicking around Edinburgh right now.

She didn't recognise him. She'd foolishly thought she would take one look and realise he was a classmate, or recognise him from campus. But that was stupid, wishful thinking.

She was sitting at the breakfast bar in her kitchen, and turned to stare out of the window. A young mum was down in her garden helping her toddler up the steps of a tiny plastic slide. In the adjacent garden, an elderly man was hanging out washing. She imagined being either of those people, having kids with Indy, being the best two mums in the world, then fifty years later Indy dying, the kids living abroad, Hannah alone in a small flat, trying to find a routine that filled the lonely day between waking and sleeping, stalling death as long as possible.

She had to square things with Indy, stop acting so self-obsessed. But there was too much to sort in her head first. The counselling was something but all the therapy in the world couldn't fix this. Her dad on the run, people dying around her, missing, homeless, lost identities, broken lives. How were you supposed to settle down and live happily ever after with all that?

She picked up the tracking bug she'd found in Bristo Square. That was the heart of the humanities schools, miles away from the science campus at King's Buildings. So what did that mean? If he was a student, which discipline? If he wasn't, how did Hugh know him? Why didn't he just speak to Wendy?

She pressed 'print' and her printer squeaked into life, the image emerging in the tray. She grabbed it and headed out the door. Twenty minutes later she was hassling passers-by outside Teviot House, thrusting the piece of paper in their faces, ignoring the looks she got.

Two hours later she was flagging, approaching fewer people, slumped against a low wall watching the skateboarders rattle and hum across the concrete. She'd already asked them, met with shrugs and headshakes. She'd been into Potterrow and Teviot, round the offices and cafes, bars and shops. Nothing.

How could you find someone in a city of half a million people with just a blurry printout? And what did it matter, Hugh was dead, this wasn't bringing him back. But there had been too many deaths recently. It was stupid to think that when your family ran a funeral home and your girlfriend was training to be a funeral director. But it was the manner of it, finding Hugh at his desk, poison for God's sake. She couldn't stand it.

She stared at the picture, it wasn't the best quality but you would recognise him if you knew him. She needed to find someone who knew him. She looked around, willing him to appear in a puff of smoke, brought into existence by sheer willpower.

It started to rain and she turned towards home.

48

DOROTHY

East Crosscauseway was a nothing street, a back alley off the main drag. In an area of sparkly new student accommodation and luxury apartments, this was old-school tenement living, rough brickwork, unfashionable shops on the ground floor, rundown flats above. Dorothy walked past a second-hand record shop, the owner sitting outside on a rickety chair examining a Bob Dylan gatefold. There was a joinery shop, and Dorothy remembered Jim saying that's how the Skelfs got started in the funeral game. It was very common, most early funeral directors were joiners first, building the coffins then eventually stepping in and organising the business side of death when no one else would. Jim's great-great-grandfather, Old John Skelf, was knocking together a casket one day and thought why not?

And now here she was, forty-five years since marrying into the death business, head of the company and family. No more Skelf men left. She wondered what Old John would make of that, a woman in charge of his legacy and a Californian to boot.

Dorothy pictured herself as a skinny teen on Pismo Beach, clue-less and hormonal. What would that naïve girl make of her now? Walking down a cold Edinburgh street searching for a father who didn't want to be found, on behalf of a girl who reminded Dorothy of herself, lost in the mayhem of teenage years, trying to find a way through.

Dorothy was a matriarch now, what a crazy idea. She imagined her dead mother raising a sardonic eyebrow at that, but maybe she was doing Mom a disservice. Dorothy moved to a foreign country as a young woman, had limited contact with her family since, something she felt a pang about. And being an immigrant was a dangerous thing these days, even a widow who'd lived here most of her life. You heard stories about the Home Office messing with people like her. Admittedly, it was brown-skinned people getting the brunt of it but she was still an outsider. She thought about Thomas, another outsider in this weird country. It was a thread that connected them across this weird city.

She found number forty-two, a main-door flat, doorbell and nameplate, Marks.

Neil Williams. Stephen Marks.

A convoy of bin lorries chugged past and turned left. What was it with the stink of garbage following her today?

She pressed the doorbell and waited.

The wind whipped along the street towards Salisbury Crags. Two young Asian women walked past. The sound of a siren somewhere in the distance.

The door opened and there he was. Dorothy pictured him closing the car door on her, the look on his face then.

'Hi,' she said. 'Remember me?'

This time he was resigned. 'How?'

'I threatened Jason. He folded pretty easy.'

'He's an arsehole.' He sighed, mouth turned down. 'You'd better come in.'

He led her to a living room like an OCD bachelor pad, everything neat and tidy, large TV on the wall above the fireplace, gaming consoles, old turntable with racks of vinyl lined up alongside.

She sat on the tasteful brown leather sofa and he sat opposite in a matching armchair. A coffee table between them had *Men's Health* and *GQ* magazines on it.

'It was never meant to go like this,' he said.

'Start at the beginning.'

He shook his head.

'Come on,' Dorothy said.

He rubbed his palms against his knees, rocked back and forth. 'I'm an actor.'

'OK.'

He stared at her for a long time, waiting for her to put something together.

Dorothy began to realise what he was getting at. 'Wait. What?'

He nodded. 'Sandra Livingstone hires me to pretend to be Abi's dad.'

Dorothy felt something creep up her spine, a weight in her stomach. Stephen looked around the room for a way to escape the truth.

'Since when?' Dorothy said.

He looked at the ceiling, counting up. 'Christ, eight years.'

'This is...'

'It's not illegal.'

Dorothy rubbed at the palm of her hand as if trying to get rid of a dirty mark. 'What the hell?'

Stephen splayed his hands out. 'I wasn't getting any work as an actor. It's impossible. I was on CTL's books but there was nothing for an anonymous guy like me.'

This was said matter of fact, not fishing for anything.

Stephen swallowed hard. 'I had a mate, another actor. She needed someone to pretend to be her boyfriend for a cousin's wedding, so I said I would do it. It started as a bit of fun, we created a character together, I enjoyed it. Afterwards, she recommended me to someone else who needed a stand-in boyfriend for a thing. I can't remember what. Anyway, she paid me.'

He rolled his tongue around his teeth. 'I told Jason, he said he could get me some work. He set up a sideline for CTL, basically renting out relatives for things. Mostly one-offs.'

'Why would folk do this?'

Stephen chewed on his lip. 'You'd be amazed how much societal pressure is still out there. It makes things easier. I've been hired as a boyfriend just to keep guys from hitting on someone.'

Dorothy shook her head. 'But this, with Abi, is something else.'

Stephen got up and went to the mantelpiece. Ran a finger along it, looked at his feet.

'Sandra came to Jason,' he said. 'I don't know how, CTL don't advertise, it's word of mouth. Jason is connected to some weird shit. Anyway, she wanted a dad for her little girl.'

'I don't understand.'

Stephen pulled at his earlobe. 'Abi was acting up at school, all sorts of behaviour issues. Asking about her dad. This was before Mike was on the scene. That's made things more complicated.'

'And this has just gone on? For years?'

'It was supposed to be short term, just to get her on an even keel.'

'But how did Sandra think this was going to end?'

'She presumed Abi would lose interest.'

'That's ridiculous.'

Stephen shook his head. 'I just do what I'm told, she pays me.'

'So Abi's life is built on a lie?'

Dorothy thought about her own life, her husband's lies, the secrets we all keep from each other. But this was insanity.

'I really like Abi, she's a great kid. I've watched her grow up.'

'You've lied to her for years.'

'Not really.'

'Jesus Christ.'

'Don't.' Stephen shifted weight from one foot to another. 'I know.'

'This is so messed up.' Dorothy stood up, couldn't bear to be seated anymore.

'Please,' Stephen said. 'You can't tell Abi, it would destroy her.'

Dorothy felt a surge of anger. 'Maybe you should've thought about that before starting this.'

'I was trying to help,' Stephen said. 'Sandra was desperate.'

Dorothy's hands were fists at her side. She felt sick, a knot twisting her guts.

'There's one thing I don't understand,' she said. 'Why not just tell Abi who her real dad was?'

Stephen stared at her for a long time. For an actor, he wasn't very good at hiding things. His face told her he knew the answer but he fronted it out, shook his head.

'You'll need to ask Sandra,' he said.

49

JENNY

The world was too harsh in the light outside the kitchen window and Jenny couldn't concentrate on what Mum was saying. The three of them were in the kitchen, their ritual, updating each other on the mess of their lives, cases, emotional states, the pressure pushing down on them. Or maybe that was just Jenny's hangover.

She spent last night trying to find Liam. Not answering his phone, not at his flat, nothing on social media. She went to visit Orla, the ex-wife, who slammed the door in her face before she could speak. The police examined his studio, there was no concrete forensics. Obviously someone had trashed the place, maybe during a fight. Had someone attacked him or simply broken in and turned the place over?

Her instinct said Craig was behind this. She knew in her heart and bones and every screaming nerve. She tried to persuade Thomas but there was no proof yet. Craig being in the pub round the corner was circumstantial. But Jenny knew him and she knew he'd done something to Liam. The fact she couldn't do a damn thing about it sent her to the wine bottle last night and she hadn't stopped until the early hours, crawling into bed and passing out, waking early with her bladder bursting and the open curtains flooding the room with sunshine. The same sunshine that was making her cringe now. Cherry blossom was falling from the branches in the park outside, a gentle snowstorm as petals drifted to the ground and turned to mulch underfoot.

Two teenage boys in school uniform were swiping at each other with rucksacks, an old woman in pink trousers and a Zimmer inching her way towards the main road, a cyclist in slipstreamed Lycra and skeletal helmet zinging past and out of sight.

Dorothy was still talking, stroking Einstein absent-mindedly. Jenny looked around for Schrödinger. Considering the cat hated that bloody dog, he was always hanging around harassing him. Jenny thought of Craig out there. He could've been anywhere else on the planet by now but he'd hung around to mess with her.

Hannah frowned and shook her head as Dorothy finished speaking.

'Wait,' Jenny said. Dorothy's words filtered through her pounding brain. 'This woman hired someone to pretend to be Abi's dad. For years.'

'That's what he told me.'

'And what does she have to say?'

'I'm going there next to find out.'

Hannah stood up, went to the whiteboards, a mess of names, acronyms, lines, scribbles and clues, links and messages, secrets and lies. 'How did she think she could get away with it?'

'That's what I asked,' Dorothy said.

'Why lie?' Jenny said. 'It's not as if being a single mum is shameful these days.'

Dorothy sighed and sipped her tea.

Jenny's black coffee was tepid but she gulped it anyway. Caffeine might cut through this head, shake her into life.

Hannah tapped a pen against the whiteboard. 'So where are we with Jimmy X?'

Jenny was amazed her daughter was so self-assured, or seemed it on the surface. She had inner steel that Jenny never had at that age. But then her daughter was undergoing therapy and had struggled with anxiety and depression, so what did Jenny know? She felt tightness in her chest at the idea of her daughter in pain. Having kids really fucked you up.

'James Dundas,' Dorothy said.

'We have a full name?' Jenny said. She tried to remember when she last had an update on that case. Fuck this hangover.

Dorothy nodded. 'From a teacher at Craighouse. I have a list of possible addresses.'

'How did he end up a homeless addict?' Jenny said.

'That's what I'd like to find out.' Dorothy tapped a piece of paper in front of her. 'Would one of you girls like to follow it up? I've got my hands full with Abi.'

Jenny looked at the paper, then Hannah, who batted her look back deadpan.

Hannah tapped the marker against the funeral whiteboard. 'I'm helping with Hugh's funeral today.'

'I'll do it,' Jenny said, taking the paper. It would keep her mind off Liam and Craig. That was a lie but she had to kid herself to keep going.

'Thank you,' Dorothy said, then turned to Hannah. 'Any further with Hugh's mystery caller?'

'Mystery caller?' Jenny said. 'Is this *Poirot*?'

Hannah ignored her. 'I tried to track him but he dropped the bug. I have his picture, went around student areas, nothing.'

'You think he's a student?' Dorothy said.

'I have no idea.'

Dorothy nodded. 'When's the funeral?'

'Twelve.'

'Indy has everything in hand?'

'I think so.'

Jenny looked at Hannah. So Indy was arranging this funeral, stepping up in the business, taking on more. Good. Hannah would need her there for support. Something about this old guy had really got under Hannah's skin.

Jenny's heart weighed her down. She didn't want to alarm the other two, hadn't told them about the ping and the business in Leith. She'd hoped she would find Liam, Craig would turn up, all this would magically resolve before she had to spill the beans. But here they were.

'I think Craig has taken Liam,' she said.

The looks on their faces killed her.

She explained through her headache about the phone trace, The King's Wark, the trashed studio. How Thomas wasn't convinced yet but she knew different. How she was just waiting for Liam's body to turn up in the Water of Leith with some fucking sick message carved into his forehead, or something equally unimaginable, but she was imagining it anyway because that's what Craig wanted her to do, he still had control of her, still pulled the strings and she hated him for it, wanted him dead if she was honest because she couldn't think of any other way to escape. And even then she wouldn't be free, his ghost would haunt her and Hannah and Dorothy, all of this would still be a part of their lives, their history and future, there would still be counselling and flashbacks and trauma and the wound on her stomach where he stabbed her, angry, pink scar tissue threatening to open up, guts spilling over the kitchen table and the dog wagging his tail beneath.

She realised she'd stopped talking. Dorothy and Hannah looked at her, all of them sharing a moment of quiet before the next piece of shit came flying at them.

50

HANNAH

Hannah guided the front of the gurney, fingertips on the edge of the open coffin, as Indy pushed it from the embalming room to the front of the house. They pushed Hugh into the viewing room to the right of reception then lined the gurney alongside the plinth in the middle of the room. Indy fiddled underneath, raising the gurney to the same level as the plinth, then on a count of three they slid the casket over. Hannah felt her biceps strain with the weight.

Indy slid the gurney against the wall and checked Hugh over, tightening his tie, smoothing the lapels of his dark suit. She ran a hand round the inside of the coffin, flattening the lining where it had ruffled up, then straightened Hugh's feet which had splayed in transit.

Hannah watched with admiration, her girlfriend's composure, attention to detail, compassion for someone she'd never met. Just three of the reasons Hannah loved her to bits. Making it all the more painful that Hannah had been lashing out at her, making everyone in her world feel as messed up as she was.

She took Indy's hand and placed her lips against it.

Indy looked weirded out. 'I'm not the queen.'

'You're *my* queen.'

Indy mimed puking into her mouth. 'Please.'

Silence for a moment, a shared sad smile.

'I want to say I'm sorry,' Hannah said.

Indy squeezed her hand. 'OK.'

That old line passed through Hannah's head, about love meaning never having to say you're sorry. What a load of rubbish.

Imagine a relationship where neither person ever said they were sorry, that would be the most disastrous marriage in history. She knew what the song intended, that two people are so close they read each other's thoughts, but it's still a load of crap. Sometimes you have to express clearly what you've done wrong and how you feel about it.

'I've been crazy,' Hannah said. 'I've taken it out on you. I think because you're the one great thing in my life. Like, I wanted to mess that up too so I could revel in misery. Or maybe because you're so strong I thought you could take it, put up with my shit forever. I'm sorry, I've been a total bitch.'

Indy took her hand away and gave Hannah a look.

Hannah swallowed. 'This is where you say I haven't been a bitch at all and you love me and forgive me.'

Indy sighed and ran her finger along the edge of Hugh's casket. 'I love you to bits, Han, you know that.'

Hannah felt her cheeks flush. 'I notice you didn't mention the bitch thing and the forgiveness.' Her voice faltered on the last word.

Indy shook her head. 'You've been a total bitch, but you're *my* bitch.'

She was trying to defuse, deflect Hannah's honesty, and Hannah loved her for that.

Hannah nodded. 'Were you serious the other day?'

Indy frowned.

Hannah looked at Hugh then at her own hands resting on the coffin. 'About leaving me.'

'I never said I would leave you.'

'You said it was possible.'

Hannah kept her head down, eyes wet, worried that a tear would drop onto Hugh's suit. She felt Indy take her hand across the chasm of the casket.

'You don't know what you've got,' Indy said.

Hannah looked up.

Indy looked around the room. 'A mum and gran who would do anything for you. Me. A whole world out there that needs you in it. Yet you focus on the bad stuff all the time. Hugh is dead, your dad has escaped. So what? You still have to live.'

Hannah felt tears now, leaned back so they wouldn't fall into the coffin.

Indy shook her head. 'My dad was the same, always catastrophising, worrying the worst would happen. It drove my mum nuts. During good times he would be terrified they wouldn't last. My mum tried to get him to enjoy himself, live in the moment.'

Indy was squeezing Hannah's hand too tight. Hannah stared at her.

'I remember once on a walk along Porty beach he was so distant. Mum and I did cartwheels and the sand squeezed between my fingers and the water lapped on the shore and terns swooped over the waves. He couldn't enjoy it.'

She cleared her throat, straightened her neck.

'Then the worst *did* happen, out of the fucking blue. So what difference did it make, all his pointless stress? It didn't mean anything, he wasted his life.'

Hannah's breath was ragged as she pulled her hand away and wiped her tears. 'I'm so sorry.'

Indy walked round the coffin, shaking her head. 'Just don't waste your life, Han.'

Hannah went for a hug, squeezed Indy's waist, buried her face in her shoulder, smelt Indy's shampoo and cocoa butter skin cream. It felt like home. She pulled away, a soft kiss on the lips turning into something more meaningful, a kiss of apology and acceptance and love and devotion.

Eventually they separated, still holding hands, and Hannah turned to Hugh in the coffin. She wondered what he would've made of two young women snogging over his body, but she thought he wouldn't have cared.

She'd been back to see Wendy, partly to say she had no luck

finding the mystery caller, partly to find out more about Hugh's life. For a terrifying moment Hannah thought Wendy was going to ask her to do the eulogy, but she already had a humanist celebrant lined up, an old friend. But she wanted to talk about Hugh, to tell Hannah about her husband's life. It helped that Hannah didn't know him well, so everything was fresh, and Wendy revelled in it.

The hiking in Greenland. More than once coming across a polar bear, scaring it off with a pistol. Eating raw seal with the Inuit, the northern lights, dancing and fizzing like spirits of the dead. Meeting Stephen Hawking early in his career. And more mundane stuff, he would have fresh flowers on the dining table every week. Their thousands of little running jokes and connections, their huge open-house parties every Halloween, loads of friends' children running around high on sugar and adrenaline, Hugh presiding over it with quiet grace, smiling in the corner of the kitchen, happy to have brought people together.

And in two hours he would be ashes. Wendy had agreed with Edward, the pair of them would take those ashes and scatter them at a remote settlement called Ittoqqortoormiit on the northeast edge of Greenland, where he proposed to her. So he could be at peace with the dancing sky spirits.

She wanted to shake him awake, ask why he killed himself, why poison, what did it mean? But maybe it didn't mean anything, just like nothing meant anything in the scheme of things. The universe will end in a few hundred billion years in a last gasp of nothingness, the big chill, and all of this will be forgotten.

Her phone rang in her pocket and she felt a flurry of shame, as if the noise might wake Hugh, make him sit up in the casket.

Unknown number.

She swallowed hard, hands unsteady.

Indy looked worried. 'Han?'

Hannah stared at the phone then at Indy. 'It's him.'

Indy's eyes widened. 'He wouldn't.'

Hannah ran her tongue around her teeth. 'He would.'

'Don't answer.'

Hannah shook her head. 'The longer he's on the line, the more accurately they can track the phone.'

'I don't think you should speak to him.'

Hannah gripped the phone, stared at the throbbing call symbol like a heart ready to burst.

'Maybe it's not him,' she said. 'Maybe it's just a scammer.'

The phone was still ringing. How long until it went to voicemail?

She pressed answer.

'Hannah, wait,' Craig said down the line, as if they were in the middle of a conversation.

Hannah swallowed.

Indy touched the small of her back. It was meant to be reassuring but Hannah imagined Indy shoving her into the coffin on top of Hugh's corpse.

'Just wait a minute,' Craig said.

He sounded exasperated, as if *he* had been wronged. He was breathing hard like he'd been exercising.

Hannah's heart hammered in her chest, pounding to get out. She bit down on her tongue to stop herself speaking.

'Han?' Doubt in Craig's voice.

'I'm waiting,' Hannah said. 'You told me to wait.'

'OK, OK. Look.'

She stared at Hugh, eyes closed in the casket, the smell of embalming fluid and the mustiness of his suit.

'This is all a big mistake,' Craig said.

'OK.'

'You believe me, don't you?'

'Believe what, exactly?'

Indy was on her phone, presumably calling Jenny or Thomas, someone who could track Craig's phone.

'I never meant for any of this,' Craig said.

'And yet here we are.'

'I'm still your dad.'

'Don't.'

'No matter what.'

It was true, there was no getting away from it.

'OK, *Dad*.' She couldn't stop the scathing tone. 'What do you want?'

'What?'

'Why did you call?'

Silence down the line, Hannah sensed hesitation.

'To talk to my little girl, of course.'

It didn't ring true, he hadn't referred to her as his little girl since the divorce a decade ago, she was too jaded, too switched-on to ever see Craig with the eyes of an innocent daughter after that.

'And say what?'

'I just wanted to hear your voice.'

'Well here I am.'

Indy finished her call, gave Hannah the thumbs up, someone was tracing this. They were on their way to break down his door, throw him back in prison.

'I'm not a bad man.'

Bile rose in Hannah's throat, she thought she might be sick over poor Hugh.

'Have you hurt Liam?' she said.

She couldn't help it, couldn't let the delusion continue.

Silence. Too long.

'I don't know what you're talking about.'

This was so deadpan it was a joke.

'I think you do.'

Hannah's hand was shaking, the phone hot against her ear, the smell of the lilies by Hugh's coffin tickling her nostrils.

'I have to go,' Craig said.

The line went dead and Hannah stood there pressing the phone against her ear, trying not to cry.

51
DOROTHY

She walked down Sylvan Place, the cold air making her eyes water, cherry blossom drifting along the gutters, ambulances lined up outside Sick Kids. She had Einstein on a lead. It was a pain in the ass looking after a dog at her age but maybe the exercise would keep her from dying anytime soon, and he was a good-natured soul. He clearly missed his owner to begin with, but that had lessened as the days went on. It helped that he had a houseful of women looking after him, plenty of dog treats. She thought about James Dundas, wondered if Jenny would find his family.

She stopped outside Abi's front door, waited a long time trying to picture what would happen. She remembered persuading Abi to come home and wondered what kind of home Abi could have now. She sighed and rang the bell. An elderly couple walked past with a basset hound, which yelped at Einstein. Einstein cowered behind Dorothy's legs and she wondered if the dog was over James after all. Maybe life on the streets made him skittish, or maybe James abused him. She'd painted this picture of a saintly young man down on his luck but an addict's life is destructive, homelessness is hard, it was easy to slide into abuse, taking it out on those around you.

The door opened and Abi stood in grey pyjama shorts and a loose LCD Soundsystem T-shirt. Dorothy's heart sank. This was a school day, she'd come to speak to Sandra presuming Abi would be at school. She'd decided she needed to speak to Sandra first, give her a chance to explain, and yet here was Abi, her life about to be ruined.

'Hey,' Abi said. 'Cute dog.'

She kneeled and stroked behind his ear.

'What happened to his eye?'

'We don't know,' Dorothy said. 'He was kind of homeless.'

'What's his name?'

'Einstein.'

She smiled. 'Hey, Einstein.'

Abi straightened up, and Dorothy thought again about teenage energy, her long, thin limbs, the buzz about her, the confusion, the effort to stay on top of hormones, emotions, the weird weight of teenage life.

'Did you find my dad?'

And there it was.

Mike appeared behind Abi, a hand briefly on her shoulder. Would Mike help her through this? Was he in on it? Dorothy didn't think so, he had a face on him like he was keen to hear what Dorothy had found.

'No,' Dorothy said. It wasn't a lie, she hadn't found Abi's dad, but that was a bullshit technicality and she felt it in her heart. She was lying to Abi for the first time and it sucked. After all the lies the girl had been told by her mum, what right did Dorothy have to add another into the bargain?

Mike lifted his chin. 'So why are you here?'

'I wanted to speak to Sandra.'

Abi's eyes widened. 'So you have found something.'

Dorothy felt sick. 'I just need to check some details with her, boring stuff, tax and national insurance.'

Abi's face fell. This was going to kill her, and it was killing Dorothy not telling her.

'She's at work,' Mike said.

Did he know? His face didn't give away anything. He didn't seem like the kind of person who was good at lying, but what did Dorothy know?

'Are you sure there's nothing you can tell me about Dad?' Abi was so keen for information, some kind of connection. But what would a connection to a real dad be if he hadn't raised you? What about Mike, stepping into her life, didn't he get a chance to connect? And what about Stephen, being there all those years, was that really as phoney as it felt?

'I just need to speak to Sandra.'

Mike nodded. 'She finishes at five but sometimes works on.'

Abi's head went down and she stroked Einstein mournfully.

'Are you OK?' Dorothy said, even though her whole body was itching to leave. 'Aren't you supposed to be in school?'

Abi rubbed her midriff. 'Stomach.'

It wasn't convincing.

Mike put a hand on her shoulder. 'It's been hard to focus. With everything.'

He waved a hand at the madness of the universe.

Dorothy wanted to hug Abi, but instead she tugged on Einstein's lead and walked away, her head throbbing.

Soderberg was like a balm for her soul, and she was disgusted it was so easy to make her feel better. She'd dropped into Warners but Sandra was doing viewings in Merchiston, wouldn't be back for hours. Dorothy left a message and number, took Einstein for a long walk round the Meadows, ended up here.

Thomas appeared from the vennel across Middle Meadow Walk, the sight of him lifting her spirits. She rose and kissed his cheek, hugged him. They'd already spoken on the phone. There was another ping from Craig's phone when he called Hannah but he was smart, made the call on the move, probably a bus or stolen car. The phone triangulated to a few different masts across the north of the city, Davidson Mains, Trinity, Granton, Newhaven. They were pulling CCTV from buses that ran those routes but chances were low. And if they got a positive ID, so what, he could be anywhere now.

Craig wasn't stupid. It was shameful to think it now, but if Dorothy was being honest she had always liked him before all this. He was sharp, funny, full of charm but also aware of the vacuous nature of that. But it had all been the deepest of lies and she, along with everyone else, had fallen for it.

'So,' Thomas said. 'You still haven't caught up with Abi's mum?'

Dorothy had told him the story on the phone, heard him sigh, pictured him pushing his glasses up, pinching the bridge of his nose.

'No.'

'That's not going to be an easy conversation,' Thomas said, scratching Einstein under the chin.

Dorothy watched people flowing up and down the street, imagined their auras, different hues surrounding them and revealing their moods. Not that she believed any of that stuff. She was a materialist, liked things concrete and provable. She didn't rule anything out, there was plenty that science didn't understand yet, and scientists would never explain why we lie to each other and ourselves.

Thomas spoke to the dog. 'And what about you, eh?' He looked at Dorothy. 'Anything more on the owner?'

Dorothy had a feeling that was going to end as badly as Abi's story. Intuition maybe, but feelings are not to be disregarded, she'd learned that over the years.

'We have a name,' she said. 'Hopefully Jenny is tracking down the family right now.'

The waitress came and took their order and Dorothy sat in silence, thinking about secrets and lies, all the pain that follows us around like storm clouds.

Gerard Way screamed in Dorothy's ears as My Chemical Romance blasted in the headphones. She pounded the kit in the studio loft at home, keeping the hi-hats tight in the verse, lifting her left foot and exploding round the toms into the choruses. This was the opposite of last time she sat on the stool, she didn't want to feel the groove, empty her mind, now she wanted to use her body to scream out of the window at all the bullcrap of the world.

The band was singing about dying, no surprise given the whole *The Black Parade* album was about death, one of the reasons Dorothy had loved it ever since a student brought it to a lesson one time, asking how to play the fills in 'This Is How I Disappear'. She loved the pure anger, thrashing guitars, pounding drums, singer on the edge of sanity.

She pummelled the kit and felt the strain in her forearm tendons, along her calf muscles, her body singing like it was on fire. The song ended and she breathed heavily, waiting for the next one. In the sliver of silence her mind flooded with images, the look on Abi's face when she thought Dorothy had news about her dad, James Dundas dead in his stolen car, Craig with his hands around her throat in the kitchen downstairs, death so close that she could feel its breath on her neck, could smell it every day when she woke, could feel its icy touch spreading from her mind to her limbs, now pounding away again as the music burst into life and her body with it, trying more than anything to hit and kick her way to some kind of truth.

52

JENNY

The first three Dundases were a bust. At least Jenny thought so, but her mind was churning over Liam so maybe she missed something. She was going round the likely Dundas addresses, mentioning James and showing a picture, seeing how people reacted. She could've done it by phone but Dorothy thought you got a better feel for things face-to-face. Plus it was good manners given that Jenny could be delivering the news that someone was dead.

So she'd driven the body van to Comely Bank, Murrayfield and Cramond, no dice. She thought again of the city as interlacing veins and arteries, the pieces of a city cross-pollinating, intertwining, spilling into each other. The differential of Edinburgh in a few hundred yards was crazy. From Cramond's seaside cottages it was three minutes through Silverknowes into Pilton and Muirhouse, *Trainspotting* territory. Then south through the huge houses and parklands of Fettes and Inverleith. She skirted the traffic chaos in the centre of town, avoided the Royal Mile that tourists were so familiar with but which was only a tiny percentage of this unfathomable city. Then east around Arthur's Seat along Duddingston Low Road, the loch below shimmering in the scudding sunshine, herons in treetop nests and swans gliding through the water, fluffball cygnets trailing in their wakes.

Then she was here in Duddingston Village, past the Sheep Heid, apparently a resting post since the fourteenth century when Duddy was separate from the city. The houses here, even in the same street, were wildly different. Compact terraced cottages one side, detached mansions with gardens on the other, a scatter of sixties pebble-dashed semis at the end. She pulled up outside 46 The Causeway and switched the engine off.

She walked up the driveway, lined by birch and oak, ravens flustering in the branches, magpies calling to each other. The house was huge, Victorian with Doric columns, plush curtains in the windows, a sporty Audi and a four-wheel beast parked outside the double garage.

Jenny felt a fire in her belly as she reached the front door. She had the list of Dundases in her hand along with the picture of James and Rachel up Crow Hill. As she stood here she realised the path to Crow Hill started just round the corner, by the loch. She felt that burn in her stomach move to her chest as she rang the doorbell.

The inner front door was old, etched glass, a swan and cygnets just like the ones she's seen on the drive here. She saw movement behind the glass. The door was opened by a middle-aged woman, apron over a yellow summer dress. She was a few years older than Jenny but well maintained, carefully arranged, short blonde hair, impeccable make-up, strong cheekbones. She wore tasteful flat shoes and small drop earrings, was clutching a tea towel in her hands. Smudges of flour were on the apron and the sleeve of her dress.

'Mrs Dundas?'

'Mary, yes. What is this about?' Her voice was posh Edinburgh, old money.

'I was hoping you could help me,' Jenny said, feeling the weight of every word. 'Do you know a James Dundas?'

Mary smiled. 'Of course, my husband. What do you want?'

Jenny shook her head as something dawned on her. 'No, I mean this James Dundas.'

She held up the picture, messy hair, smiling, briefly happy.

Mary's eyes gave her away. She reached out to touch the edge of the paper. Eventually her eyes darted away and she glanced over her shoulder, lowered her voice.

'Who are you?'

'I'm Jenny Skelf, a private investigator.' She held the paper up and it fluttered in a breeze. 'You know him.'

Mary swallowed hard, rubbed at her tea towel, twisted it into a spiral. She looked like she might pass out.

'He's my son,' she said, again looking behind then leaning forward. 'Our son.'

Jenny felt tears behind her eyes, a shiver running from her neck down her back. 'I have some bad news.'

Mary shook her head, eyes wide, she knew.

'Don't,' she said.

'I'm afraid James is dead.'

'Don't.' Mary's fingertips went to her temple like she was channelling a message from the universe, but the only message here was a broken heart.

The magpies were still making a racket in the trees behind them, and Jenny tried to remember the rhyme about them, how many were lucky or unlucky, whatever it was. As if our fate were dictated by birds.

'I'm so sorry.' Jenny wanted to reach out and hug her but the distance between them seemed overwhelming. Mary leaned against the doorframe, fingers still fidgeting at her forehead, like she was tapping out a signal in reply to the universe.

'Who are you?' she said.

'I told you, I'm a private investigator.'

'I don't believe you.'

Jenny shook her head.

Mary swallowed. 'I don't believe what you say about Jamie.'

'I'm afraid it's true.'

'No.' Mary gathered herself, pushed away from the doorframe, lowered her hand, returned to squeezing the tea towel. Her eyes were wet. 'It's not true.'

There was a noise from inside the house, a door opening, the creak of floorboards.

'Mary?' A male voice, authoritative, confident. 'Mary.'

James Senior opened the door wider. He was tall, grey hair, clean shaven, buttoned-down Oxford shirt and cream chinos. His hair was a close buzz to his head, ex-military maybe, and his chin jutted out like he wanted the world to justify itself.

'What's going on?'

Mary stayed silent, shrank into herself. Tears in her eyes but Jenny didn't think James had noticed. He turned to her.

'Who are you? What do you want?'

Jenny looked at Mary, whose face dropped. Eventually Mary turned to her husband, tears on her cheeks. 'It's Jamie.'

James stared, neck muscles tense. Mary looked down and away like a cowed beast.

'Your son,' Jenny said.

James kept staring at Mary for a long time then eventually turned to Jenny, gripping the door.

'We don't have a son,' he said.

Mary gasped and raised her head. She hesitated for a long moment and James stood, daring her to do something. She swallowed heavily, seemed to muster up some courage, held his gaze.

'He's dead,' she said, voice shaking. 'You killed him.'

53

HANNAH

The Inuit throat singers were terrifying and mesmerising. The two young women stood next to the plinth with Hugh's coffin laid on top. They wore intricately embroidered purple cloaks, bone necklaces and earrings, leather headdresses. The noise they were making was insane. Hannah was transfixed along with the rest of the small congregation at Seafield Crem.

The women faced one another and held each other's elbows, arms rocking in time with the rhythm. Their heads were close as if telling each other a secret, smiles on their faces, lost in the moment of creating something magical. Their singing was a mix of gasping breaths, low, menacing growls and higher melodies, the two of them slightly out of step, giving the syncopation an unsettling edge. They started soft, built gradually until their voices reverberated around the high ceiling and walls, the sound penetrating Hannah's mind, making her heart flutter. She was suddenly very conscious of her own breathing, how alone she was in the universe, a singular being cut adrift from the mass of humanity represented by the sisters' hypnotic chants.

She looked at Indy in her funeral-director outfit, demure black suit and white blouse, and thought about her body underneath. She hadn't felt horny or sexy in a while, and she missed that deep pleasure of sharing your body with someone else. Maybe the throat singers were turning her on.

The singers were nodding their heads, foreheads occasionally touching. It seemed deeply personal yet completely outward-looking, as if they were addressing the whole history of the planet with their primal voices. Hannah wondered if she could channel anything like that or if it was cultural, generations of women teaching their daughters this link to the universe.

She looked around the congregation. Wendy and Edward were in the front row holding hands, eyes closed, enveloped in sound. Hannah couldn't help thinking of them as a couple. What if they killed Hugh or persuaded him to take his own life so they could be together? She was an investigator now, she could investigate. Look into their lives, whether there was any evidence. Was it possible to have an affair within an open marriage? And wasn't Edward gay?

She was losing her mind. There was no evidence Hugh was murdered or that these two were in cahoots. But maybe it would explain Wendy's coolness about Hugh's death, how Edward was her rock. She stared at their hands together on Wendy's lap, let the music wash through her, felt the reverberations in her pelvis, the growls in her scalp. She imagined herself as a polar bear snarling across the Arctic tundra, ripping open a seal's stomach and feasting on the innards, seal blood smeared around her mouth and matting her fur.

Wendy opened her eyes and Hannah looked away.

The rest of the congregation was made up of Hugh's colleagues from the physics department and other academics. Hugh was in his eighties so there weren't many people here. It was a paradox of funerals, you might expect older people to accumulate friends over the years, but ceremonies for the very elderly were often quiet because some friends had died off already. Hannah found that depressing. She tried to remember when she'd last seen her therapist. She soaked up the unearthly music flowing around the room, felt her constituent atoms vibrate, a quantum entanglement that rewired her brain, turning her into someone she barely recognised.

She looked around again. She recognised some of the lecturers, heads down, sombre. A couple of post-docs and one or two undergrads, maybe they had a soft spot for Hugh.

Then she saw him.

A couple of rows behind everyone else, black hoodie and jeans, his head bowed. She wasn't sure to begin with, couldn't see his face. This guy was blond, though, cropped short, slight flick at the front, and his frame was a match too, tall and skinny. It could even be the same hoodie and jeans. Hannah hadn't spotted him on the way in but there was another entrance to the chapel, through the waiting room at the back. He must've come in that way once Hannah was inside.

The singers were still going, throbbing voices, gasping and panting, the beat of it all around.

She waited and watched, didn't blink in case she missed something. She prayed for his head to rise and up it came like she made it happen. It was him, bags under the eyes, quizzical arch to his eyebrows.

Hannah got up and walked down the aisle. Everyone watched her, the guy too, his face turning from curious to something else as he realised she was heading for him.

'Hey,' Hannah said, and the singers at the front hesitated for a moment before synching up again.

The guy got up and walked to the back of the chapel, people in the pews turning as Hannah started running and the guy did too.

'Hey,' Hannah said again, as the guy picked up pace and was out the door and through the waiting room, Hannah banging the door as she flung it wide heading after him. He was outside and turned left up the gravel drive, sprinting hard. Hannah stopped and kicked her heels off then sprinted after, feeling gravel on her stockinged feet. This was quicker, she was going to catch him.

He glanced back and saw her following, spurred himself through the graveyard, past the garden of rest and war memorial, his feet pounding. She was gaining on him, though, and he clutched at his chest. He turned into the older graves, a couple fallen down, some worn away, the forgotten dead. He was heading for the exit on Leith Links but she was getting closer.

'Stop,' she shouted between gasps of air.

He looked back but kept going, past the gatehouse and the stone exit posts. She was still closing, only a few yards away as they both sprinted along Boothacre Lane. It was a tiny street and he was near the end already, Hannah's feet burning, lungs heaving.

'Wait,' she said.

He turned and looked at her as he ran beyond the end of the street into the bend of Claremont Park, straight in front of a red Ford Ka that knocked him up and over the windscreen, tumbling across the roof in a horrible crunch, then the heavy slap of his body on the road and the screech of brakes.

'Shit,' Hannah said.

54

DOROTHY

She watched Archie embalming a Mr Bateman, checking the pressure gauge on the pump, lifting the tube to check for blockages, massaging the skin of his hand and arm, bringing him back to fake life. She tried to process the two calls. Hannah was in hospital with an unconscious man she chased into traffic from Hugh Fowler's funeral. Jenny was on her way back to the house, said she'd found James Dundas's family and the father didn't want to know. Families were hard, but standing on your doorstep denying you had a son was something else.

Archie noticed Dorothy in the doorway and smiled. She ran a hand along the fridge doors, thinking about the people inside, the lives they led, the dreams they had.

'Why do we do this?' she said.

Archie glanced up from Mr Bateman. 'What?'

'All this death.' She waved a hand. 'It seems natural to us, but it's deeply weird.'

Archie thought it over. 'If you say so.'

Dorothy walked over to where he was working. 'How are you doing?'

'Fine.'

'I mean with your mum.'

'I know what you mean.'

'If you want to talk.'

'No.'

Did talking help? That was the standard line about grief but maybe there was nothing gained from chewing it over. Maybe it just stopped the healing.

Her mobile rang in her cardigan pocket. She fished it out, a number she didn't recognise. She thought about Craig taunting them. It must be Dorothy's turn for the treatment.

'Hello?'

A pause on the line, a cigarette inhale.

'Hello.' Dorothy's voice was hard, she wasn't afraid of Craig.

'It's Sandra, Abi's mum. You left a message.'

Dorothy sensed something down the line, Sandra knew what this was about.

Dorothy smelled embalming fluid, other chemicals, a hint of decaying flesh. 'We need to meet.'

'Just tell me what you have to tell me.' There was bluster in her voice undercut by nerves.

Dorothy stepped away from Archie, back to the fridges. 'I know.'

'Know what?'

'I *know*.'

Silence down the line, another draw on the fag.

'You don't know anything.'

Dorothy leaned her forehead against a fridge door, cold metal on her skin. She imagined lying inside on a tray.

'I met Neil Williams,' she said. 'I mean Stephen Marks.'

More silence, no cigarette this time just hesitation. It went on so long Dorothy wondered if Sandra had hung up.

'Have you spoken to Abi?' Sandra said eventually.

Dorothy closed her eyes. 'I wanted to talk to you first.'

Sandra cleared her throat. 'Let's meet.'

The Earl of Marchmont was a tiny dogleg bar on the corner of Sciennes Road and Marchmont Crescent. It had fairy lights around the bottle gantry, a scatter of small tables, big windows flooding the space with light. The last time Dorothy was in here, some years ago, it was full of Bangkok Lady Boys from their Fringe show on the Meadows. They were off duty, in shirts and trousers rather than glitter and feathers, but they were still the most beautiful people Dorothy ever laid eyes on.

Today the clientele was more prosaic, an old man with a West Highland terrier by his feet, a young student couple with pints of something hoppy and cloudy. And Sandra Livingstone with a large glass of red wine already half finished. She sat in the corner, as far away as possible, and Dorothy wondered if that was deliberate. As she approached, Sandra noticed her and flinched.

Dorothy spotted the bottle of Malbec on the table and a second glass. Sandra refilled her glass and poured into the other without asking. She took a glug and nodded at a seat. Dorothy sat and sipped, her hands shaking. She didn't want to be here any more than Sandra. It was just another bunch of lies. She wondered if this was her life now as a PI, uncovering people's stupid secrets and feeling bad about it. Was that how Jim felt? The burden of knowing this stuff was overwhelming.

Sandra's eyes were red from crying.

'So you met Stephen.'

'Yes.'

'What did he tell you?'

'I know all about it,' Dorothy said. 'The only thing I don't understand is *why*.'

Sandra shook her head, picked at her thumbnail. She wore a neat blouse and skirt, the smart businesswoman with a hint of sass, it didn't hurt when letting flats to men.

'How did you find him?' she said.

'Mike gave me the address Abi had for Neil. I cased the place using an apartment opposite. That's where I found Abi.'

'What?'

'She took keys for a Warners place across the street, that's where she was holed up waiting for her dad.'

Sandra's head went down, eyes to her glass, then she drank.

'I don't think that's helping,' Dorothy said, nodding at the Malbec.

'Don't tell me how to cope.'

Dorothy sighed. 'I saw someone else using the flat, got a trace on the owners, found out CTL were using it. Both guys used the same car, owned by CTL. I put pressure on Justin there, he gave Stephen up easy enough when I threatened him with the police.'

'Too easy.'

'How did you hope to keep this a secret?' Dorothy said. 'How did you think this would end?'

Sandra drank again, half her wine gone already.

'I didn't think ahead. Obviously.'

Sandra looked out of the window. There was a seafood market across the road, corner shop, barbers, couple of tasteful bistros. Just an ordinary neighbourhood going about its honest business.

'I read about it in Japan,' she said. 'Apparently, they have businesses renting out relatives, boyfriends, even brides and grooms. Social pressure.'

Dorothy stayed silent.

'Abi started asking at nursery,' Sandra said, another swig of wine. 'All the other girls had daddies, where was hers? I thought it would go away but it intensified at school. Her behaviour was off, tantrums you wouldn't believe, back to bedwetting, refusing to eat.'

Dorothy pressed her lips together.

'I know,' Sandra said. 'Don't worry, I disgust myself. I heard there was a place in Edinburgh. A mate of a mate hired a boyfriend to get her mum off her back about being a lesbian. It was only meant to be short term.'

Dorothy sipped her wine.

'But Abi got more attached. I had to make up a job for Neil that meant he was away a lot. Stephen wasn't comfortable but I was paying him, he sucked it up. And he became genuinely fond of Abi.'

'You entrusted your girl to a total stranger.'

'I was always there at the start,' Sandra said. Her eyes were wet with tears. 'Once I knew him a bit I let Abi see him alone.'

'You trusted him?'

'He's a good man.'

Dorothy half expected her to say he was a good dad.

Sandra drank again, scratched at her cheek. 'It got harder and harder, Neil had to be away longer. I kept thinking if he wasn't around Abi would forget, realise he was fobbing her off, but she just invested more in the idea of him.'

A couple of punters came in, two young men in tight trousers and skimpy beards, headed for the bar.

'To the point where she ran away to find him,' Dorothy said.

'None of this was supposed to happen.'

Dorothy ran her tongue around her mouth, felt the red wine scuzz there already. 'I don't understand, being a single parent is no big deal. Why lie?'

Sandra looked away for a long time, a car flitted past the window.

'Because no matter what I said she would still have a real dad, and I couldn't tell her about him.'

Dorothy looked around the pub. The barman was a big man with a tight belly, shaved head, navy tattoos on his forearms. She wondered if he was a good dad to a little girl somewhere.

'Tell me,' she said.

Sandra looked at Dorothy and held her gaze. Something defiant in her face.

'Abi's dad is my dad too,' she said eventually.

She kept looking at Dorothy, eyes filled with tears, until Dorothy looked down at the table. Sandra picked up her glass and downed her wine, refilled it with the last of the bottle. Dorothy watched her chest rising and falling, thought about the heart beating inside her chest, pictured her on a slab in the embalming room, Archie treating her with dignity.

'It's as old as the fucking hills,' Sandra said, disgust in her voice. 'Daddy's little secret. I'm sure you don't need details.'

Her breathing seemed too shallow, frantic.

'I let it go on. I should've put a fucking knife in that cunt's guts, but I didn't.'

'It's not your fault.'

Sandra laughed. 'Fuck off with the therapy, you don't know.'

Dorothy touched the edge of the table, felt a sticky mark. 'No, I don't.'

Her mind immediately went to Jim playing with Jenny when she was little, patting her knee or tickling her. Jenny used to come through on mornings when there wasn't a funeral and get into bed with Dorothy and Jim. She was maybe ten at the time. Dorothy never imagined, it genuinely never crossed her mind. What if. She thought about it now and felt sick.

'He's still alive, as far as I know,' Sandra said. 'I ran away, cut off all contact. He doesn't know about Abi, I couldn't ever let him into her life. I panicked, made up a dad. Maybe I wanted it to be true, a nice guy who treated her well, bought her presents, took her for ice cream. Just a normal dad, not a fucking pervert.'

Another slug of wine then Sandra pursed her lips.

'Do you think it matters who our parents are?' she said eventually. 'I mean genetics, something in the blood?'

Dorothy tried to think what Jenny had taken from her, from Jim. What Hannah took from her mum or dad.

'No,' she said. 'I think if you raise your kids right, are honest with them, that's all you can do.'

Sandra laughed again, bitter and drunken. 'I've fucked that up, haven't I?'

Dorothy wanted to reach over and take Sandra's hand, which was twitching on the table, but she didn't move.

'What happened to you wasn't your fault,' she said. 'But you can't keep lying to Abi.'

'I can't tell her the truth either, not all of it.'

Sandra held her arms out looking for an answer.

Dorothy wished she had one.

55

HANNAH

There were no beeping machines like you saw on television hospital dramas. He didn't look injured just tired, no drip or bandages, just a young man in a hospital bed who she wanted to shake awake.

She sat by him and went over the last two hours. He'd stood up from flying over the car roof then looked around with a glazed expression. The woman driving the Ka got out and was hyperventilating, leaning against her car bonnet. A passer-by called an ambulance as Hannah took the guy's hand and led him to the pavement, where he eased himself onto a park bench like he was an old man. He closed his eyes, rubbed the back of his neck then passed out.

The ambulance took him away but Hannah had to stick around with the car driver to give police statements. Why were you chasing him shoeless from the cemetery? Good question. After half an hour they let her go, promising to be in touch. She called Indy to check the funeral went OK then jumped in a taxi to the hospital and here she was. It was easy to find him still in A&E, he hadn't been moved to a ward. She swept in, checked behind each curtain, told an orderly she was his sister. The doctor dealing with it didn't question her, barely had time to speak before he was rushed to another patient, told her the man had two broken ribs and concussion, they were keeping him in as a precaution. A nurse wheeled him upstairs and Hannah went too, so easy to bluff your way in the chaos. So now she was sitting at his bedside waiting for him to wake up, feeling terrible for running after him.

Darkness descended in her mind. People got hurt wherever she went. Hugh died, Indy got shut out, this guy was concussed and broken. She was the connection, the evil that spread across people's lives, and Indy was better off without her. This guy in the hospital bed was better off without her. The world was a better place without her.

She thought about their other cases. James Dundas, homeless and dead, his dad apparently unbothered. Abi's fake, actor dad, a mother who lied her whole life. And the worst was Craig still out there in the city.

The guy in the bed stirred and opened his eyes. Took a moment to focus then groaned when he clocked Hannah still in her funeral clothes. He wasn't much older than her. She was surprised at his eyes, beautiful blue-green, freckles on his nose, but the dark bags under his eyes made him seem sad, serious.

'What do you want?' he said, voice cracking.

She handed him a glass of water from the bedside table. He tried to take it with a trembling hand but spilled it so she held it to his lips. Something intimate about seeing his Adam's apple bob up and down.

'I want to know who you are.'

He swallowed then pushed the glass away. 'Thanks.'

'Who are you?'

He coughed, winced and held his ribs. 'Fuck, that hurts.'

Hannah nodded at his chest. 'You broke two ribs.' She looked at a graze on his head, half hidden by his hairline. 'And concussion.'

'Shit.'

Hannah had her hands in her lap. 'I'm sorry.'

The guy shook his head. 'Why did you chase me?'

'Why did you run?'

He blinked heavily. 'Because you chased me.'

He was making a joke but nervousness in his eyes suggested there was more to it. Hannah looked around. He'd somehow snagged a single room rather than a ward, maybe just luck of the draw. She'd expected a room full of patients, a comedy guy with his body in plaster, leg raised, someone else with a head wrapped in bandages, but it was just the two of them.

'How long was I out for?' he said.

Hannah looked at the clock on the wall. 'Three hours. What do you remember?'

'I got up,' he said, closing his eyes. 'I was fine.'

Hannah shook her head. 'You weren't. I took you to a bench and you passed out.'

He raised shaking fingers to his hairline. 'My brain isn't fucked, is it?'

'Not as far as I know.'

'Because that's all I need, on top of everything else.'

Hannah shifted in her seat, touched the edge of his bed, thought about the phrase 'hospital corners' that Gran used once. Not a thing people talked about anymore, something about bouncing a coin on the bed?

The guy looked around the room as if expecting someone else.

'Why are you here?' he said.

'I wanted to check you were OK.'

'Apparently I have two broken ribs.'

'I'm sorry I chased you.'

'I'm sorry I ran in front of a car, so we're both sorry.'

Hannah looked at the door as if a doctor would walk in and stop this.

'Please tell me who you are,' she said.

He pressed his lips together. 'I'm Cameron. Cammy for short.'

'Cammy who?'

'Wilson.'

She rolled it around, thought she would feel something, a spark in her synapses, an answer, but she didn't know Cammy Wilson.

Cammy rolled his neck, winced. 'And you are?'

'Hannah,' she said. 'Skelf.'

'The funeral people.'

'Yeah.'

He put out a hand and she shook it, both of them mocking the formality.

'Nice to meet you, Hannah.'

'Likewise, Cammy.' Hannah put her hands back in her lap. 'I've been trying to find you for a while.'

'Really?' Another cough, another shudder from the pain. 'Why?'

'I'm a private investigator.'

'I thought you did funerals.'

'We do both.'

'That's odd.'

Hannah shrugged. 'It is what it is.'

Cammy swallowed. 'So why were you trying to find me?'

'I've been looking into Hugh Fowler's death.'

Cammy reached for the water, lifted it to his mouth, took a drink. He was like a nervous deer in the woods. 'He committed suicide, right?'

'You visited his widow.'

He nodded. 'I didn't know he was dead the first time I went there.'

'But you went back a second time.'

He closed his eyes, touched his forehead, rubbed his neck. 'I read about it. I went to offer condolences.'

'But you ran away.'

'I got nervous, I guess.' There was something off about his tone.

'Nervous?'

'I get like that around death. You understand.'

'Not really, I'm in the funeral business.'

'Right.'

'How did you know Hugh?'

Something came over Cammy's face. 'I don't know if I should say.'

Hannah clenched her fists. 'I just want to know the truth. Please.'

Cammy sighed, shifted in bed, rubbed at his ribs. 'We were buddies at the meetings.'

'What meetings?'

'The cancer support group. We were cancer buddies. They pair you up when you first arrive.'

'Hugh had cancer?'

'Didn't his wife tell you?'

Hannah thought over their conversations. 'I don't think she knows.'

Cammy raised his eyebrows. 'Well everyone deals with this shit differently, but I'm surprised he wouldn't tell his wife he was dying.'

Hannah tried to get her head straight. 'Dying.'

'Stage four rectal adenocarcinoma.'

Hannah took a deep breath. 'Rectal.'

Cammy chewed the side of his lip. 'Yeah, nasty. Not that any of it is pleasant. But arse cancer, the symptoms are horrible.'

Hannah didn't even know how to shape what she was thinking.

Cammy went on. 'He was diagnosed very late, the prognosis wasn't exactly glowing. They offered him options, chemo and radiotherapy, even rectal surgery. But there were a lot of down sides and he was an old man. He decided to ride it out.'

Something occurred to Hannah. 'What about you? Are you...?'

'Dying? No.' He reached for the bedside table. 'Touch wood.'

He scratched at his chin and gave Hannah a look. 'Testicular.' He glanced at his crotch under the sheets. 'Both are gone, shooting blanks and all that. But I'm lucky, they caught it quickly, I'm in remission.'

Hannah couldn't help following his gaze and staring at his groin. 'I'm sorry.'

'I'm still here, right?'

Hannah tried to focus. 'When did you first meet Hugh?'

Cammy thought it over. 'He turned up about three months ago. All the old ladies loved him, he was a real sweetheart.'

Three months wasn't any time at all. And he'd planned Mel's memorial in that time, giving someone he'd hardly known a send-off when he knew he was on his own way out.

Cammy tried to get comfortable. 'I presumed Wendy knew.'

Hannah shook her head, pulled at her earlobe. 'So he killed himself because he was dying anyway?'

Cammy kept moving in bed, wouldn't settle. He looked out of the window then around the room. His energy was all wrong.

Hannah narrowed her eyes. 'There's something you're not telling me.'

Cammy shook his head. 'No.'

'Come on,' Hannah said. 'It's eating you up. Tell me, you'll feel better.'

He was vulnerable, injured, concussed, she was manipulating him but she had to find out.

He rubbed at his neck. 'I didn't know what he had planned. I mean the end is horrible, symptoms are so awful you can't imagine. Suicide is a way to avoid all that mess, inflicting it on loved ones, but I never realised that's what he was going to do with it.'

'What are you talking about?'

He came to a decision, held her gaze for a moment. 'The acid. I heard about how he did it. I mean, how was I to know, who the fuck drinks acid?'

'What?'

Cammy touched his head again, fingers fluttering at his hairline. 'The hydrocyanic acid, I got it for him.'

'How?'

'I work at the organic chemistry lab at King's Buildings. That's why the support group put me and Hugh together, because we were both at uni, had science backgrounds. I make up compounds and solutions for post-docs and post-grads when it's needed. It's shit pay but they're nice people.'

'And Hugh asked you for some hydrocyanic acid.'

'Yeah.'

'You didn't ask why he wanted it?'

Cammy shrugged. 'Said he wanted to conduct an experiment. Honestly.'

Hannah thought about Schrödinger's experiment, the cat in the box, hydrocyanic acid. She looked around again, still waiting for a doctor to come and take charge, tell her she shouldn't be here, give her a reason to get away.

She realised something. 'That's why you ran earlier.'

Cammy nodded. 'I wanted to pay respects, of course. But I looked it up, helping someone with suicide can get you done for culpable homicide, that's years in prison. When you started walking towards me with that look, I panicked.'

'That's why you ran from Wendy's house too.'

'I went to say sorry but when I was standing on the doorstep I bottled it. Saying sorry implicates me, I can't be involved, I didn't know what he had planned, you have to believe me.'

He was almost in tears, hands shaking on his bedsheets.

Hannah stared at him and felt her face grow warm. 'I believe you.'

Cammy's breathing calmed down, he nodded to himself, tried to smile. 'So are you still investigating?'

Hannah pictured Hugh frothing at the mouth, the acid bottle in his hand. She thought about Schrödinger's cat, alive and dead at the same time, a man with terminal cancer looking to die with dignity.

'I honestly don't know,' she said.

56
JENNY

She sat at Skelf's reception drumming her fingers on the desk. Hannah and Indy hadn't returned from Hugh's funeral and Dorothy was speaking to Abi's mum, so Jenny was holding the fort. She'd hoped manning the phones would distract her but she was going crazy over Liam. She'd lost count of the number of times she'd called, always voicemail. She'd gone to his flat, no answer, asked the neighbours, no one had seen him. She even went back to his ex's place, looked her in the eye when she said she didn't know where that piece of shit was. Jenny believed her.

Now she was Googling him, checking social media, snooping around his last interactions, seeing if there was anything sinister in there. She felt sick. But maybe this wasn't what she thought. Maybe he was just ghosting her, had enough of her baggage, enough of the middle-aged girlfriend with the saggy body and the killer ex-husband running loose. Maybe he was on a beach in Mykonos chatting up the cute waitress in the local restaurant, entertaining other holidaymakers with his close escape from a crazy family of funeral directors and private investigators.

The door opened and there was Mary Dundas, hair still beautifully orchestrated, haunted look on her face.

'My son,' she said. 'Is he here?'

Jenny took a moment. 'No, he's still at the morgue. They won't release the body without next of kin.'

Mary swallowed hard, leaned against the wall and tears came.

Jenny led her through to the discreet room they had for distressed mourners, tasteful armchairs, box of tissues on the coffee table, soft light through thin curtains.

Mary didn't look as if she'd slept, her eyes were red and puffy despite make-up. There was a tremor in her body, a current that felt as if it might make her explode any minute. Her son was dead and she was on the edge. Jenny flipped a tissue from the box and handed it over. Mary looked at it like it was a bomb.

'Jamie was such a sensitive boy, he took everything to heart, always thinking of others. We found a sparrow once with a broken wing, he nursed that thing for days but it still died. God, he was inconsolable.' She looked at Jenny. 'You must hear this kind of thing all the time.'

Jenny shook her head. 'Everyone has a story.'

Mary nodded as if that was some kind of obvious truth and Jenny realised it probably was.

'Do you have children?' Mary said, touching the tissue to her nose with a sniff.

'A daughter.'

'Grown up?'

Jenny thought about Hannah, all the shit thrown at her recently. 'Very much so.'

'Then you know.'

Jenny had never been convinced by the argument that only parents know what it's like to have children. Empathy put you in someone else's shoes and isn't that what society is all about, allowing ourselves to think what it's like to be someone else?

Mary shook her head. 'When they're little they rely on you for everything. Absolutely everything. They take over your life, fill every moment with their needs and destroy your sleep, your personality, your life.'

Jenny remembered Hannah as a baby and there was an element of truth to it. Then it was exponentially harder when she split with Craig, the single-mum thing.

'But then, gradually, they stop needing you,' Mary said. 'They develop their own personalities, their own friends, their own lives. And what are you left with?'

'It's not easy.' Jenny considered patting Mary's knee but kept her hands to herself.

'My life has been empty for a long time,' Mary said. 'I threw everything into looking after Jamie, I gave up my own life for him, like so many mothers. I didn't want anything back, just for him to be happy and healthy.'

Jenny heard the rumble of a truck on the road outside somewhere. 'What happened?'

Mary stuck her chin out, Jenny could see the muscles straining in her neck as she tried to compose herself.

'People change, don't they?' She looked at Jenny's left hand. 'Are you married?'

'Divorced.'

'Things didn't work out,' Mary said. 'Did your husband change?'

Jenny laughed out loud then covered her mouth. She thought about Craig, everything he'd done. What he was like at the beginning, ten years of happy marriage, for God's sake.

'You could say that.'

Mary nodded. 'My husband had a hard childhood. Boarding school. Never got on with his parents but joined the army anyway to please his father. What is it about fathers and sons?'

'I honestly don't know.'

'The army is supposed to be modern these days, inclusive. I don't know if that's true now, but it wasn't back then. It made you into a certain kind of man. Closed off, hard. I didn't understand at the beginning. When Jamie came along I thought things might change. But James never understood him. He was effeminate, creative, full of joy. My husband hated that, he was jealous. His world was full of rules, order, masculine pride.'

Mary swallowed hard, closed her eyes for a long time, a tear rolled down her cheek.

'Of course I knew Jamie was gay long before he came out. I say "came out" but he didn't have a choice after he was discovered with that teacher. But James had been blind to it all and my God it was like the end of the world. My husband threw him out the next day, the very next day, can you believe that?'

'I'm sorry,' Jenny said, though it felt worthless.

'I should've left right then, of course.' Mary stared at Jenny then looked away. 'But I didn't. I was a coward.'

'It's not your fault.'

This time Jenny did reach out and touch Mary's leg. Mary jerked her knee away like Jenny was infected.

'Of course it's my fault,' she said. 'But I was scared. I'd been with James for so long, I didn't know what adult life was without him. I was a kept woman, an officer's wife, I never had a life, never had my own personality. I was James's wife then Jamie's mother.'

Mary held her gaze. 'You think I'm an appalling person.'

'I don't.'

'You do, quite rightly. I stayed with James and gave up on my son. I managed to keep in touch with Jamie for a while but it became hard. I was secretive, didn't tell James. Jamie hated that I was sneaking around, like I was ashamed. I don't blame him.'

Jenny touched her neck and thought about Hannah, the guilt of parenthood.

'Heroin is so seductive,' Mary said. 'It's a warm bath. That's how Jamie described it, the best warm bath you'll ever have. It sounds lovely, doesn't it? But it took him. He kept moving, couldn't pay rent, lost his phone. When I met him he took all my money. I began bringing him hundreds of pounds each time. Then he just stopped calling.'

Her voice broke and she sobbed, head bowed, tissue gripped in her fist. She began rocking then an animal keening came from the back of her throat. Jenny thought of wolves howling at night, imagined early men and women on the African plains tearing at the earth in grief. Slowly Mary got herself together, straightened her hair, dabbed her nose and eyes, pulled another tissue from the box.

'Happy and healthy,' she said.

Jenny didn't follow. 'What?'

Mary gulped. 'I said before all you want is for your child to be happy and healthy. Jamie was happy and healthy when he was small. Sensitive, yes, but a happy little boy. So full of life.'

'Tell me about him,' Jenny said.

Mary smiled. 'He wasn't sporty but he loved nature and having outdoor adventures. We were lucky, we live next to Duddingston Loch and Arthur's Seat. Every Sunday when James was playing golf Jamie and I would be out spotting birds and animals, finding rare flowers amongst the gorse. We saw a red kite hunting above the trees, an otter swimming in the loch, herons catching frogs in the reeds. He was so excited and I loved seeing him like that so much. I couldn't explain to James, he wouldn't have understood.'

Jenny stayed quiet, the simple gift of the funeral director.

'And he was very arty,' Mary said, rubbing at the back of her hand. 'At primary school he would draw the animals we saw, beautiful pencil sketches, much better than anything I could've done. It's so strange, seeing someone you made develop skills you can't comprehend.'

Jenny nodded, thinking of Hannah.

Mary shook her head. 'He didn't like Craighouse. Art was the only thing he cared about, all the academic stuff went by the wayside. I tried to talk to him, but you know how teenagers are. I wondered over and over what I did wrong, if I loved him enough, if I was strong enough. Or if he needed more from someone else, from his father.'

'It's not anyone's fault.'

'He's dead, isn't he?' Mary's sharpness surprised Jenny.

'You can't play "what if",' Jenny said. 'When someone dies, we all ask if there's something we could've done, no matter the circumstances. But you can't torture yourself.'

Mary shook her head, swallowed hard.

'I've left James,' she said. 'I know it's too late but I've finally done it. My beautiful boy dying has made me realise I've wasted my life.

The one good thing I had is gone. I haven't loved James in years, kept hoping things would change. I always assumed Jamie would come back one day, want his old room back. My husband would understand, let him back in, we would be a family again. It was stupid to think things would work out, that was never on the cards. So I've left. A forty-seven-year-old woman with no skills, no husband, nowhere to live. A dead son. It's all I deserve.'

She thrust her chin out as if challenging the world to smack it with a punch.

Jenny's phone pinged in her pocket. She cringed and pulled it out to switch the ringer off, and there was a message:

Come to Ann Street now.

If you tell the police or anyone else, Liam is dead.

57

DOROTHY

Dorothy couldn't shake the image of Sandra sitting drunk in the Earl of Marchmont, contemplating the grave she'd dug for herself. She walked home along Warrender Park Road, past Abi's school where she'd bullshitted at reception with the empty lunchbox. Poor Abi, simply wanting a dad. Dorothy thought about the fathers in her life. Her own had died when she was not much older than Abi, and while it obviously had an impact, her dad was a reticent and distant figure, had fought in the Second World War and come back an empty shell. He must've gone through so much, and Dorothy never blamed him for that distance. We never know what others are going through.

She thought about Jim, a good dad to Jenny, but always so busy with the funeral business. Dealing with the dead instead of spending time with the living, a common problem in this industry. But he doted on her when he could and she was besotted with him, snatching time amongst the coffins and services, eulogies and embalmings.

And then there was Craig. The fact he left Jenny when Hannah was ten was maybe the catalyst for a lot of Hannah's problems, but that was nothing compared to the last year. Dorothy had often told Hannah that you choose your family, whatever form that takes, genes don't come into it. Find the support you need from the people around you, that's your family. She, Jenny and Hannah were family, Indy was family. Craig was just a fucked-up guy, nothing to do with her.

Dorothy walked across Bruntsfield Links and thought about Jim's ashes scattered there, making the grass grow, feeding the worms. And she thought about Craig running bleeding across the same piece of ground, chased by Hannah. Maybe everything Dorothy thought about family was bullcrap, maybe you couldn't escape your blood.

She was surprised to see no lights on in the house. She walked through the garden and saw the van was gone from the garage, Jenny must've taken it. Hannah was still at hospital with her funeral interloper, but was due back soon for the Skelf round-up. Dorothy loved their kitchen meetings. Despite the talk of deaths and the nefarious dealings of their investigations, she loved the time with her daughter and granddaughter, a bond that tied her to them both.

Dorothy wondered what Sandra was going to say to Abi. Jesus, she didn't envy her. She opened the front door and Einstein came tumbling down the stairs, tail thumping against the banister.

'Good boy,' she said, kneeling to cuddle him.

Another stray brought into the big house, another victim of loss looking for a family.

'Where's Jen, eh?' she said, standing up.

She looked around reception in the gloom. She loved this place, so much a part of her, so peaceful, something reliable in her life.

'Jenny?'

No answer. She went upstairs, Einstein behind, into the kitchen and switched the light on. She got her phone out and called. Voicemail. 'Hi, it's me, just wondering what you're up to, give me a call.'

She hung up and stared at her phone, then made another call.

Hannah picked up after two rings. 'Hey, Gran.'

'Hi, darling, where are you?'

'On the bus, just left the hospital.'

'How did it go?'

A sigh down the line. 'I'll tell you when I get there.'

'Do you know where your mum is?'

'She's not at home?'

'And not answering her phone.'

Silence down the line, something unspoken between them. Normally they wouldn't be worried but this wasn't a normal time.

'I can track her phone,' Hannah said.

Dorothy smiled. 'OK, see you soon.'

She hung up, thinking about mothers and daughters. Sandra and Abi, Jenny and Hannah, her and Jenny. The symbiotic nature of it, how we all need someone to rely on. Speaking of relying, she went to get Einstein some food. The dog trotted after her, nose in the air, eager for what was coming.

58

JENNY

The house on Ann Street was dark. There was a police car parked across the road, no one inside. Jenny thought about that, then Craig's message, no cops. She went to the car, tried the door, locked. She looked along the road at all the family homes, lights on, food being eaten, homework getting done, games being played. She looked back inside the car then turned to number eleven. She got her phone out, saw a missed call from Mum. She didn't listen to the voicemail. She read the text for the hundredth time. It was stupid not to tell anyone but she knew he was serious, Liam was in trouble. She knew what Craig was capable of, had seen it first hand. Her fingers went to her belly, touched the scar.

Her hand moved to the back of her jeans at the waistband. She pulled out the kitchen knife she'd brought after she packed Mary Dundas off, making thin excuses about other appointments. She ran a finger along the blade. It was just like the one Craig plunged into her guts six months ago. She replaced it, felt the cold metal against her skin. She tried to be prepared, second guess what Craig would do, how this would end. But no final scenario came to mind, she couldn't see a way out of this. She got on her phone and sent a message:

I'm outside now.

Waited a few minutes then the door of number eleven opened.

Just a dark doorway, he must be behind the door. She looked at the blackness waiting for a sign, the face of evil, a stupid jump scare. Any fucking thing.

She started up the steps, was almost at the door when he emerged from behind it, standing there like nothing was wrong.

He wore jeans and a loose shirt, black loafers. He seemed at ease with himself, comfortable in his skin, even after all of this.

And he was pointing a gun at her.

She couldn't stop the surprise on her face.

'Hi,' he said, like she just dropped by for a drink.

She nodded at the gun. 'Where did you get that?'

She tried not to show she was trembling. Casually reached round to her back, pretended to scratch herself, touched the handle of the knife.

He smiled, watching her.

'I've always been a resourceful man,' he said. 'You don't spend six months in prison without making contacts.'

'This has been some slippery slope for you, huh?'

He shrugged, waggled the gun. Jenny gauged how close she was, if she could grab it. His grip seemed loose.

'We are where we are,' he said.

Jenny looked inside the house. 'Where's Liam?'

'Why don't you come and see?' He was focused now, gun pointing at her chest.

Jenny stood judging the distance between them, thinking about the knife. Her hands were at her side, loose, ready.

'Do you have your wife and daughter tied up in there too?'

Craig actually smiled. 'I knew they would go to her mum's after the break-in. I knew the place would be empty, and it's my home, after all.'

Jenny nodded at the patrol car across the street. 'Where's the cop?'

Craig looked up and down the street. Waved the gun at her. It was small and black, she knew nothing about guns, for all she knew it was a starting pistol.

'Inside,' he said, voice hardening.

He stood aside.

She would have to pass him, an easy reach with the knife. Her heart was a drum, limbs shaking, as she took the last few steps towards the house. She forced a smile, thinking of all the times she charmed him round when they were married, got her way by distracting him with sex, turned an argument into making up like flicking a switch. She used to be able to manipulate him or so she thought, then she found out he was playing her all along, he was the one having an affair, he won in the end.

She was at him now, could smell him, was surprised he smelled fresh but he'd had time to wash, get changed into normal clothes, do whatever it is escaped prisoners do in their expensive Stockbridge homes when nobody seems to be after them.

She held his gaze in the doorway, reached behind her back and grabbed the knife, pulled it from her trousers then felt his grip on her wrist, a sudden shock of violence, pulling her arm in front of them both with the knife still in it, shaking the wrist until the knife flopped and clattered on the tiles.

'Fucking devious bitch,' he said, holding her wrist with one hand, pushing the barrel of the gun into her cheek with the other. 'Little cunt.'

He shoved her against the wall, pressed himself against her crotch and breasts, his breath on her face, the gun stretching the skin of her cheekbone. She craned her neck to get away, she could see the knife on the floor next to Sophia's welly boots, yellow with red flowers. She thought about Hannah, whether she would ever see her again.

'Inside,' Craig said, shoving her through the doorway into the hall.

He kicked the door closed and followed, pushed her towards the stairs.

'Down,' he said, looking at the stairs to the basement. 'Let's go see lover boy.'

She stepped downstairs, worried about what she would see, thinking about her phone in her pocket, the missed call from Mum. Fucking stupid, should've answered, should've said where she was. But Liam, what if?

The basement was open plan, a man-cave feel to it. Big-screen TV in one corner, games console, electric guitar and amp, two old sofas. Two thick pillars in the centre of the room, Liam tied to one, slumped on the ground, arms behind him, face covered in blood.

Jenny gave Craig a look and he pushed her into the room.

'Liam,' she said.

His face was swollen, one eye completely shut, cuts and scrapes around his mouth, his cheek and eyebrow split open, blood down his shirt, dried in places. He looked like a defeated boxer.

'Jesus.' Jenny kneeled and touched her hand to his bruised face.

He opened his functioning eye, coughed, a bubble of blood popping at the corner of his mouth. He shook his head, swallowed hard.

'You shouldn't have come,' he said.

Jenny stroked his hair, let her fingers rest on his temple. 'I had to.'

'No.'

'It's OK,' she said, like she was reassuring a toddler.

She stood up. 'You sick fuck.'

'Takes one to know one.'

'Let him go.'

Craig laughed. 'That doesn't seem likely, does it?'

Jenny put her hands on her hips. 'I'm here now. This has nothing to do with Liam. You said—'

'I said if you told anyone, I'd kill him,' Craig said. 'That doesn't mean I let him go.'

He stepped towards her and she backed away to one of the sofas.

'What's the plan, here?' Jenny said. 'What's your endgame?'

Craig hesitated briefly then took another step.

Jenny's hands were fists at her side, ready to fight him off. She thought about the knife upstairs, the gun in his hand. 'I mean, you're fucked, right? An escaped prisoner, a murderer, now this?'

She waved at Liam slumped against the pillar. He seemed to have passed out, head to the side, hands loose.

'It's so exhilarating,' Craig said. 'When you're at the bottom you have nothing to lose. I can do anything now, I'm untouchable.'

Jenny had backed round the sofa, was edging towards the stairs. Craig stepped across to cut her off.

'Do you think I'm fucking stupid?'

Jenny looked at Liam pointedly and Craig followed her gaze.

She bolted in the other direction, squeezed past him and reached the bottom step, but she only managed two strides when her leg was pulled from under her, smacking her chin on a step and being dragged backwards. She felt a kick to her stomach, a bright flash of pain shuddering through her body. Her hands went to her belly then there was a fist in her face, then the butt of the gun on her cheek, slicing the skin, blood spurting down her face. She raised her arms to cover her face and felt her hair grabbed, yanked upwards, a clump of it coming out in Craig's fist as he lifted her to her knees and spat in her face. She was fucked from pain, her breath ragged, Liam groaning behind her, Craig panting in her face.

'Fuck you,' she said between breaths.

'No,' Craig said, lifting the gun above his head. 'Fuck you.'

He swung it down on Jenny's temple and she felt sick and dizzy from pain, then she saw spots in her eyeline, flashing brilliantly, then she was gone.

59

HANNAH

Voicemail.

Hannah looked out of the bus window as she listened to her mum's brusque voice: 'Leave a message.'

'Hey, Mum, where are you?' Her bus passed Grange Cemetery and she had a great view of the old Victorian mausoleums inside, ornate carving and flamboyant designs. 'Call me.'

She hung up as the bus turned into Marchmont Road heading for the Meadows. She opened her phone-tracker app, picked Jenny's number. Watched the blob as it focused on screen, floated around Stockbridge for a moment then settled. She zoomed in. Ann Street. Fiona's place. Weird. She had Fiona's number from one time when she had to do the school run for Sophia, Craig and Fiona stuck at work. She called. Rang six times, then was picked up.

'Hey Fiona, it's Hannah. Listen, is Mum there, she's not answering her phone.'

The sound of Fiona taking a sip of something. 'I'm sorry?'

'Jenny,' Hannah said, as if explaining to a simpleton. 'She's with you, right?'

There was sound in the background, the clink of cups. Then the grind and scoosh of an espresso machine. 'What makes you think that?'

'Wait,' Hannah said. 'Where are you?'

'In a café in Cramond,' Fiona said. 'I'm staying with my mum for a while, she lives out here.'

Cramond was miles away from Stockbridge.

'So you're not at Ann Street?'

Fiona hesitated again before speaking. 'It's on the market, we're selling it.'

The bus was on the corner of Lothian Road and Princes Street, tourists crossing the road at a snail's pace, eyeballing the castle behind her. A shiver ran through her.

'So it's all locked up?'

'Of course.'

'I have to go.'

She hung up and checked the tracker again. The bleep still throbbed in the same spot. It was definitely at number eleven, Fiona's place.

Fiona and Craig's place.

She checked her bus app, to see where the twenty-four took her, realised it went to Stockbridge, they were only a few minutes away.

She phoned Jenny again, voicemail. She didn't leave a message.

She called Thomas. 'Do you still have an officer at Ann Street?'

'What?'

'You had someone posted at Ann Street after the break-in, are they still there?'

Confusion in his voice. 'Yes.'

'Call them now,' Hannah said. 'I think Mum is there.'

It took Thomas a moment to put it together, as the bus trundled down the hill over the cobbles of Howe Street.

'Craig wouldn't go back there,' he said.

'Just do it.'

'Hang on.'

Static on the line for what seemed like forever. Hannah was jostled as the bus turned into Circus Place.

'Hannah,' Thomas said. 'I can't get hold of him. We're sending backup units. Where are you?'

Hannah laughed as she pressed the button for the bus to stop. 'I'm almost there.'

'Do not go in, do you hear me? Wait until we arrive.'

She hung up and got off the bus, ran across the bridge over the Water of Leith, turned up Dean Terrace, her feet thumping. Ann Street was the third off to the right and she was there in no time.

She glanced inside the empty police car, tried the door, then went up to the dark house. She stood at the door, looked at her phone. Jenny's bleep still throbbing. She was almost on top of it. She raised a finger to the doorbell but hesitated. Lowered it. She pushed at the front door and it opened. On the floor in the doorway was a knife. She knelt and looked. She recognised it from Gran's kitchen.

She looked behind her at the street in the evening gloom. She listened for sirens, imagined flashing lights appearing round the corner, the screech of tyres as police cars arrived. But there was just birdsong, leaves rustling.

She picked up the knife, weighed it in her hand, gripped the handle. She went along the hall, trying to get her eyes accustomed to the darkness, blinking heavily, opening them wide, listening for noises. She stared up the spiral stairs, three floors, skylight at the top.

She went into the living room, empty, dark. Same with the connected kitchen. She took light steps, her breathing hard in her ears, the tingle of electricity flowing from her brain through her body to her fingertips and into the knife. She imagined it glowing, but the blade was dull in the dark.

She went back into the hallway and looked upstairs again. She was about to put a foot on the first step when she heard something. A scraping noise. She noticed the stairs down to the basement. She looked up the three flights, then down. Thought about her dad. Liam missing. Jenny's phone in the house.

She walked towards the basement steps and began down, wishing she could float. The sound of her footsteps on the carpeted stairs seemed impossibly loud in her ears. The knife trembled in her grip but she followed it like a divining rod, the blade leading her into the depths. She was halfway down now, turning the corner, and she saw a low light in the corner of the room. Two more steps and she had a better view.

Liam, face beaten to a pulp, tied to a pillar. Unconscious.

She swallowed.

Two more steps.

And there was Mum, tied to the second pillar in the room, blood on her face. She seemed unconscious too.

Another step.

Then another.

And there was Dad. Pacing along the wall, running hands through his hair, shaking his head, his tongue poking from the corner of his mouth, something she knew meant he was thinking. She knew so much about him, had spent half her life with him, shared DNA, maybe shared an outlook on life. Girls are supposed to have a special relationship with their dads, right?

He hadn't spotted her.

She took another step, the knife hot in her sweaty fist.

Jenny lolled her head to the side but didn't wake up. Liam's rattling breath sounded bad.

She looked around the room. There was a gun on the arm of the sofa. It was four metres away, about the same distance from her dad.

She stood still, thinking. Then in a single motion she bolted down the remaining stairs and across the room, the sound making Craig turn. It took him a moment to realise what was happening before he also headed for the gun, but Hannah was quick and she reached it while he was still only halfway across the room. She picked it up, surprised how cold and heavy it was, pointed it at Craig with a shaking hand. He reared up and took a step backwards, his hands low, palms spread out as if he'd just performed a magic trick.

She stared at him, tried to work out something from his face. She seethed with hatred, that he could do this to all of them. She would never be the same again.

He widened his eyes, angled his head, threw on a sad smile to see if it would land.

'Hannah.'

'Dad.'

Jenny gave out a groan and they both glanced at her.

'I never meant for any of this,' he said.

'Save it.'

'Let me explain.'

She shook her head, couldn't believe what she was hearing. 'Fuck you.'

He sighed, like he was disappointed in her.

'I wouldn't survive in prison,' he said.

'Good.'

'I'm just trying to start again.'

Hannah laughed. 'Then why are you still here? You got your passport, you could be anywhere in the world right now. Why are you still hanging around like cancer, eating away at us?'

Craig looked at Jenny, then back at Hannah.

Hannah shook her head, waggled the gun towards Jenny and Liam. 'You're just a sad old man.'

A steely look came over his face. 'I don't expect you to understand. But I never wanted you involved, I never wanted to hurt you. You're my daughter.'

Hannah felt tears in her eyes. 'I'm not.'

'You can't deny it,' Craig said. 'No matter what, you'll always be my little girl.'

'No.'

He took a step towards her.

She tightened her grip on the gun. 'I will shoot you right here.'

'No you won't.' He took another step. Reached out a hand.

Hannah felt sick, tears on her face, gun wavering in her hand, the knife in the other. She remembered Dad cleaning her scraped knee, putting a plaster on it, kissing it better, encouraging her into the swimming pool with her armbands on, reading *The Cat in the Hat* to her at bedtime, a lesson in letting chaos into your life. She knew this wasn't that man, this was a monster, but she couldn't untangle them, they were in the same body, the same mind, the same collection of atoms moving through energy fields, interacting with her, intermingling with her own energy.

He took another step, was nearly at her now.

'You won't shoot me,' he said. 'You don't have it in you. You're my daughter.'

She let out a sob, the gun trembling.

He reached for the gun and she squeezed the trigger, the shocking crack as it went off making her jump. Blood spurted from Craig's hand as his index finger exploded. His face whitened and he staggered backward clutching at his hand, blood throbbing between his fingers onto the floor, the smell of burning from the gun barrel in Hannah's nose making her feel sick. She stepped back herself, as if she could walk away from what she'd done. She heard her mum moan on the floor.

'Shit,' she said.

'Fucking hell.' Craig looked up at her. 'You shot me.'

'Sorry.' Hannah's voice sounded alien in her ears. 'I didn't mean...'

'You fucking shot me.' He straightened up, examined the bloody mess of his hand and grimaced. 'You shot your own dad.'

Hannah shook her head, the gun at her side now. It felt hot in her fist, the knife too, like she had her hands on a radiator. She wanted to drop them both and run, she wanted to run all the way home to Indy and safety, but nowhere was safe, nowhere was ever going to be safe again.

Craig stared at her, breath ragged. 'How does it feel?'

'What?'

'Do you feel powerful?'

Hannah shook her head, crying. She thought she would be sick, put a hand to her face. She wasn't strong, she was weak, too weak to be here and he knew it.

Craig took a step towards her, still holding his bloody fist. The colour had returned to his face, the smile too.

'Go on.' He spread his arms out, blood dropping on the carpet. 'Finish the job.'

Hannah tried to swallow, couldn't.

Craig took another step.

'Come on,' he shouted. 'Do it.'

'Stop,' Hannah said between sobs.

'Hannah.' This was Jenny speaking from the ground.

They both turned and stared. Hannah waited for something, a sign. Her mum wasn't even focusing, didn't seem to know where she was. Hannah was about to speak when Craig lunged at her, pushed her against the wall, knocked the knife from one hand and grabbed the gun from the other. He stepped back, holding the gun loosely at his side. It was all too easy.

She put a hand to her head, felt where it had banged the wall.

He looked around the room and laughed.

'This is something, eh?'

He shook his head like he'd just heard a bizarre joke. He looked at Hannah and she tried to work out what he was thinking. He stepped towards her with the gun raised, reached out and brushed hair from her face, took her hand and held it for a moment. She faced the floor, couldn't stand to look at him.

He held up his hand, the finger stump pulsing blood over his knuckles. He smiled. 'You're just like your dad.'

Sirens.

He heard it too, looked at the ceiling, then back around the room, at Hannah, then Jenny and Liam.

'Of course, you called them,' he said, smiling. 'You're my smart little girl.'

He touched her cheek and she felt sick, then he turned and ran upstairs, leaving her in the basement, the sirens getting louder.

60

JENNY

It looked like winter outside, threatening snow clouds, wind whipping the cherry blossom from the branches, people huddling against the chilly squalls as they trudged across the Links. Jenny's face hurt as she looked out. Schrödinger sidled past her, leapt into the armchair and closed his eyes. Einstein padded over and gazed up at Jenny. She tickled him under the chin. She straightened up, feeling the ache of her bruised stomach muscles. She felt the puckered skin at her temple, ran a finger along the stitches, then did the same with the cut on her cheek. Twenty-five stitches over three cuts, she was lucky. She placed her hand under her T-shirt, pushed her fingers against the bruises. This was getting to be a habit.

The missing police officer was equally lucky. When backup arrived they found him unconscious in the boot of the patrol car, tied up with his own restraints. A hard knock to the head with a blunt object left him with concussion and a certain amount of wounded pride, but he was otherwise fine.

Liam was much worse. Several broken ribs, some internal bleeding, one of his lungs had collapsed and was still being drained. He was wheeled into theatre for an operation to save his right eye. Jenny tried to wait it out but Dorothy insisted she come home and rest. So here she was. Exhausted, in pain, totally fucked in the head but still alive.

She heard footsteps then voices as Dorothy and Thomas came in, Hannah behind. Jenny felt a pang at the sight of her daughter. Hannah had saved her life, which gave her a weird mix of relief and guilt. Guilt that Jenny's actions had forced Hannah into a situation where she had to confront her dad. Guilt for everything.

Being a mum was great. But Jenny was also proud, felt her chest swell. Her daughter was a stronger woman than Jenny would ever be.

'Well?' she said to Thomas, who had taken a seat at the table. Dorothy busied herself with the kettle, Hannah skulked at the whiteboards looking at the hotchpotch of cases they'd been working on. On TV dramas everything gets tied up, they catch the killer and get resolution. They have a chuckle and make a quip, end credits, tune in next week.

If only.

They had a dead homeless addict whose father refused to acknowledge him because he was gay. They had a woman who lied to her daughter her whole life. A suicide to end the horror of terminal cancer. And a killer still on the loose.

Tune in next week, folks.

Thomas looked sheepish. 'We're doing everything we can.'

Jenny knew it was no use, Craig had vanished. His face was in the news, the most wanted man in the country, but that didn't make a difference. There had been a bunch of sightings which all turned out to be mistaken identity or cranks or just lonely people wanting a blether.

There were roadblocks around the city but that was only tenable for a day, too much traffic disruption. Better to let a dangerous killer run free than make commuters five minutes late for work. Airports were on high alert but his passport hadn't been used, and police were watching train stations too. But Craig was smart, he would think of something else. Despite what folk think Edinburgh is a big city, an easy city to get lost in. As they'd found with James Dundas, it was easy to disappear, to slip between the cracks, to live in the shadows. The cops had also gone round homeless hostels and shelters but he wouldn't be that stupid. Maybe he would take a leaf out of James's book and steal a car, live in that.

Maybe he would show up, maybe he wouldn't. In a way it didn't matter, he'd already fucked them all up. Did he really plan to kill her and Liam?

Dorothy made tea for everyone as if that would make a difference.

Jenny didn't move. Hannah stared at the whiteboards, her finger in the air as if trying to find connections.

'So what now?' Jenny said.

Thomas blew on his tea, shook his head. 'We keep looking. He'll turn up.'

'You think so?'

Thomas gave her a sincere look. 'Yes, I do.'

'I wish I shared your confidence.'

Thomas looked around the room. 'We'll keep a police presence here as long as you need it.'

Dorothy nodded. 'Thank you.'

'It's not a good look,' Jenny said. 'A cop car parked outside a funeral home. Could be bad for business.'

'Jenny,' Dorothy said.

Her name on her mother's lips made Jenny tear up. She fanned her face, tried to swallow it down, made her eyes go wide.

Hannah's eyes darted around the PI whiteboard like a cat watching a butterfly. She hadn't spoken since she came in. Jenny had hugged her so hard in the ambulance that the pain in her chest and face was almost beautiful, delicious. She didn't ever want to let her daughter go, but the truth was she did that a long time ago, like all mothers.

'Han, are you OK?' Jenny said.

Hannah made a motion with her head and Jenny didn't know if it was a shake or a nod.

'We just need to keep going,' Dorothy said.

Jenny looked around the room then out of the window. Dark skies, cowering trees, wet streets.

'People need us,' Dorothy said. 'We have funerals to perform. We have to be here.'

Jenny sighed and wondered who was here for the Skelfs.

The sight of Liam in the hospital bed made her feel sick. His right eye was bandaged, the rest of his face a mess of purple and black bruising, a long cut across his cheek, a gash on the edge of his mouth sewn up, his other eye swollen so that it only just opened. A tube emerged from his side into a bag of cloudy yellow liquid. The skin around the tube was discoloured. The room was gloomy, grubby windows, the view outside to a delivery entrance where a waste truck was backing up.

Jenny stood in the doorway and thought about leaving. She touched the edge of the doorframe, looked behind her then back into the room. His breath was a shallow wheeze. He turned and saw her, raised his head. She swallowed and put on a smile, went and stood by his bed.

'Jesus,' she said.

He shifted his weight, hand going to the tube taped to his midriff. 'I'm supposed to say, "you should see the other guy", but...'

He trailed off and she took his hand.

The other guy was gone, vanished like a fucking ghost. And this was left behind, a good man beaten to shit.

Liam tried to open his eye. 'How are you?'

Jenny laughed. 'I'm fine.'

Her hand went to her bruises. He saw her touch her ribs and nodded. 'Hurts like fuck.'

'Yeah.'

All of it hurt, their bodies, of course, but the rest too.

Jenny felt tears building inside her, her face redden. 'I'm so sorry.'

'You have nothing to be sorry for.'

'Of course I do.' She tried to take her hand away but he squeezed it and that made the tears come. 'Look at you.'

He coughed out a laugh. 'Thanks.'

'You know what I mean.'

He swallowed, his tongue touching the scab on his lip where the stitches were.

Jenny shook her head. She'd allowed Craig to control her life for years and he was still doing it, still pulling her strings.

'I brought this on you,' she said.

She felt another squeeze of her hand.

'You can't think like that,' he said.

Jenny had tears on her cheeks, wiped at them with her sleeve, sniffed loudly. 'What did the doctors say?'

He let go of her hand, rubbed at his chest. 'No permanent damage.' He lifted his fingers to the bandages on his head. 'The operation went well, should get these off in a couple of days. And the lung is on the mend. The ribs will take time to heal, same with the face.'

Jenny reached out and touched his cheek. He flinched and lifted his hand up, moved hers away.

'Sorry,' Jenny said.

He coughed and winced. 'Please stop saying you're sorry.'

Jenny didn't know how to explain that she was a dangerous person to be around.

'Listen, Liam...' She felt another squeeze of her fingers and gently pulled her hand away, gripped the edge of the mattress. She shook her head and looked around the room, waiting for a nurse to save her. 'I don't think we can see each other anymore.'

He breathed, trailing into a cough. 'Jen, this is a mistake.'

She gripped the mattress, fingers red, knuckles white. 'You can't be around me.'

'He wins if you do this,' Liam said.

Jenny let go of the bed and straightened her shoulders. 'He's already won.' She had to look away from his hurt face. 'You don't know how hard this is.'

'Then don't.'

She rubbed her hands on her thighs as if trying to get rid of an invisible stain. 'Don't call.'

'Jen—'

'I hope you feel better soon.'

He reached out and grabbed her hand, tried to hold it but she pulled free and stepped away. 'I have to go.'

He stared at her with his swollen eye. She turned away, tears on her cheeks, fists by her side, pulse pounding in her throat.

61

HANNAH

Hannah and Indy sat in Wendy's living room staring at the ashes casket on the coffee table. As the funeral director in charge of Hugh's ceremony it was Indy's job to deliver them and Hannah had tagged along. Wendy sat in the same chair as before, cocktail glass in hand, twirling the onion on a stick and making ripples in her Gibson. Edward sat in the chair opposite, sipping his drink and pursing his lips.

'So this is him,' Wendy said, staring at the container.

It wasn't like the fancy urns you saw in movies, the ones that get smashed in slapstick comedies, the lead actor getting a relative's ashes up his nose. It was just a simple, unvarnished wooden box.

Hannah looked at Indy, neither of them said anything.

Wendy looked at the giant maps on the wall. 'We're going to scatter him in Greenland.'

Hannah remembered the plan, the two of them.

Edward nodded. 'We're taking a cruise.'

'It'll be lovely this time of year,' Wendy said.

Hannah looked out of the window. Trees were bending in the wind, icy blasts and swirls reminding everyone that summer was still a way off. She was about to speak when Indy touched her knee.

'I'm sure it will,' Indy said.

Hannah looked from Wendy to Edward, was this a thing now, the two of them? They had an open marriage and now one was gone, maybe they were coming together. But she was being unfair, they both lost someone they loved, why not take a fancy cruise together up the Greenlandic coast in springtime?

Wendy cleared her throat and looked at Hannah. 'So, was that him?'

'Sorry?'

Wendy pressed her lips together. 'The last time I saw you, you were chasing a young man out of my husband's funeral. Was he my mystery caller?'

Hannah hadn't decided how to play this so she just opened her mouth to see what would happen.

'Cammy Wilson,' she said. 'He was a friend of Hugh's.'

Edward perked up. 'Friend?'

Wendy's hand trembled, ripples across the surface of her cocktail.

'Not like that,' Hannah said. 'Is that what you both thought?'

Wendy swallowed. 'We didn't know what to think, that's why I hired you.'

'But you presumed he had a younger boyfriend.'

'He wouldn't be the first man in the world to take a young lover.'

Hannah shook her head. 'He was dying of cancer.'

She'd thought about Hugh keeping it a secret, Cammy's worries, but Wendy's presumptions pissed her off.

Wendy flinched. 'I beg your pardon?'

Indy gave Hannah a look.

Hannah spoke to Wendy. 'He had stage four rectal cancer, Cammy met him at a support group, they were friends.'

'He was dying?' She glanced at Edward. 'Did you know?'

Edward shook his head, stared at his drink.

'Why wouldn't he tell us?' Wendy said, voice wavering.

Hannah thought about saying something, maybe these two didn't know him, maybe they weren't all soul mates, maybe we never really know anyone.

'He was protecting you,' she said. 'He didn't want you going through it with him. That's why he killed himself, to protect you both from the worst.'

Wendy's shaking hand went to her mouth. Her breathing got louder then she coughed out sobs, tears in her eyes, the first time Hannah had seen anything in her. The cocktail glass fell from her hand, smashed on the floor, the onion rolling under her chair, clear liquid running into the gaps between floorboards.

'My God,' she said. 'Why didn't he tell me?'

She looked around for an answer, just Indy and Hannah on a sofa, Edward looking concerned in his seat, the clock on the mantelpiece ticking loudly. She shook her head, tried to compose herself.

'How could he talk to complete strangers about it, but not us?' She looked at Edward, confusion and something else, a flicker of self-loathing maybe. 'Sixty years I was with that man. Sixty years.'

Hannah imagined talking about Indy's death sixty years from now. It was unfathomable. She would tear her hair out, scream from the rooftops, rip her clothes in fury. Indy looked at her like she was a tripwire. She wanted to grab Hugh's ashes and sprint out of the room.

Edward addressed Hannah. 'Why did he run? From the funeral.'

Hannah pictured Cammy at work, carefully measuring beakers of liquids, squeezing pipettes, mixing bottles of solutions. She had no idea if any of that was realistic, but it's how she imagined him. She pictured a cloud of guilt following him for the rest of his life, a twinge in his heart every time he made up an order of hydrocyanic acid.

'He was just upset,' Hannah said. 'When I went for him, he panicked and ran.'

Hannah chewed her tongue.

Wendy composed herself, stared at the smashed glass on the floor but didn't move. 'Is he dying too?'

Hannah breathed in and out. 'He's in remission.'

'I'm glad.'

Edward stood up. 'Thank you for everything.'

Wendy seemed surprised by this. She stared at Edward as if she didn't recognise him. Hannah saw the grief in her eyes for the first time, that bewildered look when someone is gone and you don't know what to do next. Hannah was relieved to see it, made her feel better for Hugh.

'Yes,' Wendy said, hand at her neck. 'Thank you for everything.'

So this was it. Hugh was dead, cremated, gone. He'd taken control of his own death, a luxury we don't all get. There was no conspiracy here, no murder or subterfuge, just an old man choosing how to die.

Indy got up and Hannah did likewise. She couldn't take her eyes from Hugh's casket. Edward walked the two of them to the front door. She followed Indy with her hands in her pockets, where she felt the ziplock bag holding the small amount of Hugh's ashes she'd siphoned off for herself. She rubbed at it like a lucky charm and thought about her own death.

Rita's face was a picture. Hannah laughed, shocking herself with the sound of it. She'd spent half an hour talking about what happened since the last counselling session.

'You've been through a lot,' Rita said eventually.

'No shit.'

Hannah got up and looked out of the window. Wet, squally showers swept across the Meadows, sleet and snow, ice particles slapping against the window and sliding down. It was supposed to be springtime, new life budding in the world.

'But talking about it can still help,' Rita said.

This was way above her pay grade, but annoyingly she was right. Saying out loud what had happened made Hannah feel lighter, somehow. She and Indy were a little better too, now the whole Hugh thing was done. But her dad was still out there, a shadow over everything. She stared at the weather, trees dancing in the wind, sleet swirling around their branches, and wondered where he was. Scotland wasn't an easy place to be homeless in these conditions. She turned back to Rita, sitting with her notebook on her lap. She almost looked scared of Hannah, now she knew what Hannah was carrying.

'Remember last time, I talked about cosmic rays,' Hannah said.

Rita flicked through her notebook. 'Neutrinos, right? Passing through us.'

Hannah wondered if she would ever go back to uni, if she could handle it. 'There's so much about the universe we don't understand, so many mysteries.'

Hannah looked at a picture on Rita's desk, two young boys with melting ice creams in their fists.

'Do you know how all this will end?' she said, waving her hand.

Rita frowned. 'All what?'

'Life, the universe and everything.'

Rita shook her head. She didn't get it.

'A quadrillion years from now, in what they call the degenerate era, stars will stop forming, the sun will wink out, the solar system will collapse. Then in the black-hole era galaxies disband, all proton matter decays, supermassive black holes swallow everything, then they'll evaporate too, all the energy and matter in the cosmos gone. In ten to the power of a hundred years the universe will just be cold, empty nothingness. It's the end of the dark era. It's called the big chill.'

'That's all a long way in the future, Hannah.'

Hannah rapped a knuckle on the desk. 'Sounds like a nice way to go, doesn't it?'

62

DOROTHY

She was never sure why we dress the dead up for their final appearance. How often do we wear suits in everyday life? For most people it feels ill fitting, unfamiliar. Why make your dearly beloved uncomfortable as they go into the afterlife?

James Dundas looked smart. His mother had brought in a suit, shirt and tie, polished black shoes. She had a picture of him from his school days wearing the same outfit, some formal dance. But now, lying in the casket in the viewing room it seemed like it wasn't really him at all. That was crazy, Dorothy never met him, didn't know a damn thing about him. But she pictured his clothes on the day he died, his unkempt hair, scraggly beard. The blood coming from his ear, the cut on his forehead, the stare of his eyes.

What must it be like for Mary? It snagged at Dorothy's heart. She imagined Jenny lying here instead, a brief flash of gut-sinking heartbreak. Mourning your child was unthinkable yet she saw it all the time, the confusion and anger, the pain, impotent fury at the universe.

She reached in and lifted the lapel of his suit jacket, brushed a piece of lint from his trousers, rubbed at a fingerprint smudge on one of his shoes.

Dorothy had wanted answers, who he was, what kind of person he was. She'd found out the first but really had no idea about the second. Did anyone? His mum and Rachel were probably the people who knew him best, and they didn't know much. Did he ever fall in love or have his heart broken? Was he ambitious, angry, depressed? Drugs sometimes hide pain, maybe that was the case with James. His father's rejection, his own rejection of the life his parents chose for him. But really, who knows any of it? James didn't have any answers now. She realised part of this was her own grief for Jim, the need for resolution. But grief doesn't have answers, there is no resolution, it just goes on until it doesn't.

She touched James's face, felt intrusive. She didn't have permission, no right to invade his personal space. The back of her hand ran down his shaved cheek. He was a handsome man, a catch for someone. Archie had done a good job as usual, he looked peaceful.

The door to the viewing room opened and Thomas came in, stood across the coffin from her.

'Thought I might find you here,' he said.

Dorothy was supposed to be on the front desk but had slipped through to commune with James. She reached out a hand and Thomas took it. The light in here was like twilight, thin gauze curtains and uplights making it feel like a dream.

'I'm sorry,' Thomas said.

Dorothy squeezed his hand. 'For what?'

'Not being more help. With Craig, and everything else.'

'You've done everything you can,' Dorothy said. 'I know it's not easy, having to come running every time a Skelf woman calls.'

He smiled and took his hand away, rested his fingers on the edge of the casket.

'I don't do that.'

She returned his smile. 'You do and I appreciate it.'

Thomas looked down at James and sighed. Dorothy stared at him, greying hair, kind eyes, his gentle way. Such a calm presence since Jim died. She needed stability back then but Jim wasn't coming back and she was lonely. She wanted to feel like a woman again.

'Remember in Soderberg?' she said.

He looked up, knew what she meant. 'I remember.'

She glanced down at the coffin. 'You said you'd go out on a date with me when things calm down.'

'I did.'

Dorothy shook her head. 'I don't think things will ever calm down.'

'Oh.'

'I mean I think we should go out anyway. How about dinner tomorrow night?'

A look came over his face. 'I would love to.'

'OK, then. Great.'

'Great.'

They both laughed, holding the coffin, looking at each other.

The doorbell rang.

They held each other's gaze for a moment then Dorothy went to the front door and opened it. It was Abi, rucksack on her back, in an orange sweatshirt and black leggings, face crumpled from crying.

'I spoke to Mum,' she said, catching her breath in gulps.

'Come in.'

Abi dumped the rucksack on the floor and threw herself into Dorothy's arms, squeezing tight around her waist, crying into her shoulder. Dorothy felt her lean frame as she shuddered. She smelled of sweat and shampoo, stress oozing from her pores.

'It's OK,' Dorothy said, as Thomas came into the hall.

He gave Dorothy a look and she returned it.

Eventually Abi's breathing settled and she pulled away, wiping at her eyes with the backs of her hands. She crossed her arms, shook her head.

'I can't believe that bitch,' she said.

Dorothy breathed in and out. 'Don't be too hard on her.'

Abi's face was stone. 'If you hadn't found out she would still be lying to me.'

Dorothy wondered how much Sandra had told her, whether it was just the fake dad, or maybe her real dad too.

'I've left,' Abi said.

'You're fourteen, Abi.'

'I can't stay in that house another minute.'

Dorothy nodded. The scent of lilies was in the air, an arrangement in the corner of reception waiting for a coffin.

'OK.' Dorothy kept her voice calm. 'So where are you going?'

Abi shook her head, avoided eye contact. 'I've got nowhere.'

Dorothy knew where this was heading from the moment she opened the front door. 'You can stay here.'

She put steel in her voice so Abi wouldn't have to make a song and dance about accepting. Abi smiled and Dorothy saw the little girl in her still. She didn't know how long this was for, what it would bring, but this was the right thing to do and sometimes you just have to do the right thing.

'Thanks,' Abi said and came in for another hug.

The view from the top of Crow Hill was beautiful. Dorothy had been up Arthur's Seat before but never this neighbouring hill. It was slightly less high so tourists always passed it by. She looked at Arthur's Seat now and fifty people were straggled across its craggy top, selfie sticks and fleeces, gangs of foreign teens in matching outfits, couples with kids clambering the last few feet to the trig point.

Crow Hill was empty, just the four of them. The funeral earlier was a little busier but not much, which saddened Dorothy. Mary was there but not her husband. Dorothy couldn't imagine not attending her child's funeral, imagine having that in your heart. But she'd experienced plenty of narrow-minded people in her time in the funeral business, so James Dundas wasn't so unusual. She tried to give him the benefit of the doubt, maybe he was grieving in his own way. She hoped he wouldn't regret it.

Hannah and Jenny were behind Dorothy, hands clasped in front of them. Mary stood to the side, biting her lip, shaking her head, gazing at Duddingston Village below, her big house.

Dorothy looked at the ashes casket in her hands then at the view. The snow flurries of earlier had slipped away, high grey clouds remained, a bite in the air as the wind swept in from the west. She saw the three bridges over the Forth in the distance, a jumble of supports jutting into the sky. Then the spread of the city from the sea to the Pentlands, her own house in there somewhere. She turned and took in the east side of the city, Leith Docks and Porty Beach, the islands sitting out there like giant whales, the bump of Berwick Law and the white stump of Bass Rock. Hundreds of thousands of people putting one foot in front of the other, trying to carve out some peace amongst the mayhem and madness, secrets and lies, violence and pain. Jamie Dundas in her hands was beyond all that now. Whatever led him to drive away from the police into the graveyard that morning, it was over.

Einstein followed scents around the rocks and moss, tail low and swinging, padding over the uneven surface.

Dorothy caught Mary's eye and offered the casket to her.

Mary burst into tears, pressed a handkerchief against her nose and mouth like she was inhaling ether, something to make her forget.

Hannah stepped forward and put an arm around her and Mary pushed herself into a full embrace, shaking and sobbing, her face pressed into Hannah's chest. It was strange to see a middle-aged woman take comfort from a twenty-year-old, but Dorothy had seen plenty of strange things.

She thought about Abi back at the house. She was playing with Schrödinger in the kitchen when they left, another moment of peace carved from the turmoil. She still hadn't told her mum where she was staying but Dorothy would make her do that.

Dorothy looked at Jenny, staring at the city. Craig was out there. It was unbearable but they had to bear it.

Mary composed herself and looked at Dorothy and the casket. 'You do it,' she said.

Dorothy raised her eyebrows. 'Are you sure?'

Mary swallowed and nodded.

Dorothy checked which way the wind was blowing and turned so the ashes blew away from her. She opened the casket and looked at the grey dust. She'd seen cremated remains countless times but she was always moved.

'Goodbye, Jamie,' she said. 'I hope you've found peace.'

She looked at Mary, who nodded, a tiny movement like a pecking bird.

Dorothy turned the casket upside down and emptied the ashes out, watched as the dust blew and spread, disappeared into the grass and the rock. She shook out the last of him then closed the casket.

Einstein came up and snuffled at her hands.

She couldn't think of anything to say so she stayed quiet. Eventually Mary nodded to herself and turned away, began picking her way down the path from the summit. Jenny and Hannah followed in silence.

Dorothy watched for a moment. She wanted to scream into the wind but she just took a last look at the city that was her home and followed the rest of them down the hill.

ACKNOWLEDGEMENTS

Huge thanks to Karen Sullivan and everyone else at Orenda Books for their constant hard work and love. Thanks to Phil Patterson and all at Marjacq for their dedication and support. Thanks to all the readers, writers, bloggers, booksellers, librarians, teachers and everyone else who has championed my books over the years. And a special thanks to fellow author Katerina Diamond who gave me the idea for one of the plots here. The biggest thanks as always go to Tricia, Aidan and Amber, for everything.